The Things That Answer

Volume Two

by
Christopher Winterberg

Published by fu-X Publishing Company.

This is a work of fiction. Names, characters, places, and incidents are either products of the author's imagination or used fictitiously. Any resemblance to actual persons, living or dead, events, or locales is entirely coincidental.

First edition. Volume Two.

ISBN: 978-0-9894483-2-1

Dedication

For those who believed in and appreciated my writing along the way. You know who you are.

And, for those who read.

Contents

The Station

The last train leaves Ashbury Station at 12:07 a.m. without stopping.

It doesn't slow. It doesn't screech. It screams past the platform in a silver blur, windows flashing bright enough for Lena Carrick to see four versions of herself stutter across the glass.

One standing.

One turning.

One already running.

One with her mouth open like she sees something on the other side of the train that the real Lena does not.

Then it's gone.

The wind hits.

Old newspapers lift off the platform. Dust snakes along the yellow safety strip. Somewhere overhead, a light bursts with a flat little pop, and Jalen Cross ducks like someone fired a gun.

"Shit," he whispers.

Theo Latch steps to the platform edge, broad shoulders hunched inside his work jacket, staring into the tunnel after the train. "That one wasn't on the board."

Priya Sen gives the departure screen a look. The screen still says:

NO DELAYS

NEXT TRAIN: 6 MIN

"Fantastic," she says. "The lying rectangle says everything's fine."

Lena doesn't answer. She's looking at the stairs.

Or where the stairs were.

Ten seconds ago, the stairs to street level rose between two tiled walls plastered with ads for injury lawyers and meal kits. Now there's only a wall. White tile. Black grout. Wet shine. Perfectly seamless.

Lena walks to it and presses her palm flat against the surface.

Cold.

Not normal cold. Not old-station-at-midnight cold. Meat locker cold. Buried-in-January cold.

"No," she says.

Theo turns. "What?"

"There were stairs here."

Jalen laughs once, high and thin. "Yeah. Yeah, there were. That's kind of the headline."

Priya comes closer, her sarcasm slipping for half a second. "Please tell me there's a maintenance thing. A secret transit goblin hallway. Whatever."

Lena runs her fingers along the grout lines. "There's no seam."

"You're sure?" Theo asks.

"I'm a civil engineer. I know what a wall is."

"Congratulations," Priya says. "We're saved."

Jalen backs away from the tiled wall and looks up at the station sign.

ASHBURY.

His camera hangs from a strap around his neck. Old thing. Heavy. Too professional for a tourist and too battered to be new. His thumb rubs along the side of it like he's checking that it's still there.

"I knew I shouldn't have come back here," he says.

Lena looks at him. "Come back?"

He shakes his head too quickly. "Nothing."

Before she can press him, the PA system crackles.

It starts as station static, that familiar dirty electrical breath. Then guitars detonate overhead.

Death metal floods the platform.

The volume is obscene. Drums hammer through the tiles. Bass crawls up through their bones. A vocalist roars behind layers of distortion, a voice buried so deep it sounds less like singing and more like something being fed into machinery.

Jalen clamps his hands over his ears. Theo curses. Priya shouts something that gets eaten by the noise.

Lena looks up at the speakers.

The music cuts off.

The silence afterward feels worse.

A smooth automated voice fills the station. Not male. Not female. Too polished to be human. Too patient to be kind.

"Welcome to Ashbury Station. For your safety, remain with your party at all times."

The four of them go still.

The PA clicks.

"First rule," the voice says. "Stay together."

A pause.

"Or else."

"Or else what?" Theo calls.

The PA crackles like it's considering him.

The death metal comes back for half a second. One violent guitar shriek. Then silence.

"Second rule," the voice says. "One for all. All for one."

Priya slowly lowers her hands from her ears. "That's not comforting. That's never comforting."

"If one member of your party suffers," the voice continues, "all members of your party suffer."

Lena looks from Theo to Priya to Jalen.

Jalen's face goes pale under the red emergency lights. "That sounds metaphorical, right?"

Theo grunts. "Nothing's metaphorical after stairs turn into walls."

The PA clicks again.

"If one member of your party dies," the voice says, "all members of your party die."

Nobody speaks.

The air seems to drain out of the station. Even the tunnel goes quiet, as though the city above has been unplugged.

Priya swallows. "Okay. So it's a team-building exercise from hell."

"Third rule," the voice says. "Do not, under any circumstances, open a door with the words in red… WRONG WAY."

On the wall behind them, the departure screen flickers.

NO DELAYS disappears.

A new message appears in yellow-green letters.

STAY TOGETHER

Then:

BEGIN

The platform lights snap brighter.

Not all of them. Just the ones at the far end.

They illuminate a section of wall Lena would swear wasn't there before. An old service corridor opens between two support columns, framed by cracked tile and rusted metal trim. A red sign above it reads AUTHORIZED PERSONNEL ONLY, though someone has scratched the word PERSONNEL until it looks more like PERSON.

Theo stares at it. "That's new."

Priya points at the seamless wall where the stairs should be. "Everything's new, Theo. Reality's renovating without permits."

Lena starts toward the corridor.

Theo grabs her sleeve.

She spins on him. "Don't."

"Don't what? Stop you from walking into the murder hallway?"

"We need to move."

"We need to think."

"I'm thinking faster than you."

His eyes harden. "That a fact?"

Jalen steps between them, palms up, camera swinging from his neck. "Guys. The creepy voice literally just said stay together. Maybe we don't start with a workplace dispute."

Priya lifts a finger. "He's right. I hate that he's right, but the scared kid with the camera has the floor."

"I'm not a kid," Jalen says.

"You're right. Sorry. The terrified young adult with the camera."

"Better. Still rude."

The speakers hum.

"Warm," says the voice.

All four freeze.

Lena turns toward the service corridor.

The voice says nothing else.

Priya's eyes sharpen. "Oh. It's playing hot and cold."

"Lovely," Theo mutters. "The subway's possessed by a kindergarten teacher."

"Warm means we're near something," Priya says.

"Near what?"

"A clue, probably. Or a trap pretending to be a clue. Or a clue inside a trap. The genre's flexible."

Lena looks back at the corridor. The walls inside sweat black water. A thin strip of fluorescent light buzzes overhead, stuttering just enough to make the passage seem to breathe.

"We go together," Lena says. "Slowly."

Theo lets go of her sleeve. "Fine. But you don't run ahead."

"I wasn't going to."

"You absolutely were."

She doesn't answer because he's right.

They enter the corridor in a crooked line, none of them wanting to be first but all of them wanting to get away from the platform. Lena takes the lead because she understands tunnels. Theo follows close enough that his bootsteps keep brushing hers. Priya walks behind him, eyes scanning pipes, screws, peeling paint, anything that might hide a mechanism. Jalen brings up the rear and keeps looking back.

After twenty feet, the death metal fades in again.

Not loud this time. Low. Grinding. A distant engine made of guitars.

"Do you think the music matters?" Jalen asks.

Priya says, "Everything matters. That's the problem."

The corridor bends left.

Then left again.

Lena stops.

Theo bumps into her. "What?"

"This shouldn't fit."

"Meaning?"

"Meaning this corridor turns back under the platform."

"So?"

"So we should be seeing the track access gate. Or a pump room. Or a wall. Not this."

Ahead, the corridor stretches farther than it should. Twenty yards. Maybe thirty. The emergency lights continue down it in a red dotted line.

At the far end stands a vending machine.

It glows blue-white in the dark.

Jalen laughs under his breath. "No. Nope. That's worse than a monster."

The machine is old, with a scratched plastic front and rows of snacks that look sun-bleached and wrong. Candy bars without labels. Water bottles filled with something cloudy. A slot for coins. A card reader. A keypad.

Across the glass, written in black marker, are four words:

FEED ME ONE SECRET

Priya moves closer. "That's charming."

Theo says, "Don't touch it."

"I'm looking."

"People say that right before they touch it."

Lena studies the machine. "The voice said warm."

The PA above them crackles.

"Warmer."

Priya smiles tightly. "See? Vending machine of emotional damage is definitely important."

Theo folds his arms. "So what? It wants us to confess?"

Lena looks at the keypad. The buttons have letters as well as numbers, like an old phone. "Maybe we type something in."

"Or maybe we don't play," Theo says.

The lights behind them shut off.

One by one.

Red bulbs pop into darkness down the corridor they came from.

Jalen turns. "Uh."

The dark creeps closer in sections, each light dying with a small electric tick.

Priya's voice drops. "We play."

Theo pounds a fist against the vending machine glass. "Hey! Conductor! What's the clue?"

The speakers hiss.

"Cold," says the Conductor.

Theo looks up, furious. "Excuse me?"

Priya points at him. "That's not how hot and cold works, big guy. It's telling you violence is the wrong answer."

"Wonderful. The murder station has manners."

The darkness reaches the bend behind them.

Lena steps to the keypad. "One secret. It says one secret. Maybe one of us enters something."

The lights flicker.

"Colder," says the Conductor.

Lena pulls her hand back.

Priya tilts her head. "Not one of us. One secret from all of us?"

Jalen hugs his backpack strap. "I don't wanna do that."

"Nobody wants to do that," Priya says. "That's why it's a challenge."

Theo shakes his head. "I'm not telling a vending machine my private business."

The light nearest them dies.

Now there's only the vending machine glow and three red bulbs overhead.

Lena exhales. "The rule says one for all, all for one."

Priya nods. "A shared secret."

"No," Theo says immediately.

Lena looks at him. "You don't even know what I'm going to say."

"I know I don't like it."

"We need a secret that belongs to all four of us."

"We met five minutes ago."

"Then we make one," Priya says.

Jalen looks at her. "What?"

Priya's face has gone very still. Her game-designer brain is moving fast now, maybe too fast. "A secret doesn't have to be old. It just has to be hidden. We choose something all four of us agree not to say out loud again."

The Conductor says, "Warm."

Theo stares up at the speaker. "I hate that you're encouraging her."

Lena steps closer to the vending machine. "What secret?"

Priya looks at each of them. "We're scared."

Jalen blinks. "That's not a secret."

"It is if we've all been pretending otherwise."

For a second, none of them speaks.

The music gets lower. Slower. The drums thud like a heartbeat under concrete.

Lena's jaw tightens. "Fine."

Theo looks away.

Priya says, "Say it."

Lena glances at the darkness behind them. "I'm scared."

The vending machine hums.

Priya nods once. "I'm scared."

Jalen's voice cracks. "I'm really scared."

Theo doesn't say anything.

The last red bulb before the vending machine flickers.

"Theo," Lena says.

He glares at the glass. His reflection glares back, warped and huge.

"I'm not doing confession circle."

The bulb flickers harder.

Jalen whispers, "Please."

That does it. Not Lena. Not Priya. Jalen.

Theo's shoulders drop half an inch.

"I'm scared," he says, the words rough as gravel. "Happy?"

The vending machine dings.

A candy coil turns.

Something drops into the retrieval tray with a heavy metallic clunk.

Priya reaches for it.

Theo catches her wrist. "Slowly."

She gives him a look. "See? Teamwork. Hate it already."

She pulls open the plastic flap and takes out a brass token the size of a poker chip. One side shows a train tunnel. The other side has an engraved number:

4

Under it, in tiny letters:

NOT ONE LESS

The corridor lights blaze back to life.

Then all four of them scream.

Lena drops first, clutching her hand.

Theo swears and stumbles into the vending machine. Priya doubles over. Jalen falls against the wall, camera cracking against the tile.

A line opens across Lena's left palm.

Not a scratch. A clean, deep slice, as if an invisible blade has drawn itself through her skin.

Blood wells.

At the same moment, Theo's palm splits. Priya's palm splits. Jalen's palm splits.

Same place.

Same length.

Same blood.

Jalen makes a small, panicked sound. "No, no, no…"

Theo grabs his own wrist and stares at the cut. "What did you do?"

Lena looks at him, pain bright in her eyes. "I didn't do anything."

The PA clicks.

"One for all," the Conductor says.

Priya breathes through her teeth, staring at her bleeding hand. "All for one."

Theo turns in a circle, looking for a camera, a person, anything he can hurt. "Show yourself!"

The death metal slams on full blast.

This time the vocals are clearer.

Not words.

Laughter.

Or something close enough.

Lena wraps her bleeding palm with the scarf from her neck and keeps moving because stopping feels like accepting the station's terms.

Theo tears a strip from the bottom of his shirt and ties it around Jalen's hand first. Not his own. Jalen notices. Priya notices too, though she says nothing because she's busy trying not to pass out.

The corridor ahead of them flickers between red and white. With every pulse of light, the vending machine behind them seems farther away than it should. Ten feet. Twenty. Fifty. Then gone completely, swallowed by a bend that wasn't there a second ago.

"Everybody good?" Theo asks.

Priya laughs through clenched teeth. "That's adorable."

"I mean, can everybody walk?"

Lena flexes her fingers and immediately regrets it. "Yes."

Jalen nods, though his eyes are wet. "Yeah."

The music fades again, dropping into a low distorted churn under the PA static.

"Proceed," says the Conductor.

Priya looks up. "Can we request something softer? Jazz? Elevator music? The sound of you dying in an electrical fire?"

The speakers crackle.

"Cold."

She points upward. "Rude."

Lena leads them deeper into the service corridor. She wants to understand the geometry, but the station keeps refusing to be a station. Pipes run into walls and come out of ceilings. Exit signs point down. Fluorescent tubes buzz behind tile instead of overhead.

They pass three identical posters for a missing woman named Diana Rook, each poster older than the last.

In the first, Diana is twenty-eight.

In the second, her face is faded and her smile is nearly gone.

In the third, someone has scratched out her eyes.

Jalen stops in front of it.

"Don't," Theo says.

Jalen lifts his camera anyway.

"I need proof," he says.

"Proof for who?" Priya asks.

Jalen doesn't answer.

The flash fires.

The whole corridor goes black.

"Jalen," Lena snaps.

"I'm sorry," he says. "I didn't mean to. It was automatic."

They stand in darkness, breathing too loudly.

Then the photo prints from the bottom of Jalen's camera.

He doesn't own that kind of camera.

He holds it in shaking fingers as the image develops. At first it shows the poster. Then the wall. Then four figures standing in front of it.

Then a fifth.

Behind Theo.

Tall. Thin. Blurred by motion.

Jalen turns with a strangled sound.

There's nothing there.

The PA hums.

"Warm."

Priya leans over the photo. "Nope. Hate that. Deeply hate that."

Lena takes the photo from Jalen carefully. The fifth figure has no face. Its head tilts toward the missing poster, as if it's reading.

Theo looks back down the corridor. "We're not alone."

"We knew that," Priya says.

"No. I mean something's in here with us."

The corridor lights return, but dimmer now.

The fifth figure is no longer in the photograph.

Instead, words appear across the bottom in cramped black letters.

THE ONES WHO LEAVE WALK BEHIND

Jalen's breathing turns thin.

Lena folds the photograph and puts it in her coat pocket. "Nobody leaves."

Theo looks at her. "You don't get to say it like it's easy."

"I didn't say it was easy."

"You sound like it is."

"We don't have time to argue."

Priya gives a sharp little laugh. "Actually, based on the architecture, we might have infinite time to argue."

A door slams somewhere ahead.

All four of them flinch.

The lights at the end of the corridor blink on, revealing a maintenance room with its door hanging open. Above it, another speaker dangles by one wire, swaying though there is no wind.

"Warmer," says the Conductor.

They approach as a group.

Inside the room are four chairs bolted to the floor.

Four metal helmets hang from cables above them.

On the far wall is a square steel door with no handle. Beside it is a panel with four green lights, all dark. Painted above the panel in careful black letters:

ONE MEMORY EACH

Priya takes one step backward. "Absolutely not."

Theo's shoulder bumps hers because he's stepping back too. "No."

Lena studies the helmets. "It's a mental challenge."

"It's a brain blender," Priya says. "I build games. I know a brain blender when I see one."

The Conductor's voice drops from the speaker above them.

"Please be seated."

"No," Theo says.

The steel door on the far wall thumps.

Once.

Then again.

Something behind it drags along the metal.

Jalen backs into Lena. "What's in there?"

The door bulges outward.

Priya whispers, "Something that wants us to waste time."

The door bulges again. Bigger.

Theo grabs one of the chairs and pulls. It doesn't move. "Fine. Sit. Everybody sit. But if this fries my brain, I'm haunting all of you."

They sit.

The helmets descend.

Lena's settles over her head like a cold hand. The metal smells of pennies and old rain. Across from her, Jalen trembles so hard his helmet clicks against the chair back.

"Hold on," Lena says.

"To what?" Priya asks.

Lena reaches out her bandaged hand. Theo takes it. After a second, Priya takes Lena's other hand. Jalen takes Priya's.

The circuit completes.

The room vanishes.

Lena stands on a platform eight years earlier, smelling hot brakes and blood.

A man lies twisted beside the tracks. Transit workers shout. Someone is crying. She sees herself younger, cleaner, holding a clipboard she shouldn't be holding because she knows the crack in the support beam is worse than the report says. She knows the vibration tolerance is bad. She knows the city wants the line reopened before morning.

She signs anyway.

The memory tears.

Now she feels Theo.

Not sees.

Feels.

Cold beer in his hand. Phone ringing. His brother's name on the screen. Theo ignores it because they fought that morning, because he's tired of rescuing a grown man from his own bad choices. The voicemail comes ten minutes later. Screams. Track noise. Then nothing.

Theo's hand crushes Lena's.

The memory rips again.

Priya.

A warehouse escape room. Screams that are supposed to be part of the show. Smoke machine running too hot. A guest coughing behind a locked prop door. Priya at the control desk, staring at a warning light, telling herself the sensor glitches all the time. Telling herself opening the room ruins the experience. Telling herself one more minute.

One more minute is enough.

Then Jalen.

A blackout. Rain. He is nine years old, standing at the top of subway stairs while his father kneels in front of him and says, "Stay here. I'll be right back."

His father smiles like he believes it.

Then he goes down into Ashbury Station with a flashlight in his hand.

He never comes back.

The room returns.

All four of them gasp at once, as if surfacing from dirty water.

The helmets retract.

The green lights on the panel glow one by one.

The steel door behind them stops bulging.

For a moment, no one moves.

Then Priya pulls her hand away from Lena's. "So we're doing involuntary trauma sharing now. Great. Love the intimacy."

Jalen stares at Lena. "You signed off on a bad station?"

Lena's throat tightens. "It wasn't this station."

Theo looks at Priya. "You left somebody locked in?"

Priya's face twists. "She lived."

"That wasn't the question."

She stands too fast. "Don't look at me like that. You ignored your brother."

Theo rises so quickly his chair scrapes the floor.

Lena gets between them. "Stop."

"No," Theo says, voice shaking. "No, she doesn't get to throw that at me."

"You don't get to throw mine either," Priya snaps.

The PA clicks.

"Cold."

Lena looks up. "It wants this."

Theo's breathing is heavy. Priya's eyes are bright with tears she clearly hates. Jalen has gone quiet in the corner, folding into himself.

"The memories are bait," Lena says. "It showed us the worst thing and waited for us to do the rest."

Theo stares at Priya.

Priya stares back.

Then she says, smaller, "I'm sorry."

Theo's jaw works. "Yeah."

"I mean it."

"I know."

The steel door on the far wall slides open.

Beyond it waits a stairwell.

Not upward.

Down.

Jalen gives a bitter little laugh. "Of course."

They descend together.

The stairs narrow as they go. At first, they can walk two abreast. Then single file. Then shoulder-turned, bodies brushing tile on both sides. The walls sweat. The music grows louder beneath them, not from the PA now but from below, like a band is playing somewhere deep underground for an audience of worms.

Halfway down, the stairs split.

Left and right.

Two identical tunnels.

Between them stands a sign.

FOUR MAY ENTER
TWO LEFT
TWO RIGHT

Theo reads it and shakes his head. "No."

Priya exhales. "It's forcing a split."

Lena steps closer to the sign.

The PA whispers from a tiny speaker in the ceiling.

"Warm."

"No," Lena says.

The sign changes.

TWO LEFT
TWO RIGHT
OR THE BOY STOPS BREATHING

Jalen touches his throat.

At first, he only looks confused.

Then he chokes.

Theo grabs him as Jalen doubles over, clawing at his own neck. Lena feels it a second later, a tightening around her windpipe. Priya coughs. Theo's face purples.

"All for one," the Conductor says softly.

Lena staggers toward the left tunnel, dragging Jalen with her. The choking eases a fraction.

"Warmer."

Theo points right while coughing. "It wants two and two."

Priya's eyes water. "Rule one says stay together."

The pressure clamps down harder.

Jalen drops to one knee.

Lena looks at the two tunnels. There has to be something. A seam. A trick. The sign says two left, two right because the maze wants them thinking in corridors. It wants compliance. It wants them to forget the words that matter.

Stay together.

She looks down.

The floor between the tunnels is painted black, a triangular wedge of concrete where the sign is bolted.

"Lena?" Theo rasps.

She grabs the sign pole with both hands and pulls. "Help me."

Theo understands. He wraps his big hands over hers and yanks.

The pole doesn't move.

Priya sees it then. "Together. All of us."

Jalen, still choking, crawls forward and gets one hand on the pole. Priya adds hers.

Four bodies. One pull.

The pole gives with a wet, rootlike sound.

The sign tears from the floor.

Beneath it is a narrow hatch.

The choking stops.

The PA says nothing.

Theo coughs hard, then laughs once. "That's right, you piece of shit."

The Conductor answers.

"Hot."

They open the hatch.

A ladder drops into darkness.

At the bottom is another platform.

Not Ashbury. Not any station Lena knows. The walls are raw concrete. The tracks are missing. Instead, two trenches run where rails should be, filled with dark water that reflects lights no one can see.

The music is deafening here. It pumps through massive old speakers bolted to the walls. The sound is physical. It pushes at their chests, rattles teeth, turns thought into sludge. The water trembles with it.

At the far end of the platform is a turnstile.

One turnstile.

Beside it sits a glass booth.

Inside the booth is a transit worker in a blue uniform.

He sits with his back to them.

Jalen stops breathing for a different reason.

"Dad?" he says.

The worker slowly turns.

His face is wrong in the way old wax is wrong. Familiar features softened, melted, almost remembered. He's got Jalen's eyes. Or something wearing them.

Jalen takes a step forward.

Lena grabs his jacket. "No."

The thing in the booth smiles.

"Jay," it says through the booth speaker, voice warm and cracked and human. "You got so tall."

Jalen makes a wounded sound.

Theo moves beside him. "That isn't him."

"You don't know that."

"Yes, I do."

Jalen tries to pull free. "You don't."

The Conductor cuts through the music.

"Challenge three. One ticket. Four passengers."

The booth drawer slides open.

Inside is a single black ticket.

Lena can see red lettering on it from where she stands.

ADMIT ONE

Priya wipes tears and sweat from her face. "No. No, we don't take that."

The thing wearing Jalen's father looks at him. "I can get you out. Only you. That's all I can do."

Jalen shakes his head. "Where did you go?"

The thing's smile trembles. "I got lost."

That lands harder than any scream could have.

Jalen's face crumples. He is nineteen and nine years old at the same time.

The booth speaker crackles.

"You stayed," the thing says. "Good boy."

Jalen pulls against Lena. "Let me talk to him."

Lena holds on. "He wants you alone."

"I said let me go."

Theo steps in front of him. "No."

Jalen shoves him. "Get out of my way."

The shove isn't hard, but Theo's temper is already stripped down to bare wire. He grabs Jalen by the shoulders and pushes him back.

Jalen slips.

His heel hits the platform edge.

For one horrible second, he windmills.

Then he falls into the trench.

The dark water takes him with a slap.

All three of them scream his name.

And all three feel the cold.

It swallows them from the feet up. Lena collapses, her lungs locking as black water fills her mouth though she is still on the platform. Priya drops beside her, gagging. Theo goes to his knees, eyes bulging.

In the trench, Jalen thrashes like a feeding shark.

Something under the water pulls him down.

Theo lunges flat on his stomach and plunges both arms into the trench. "Grab me!"

Jalen's fingers break the surface.

Theo catches him.

The moment he does, Lena can breathe again. Priya vomits water onto dry concrete. Theo roars and hauls Jalen up with both arms, dragging him onto the platform.

Jalen comes out with something wrapped around his leg.

A hand.

Gray. Long-fingered. Human enough to be obscene.

Theo stomps it.

The fingers snap.

A scream rises from every speaker at once.

Not death metal. Not the Conductor.

A real scream.

The hand releases.

Priya grabs the black ticket from the booth drawer, crumples it, and shoves it into the mouth slot of the booth speaker. "Admit that, asshole."

The glass booth lights burst.

When the dark clears, the worker is gone.

So is the ticket.

The turnstile unlocks.

Lena helps Jalen stand. He's soaked, shaking, lips blue. Theo won't look at him.

Jalen looks at Theo anyway. "You saved me."

Theo's voice is hoarse. "I almost knocked you in."

"But you didn't leave me."

Theo nods once, like it costs him.

They pass through the turnstile together, awkwardly, all four squeezing through one metal cage while the bars clack against their hips and shoulders.

The next room is white tile.

Hospital white.

Too clean. Scrubbed, gleaming, wrong.

At the center is a door.

On the door, in red letters, are the words:

WRONG WAY

Everybody stops.

The Conductor speaks at once.

"Cold."

Priya laughs weakly. "For once, we agree."

They back away.

The room changes.

Another door appears behind them.

Same shape. Same size.

White letters this time.

WRONG WAY

The music dies completely.

The silence is immense.

Lena looks from the red-letter door to the white-letter door.

Jalen whispers, "Rule three said red."

Theo says, "It said don't open a door with the words in red WRONG WAY."

Priya's eyes are fixed on the white letters. "These aren't red."

"Could still be a trick," Theo says.

"It's definitely a trick," Priya says. "The question is what kind."

The Conductor says, "Warm."

Lena's skin prickles.

Theo points at the red-letter door. "That one is cold, right? So this one's the clue."

"Or it wants us to think exact wording matters," Priya says. "Game masters love exact wording. Evil ones love it more."

Jalen hugs himself, still dripping. "What happens if we stay?"

Nobody answers.

The room's ceiling lowers an inch.

A soft grinding sound fills the tile chamber.

Theo looks up. "That answers that."

Lena studies the white-letter door. There is no handle. Just four circular depressions in the tile at chest height.

Hands.

Four hands.

"Of course," Priya says.

Lena lifts her bandaged palm. Blood has soaked through the scarf. "One for all."

Theo flexes his cut hand.

"All for one," he says.

Jalen steps closer but doesn't touch the door. "Wait."

The ceiling lowers another inch.

"What?" Lena asks.

Jalen points at the letters.

The words are white, but the grooves around them are wet. Not paint. Condensation, maybe. Or something thicker.

He leans in, squinting.

"No," Lena says. "Don't get too close."

"They're not painted white," Jalen says. "They're covered."

Priya moves beside him. "Covered with what?"

Jalen wipes one letter with the edge of his sleeve.

The white smears away.

Under it is red.

Priya goes still.

Theo whispers, "Son of a bitch."

The Conductor says, very softly, "Warmer."

Lena feels the room tilt. "It wanted us to clean it."

The ceiling drops another inch. Faster now.

Jalen backs away from the door. "So what do we do?"

The red-letter door remains behind them, waiting like an obvious death.

The white-letter door is no longer white where Jalen touched it. One red streak shines through.

Priya starts pacing. "If the words are in red underneath, is it already a red WRONG WAY door? Or only if we expose it? Is color about appearance or truth?"

Theo slams his fist against the wall. "Stop playing lawyer with paint."

"I'm trying to keep us alive."

The ceiling drops again.

Lena stares at the four handprints. Something is wrong. The handprints aren't on the white-letter door. They're on the wall beside it.

No.

Not beside it.

Between the two doors.

Four depressions in the tile.

She steps backward until she can see both doors at once.

"Not the doors," she says.

Priya stops pacing. "What?"

"The clue isn't either door."

The Conductor says, "Cold."

Lena smiles, and there is no humor in it. "Liar."

The PA hisses.

Theo looks at her. "Lena."

"Both doors are wrong. The red one breaks the rule. The white one becomes red when touched. It's a false choice."

The ceiling drops faster. Tile dust rains down.

Jalen points to the four depressions. "Then what're those?"

Lena presses her injured palm into one.

Pain flashes.

The wall groans.

"Hot," says the Conductor.

Theo, Priya, and Jalen move at once.

Their palms hit the remaining depressions.

The wall between the doors splits open.

Not a door. A seam.

A narrow gap appears, black and breathing cold air.

The ceiling stops six inches above Theo's head.

The Conductor does not speak.

For the first time, it feels surprised.

They slip through the gap together.

On the other side is Ashbury Station.

The real platform.

Maybe.

The stairs are back. The departure board glows. Ads peel on the walls. A train waits with its doors open, interior lights humming.

For one beautiful second, none of them moves.

Then Priya says, "No. Too easy."

The PA crackles.

No death metal.

No static.

Just the voice, calm as ever.

"Final transfer."

The train doors chime.

Lena looks down the platform.

Dozens of people stand there.

Silent.

Motionless.

A woman with scratched-out eyes from the missing poster. A transit worker with melted features. A man in a torn suit with both hands bandaged. A little girl holding a brass token. More behind them. Too many. All watching.

Jalen whispers, "They failed."

The people open their mouths at the same time.

The Conductor's voice comes from all of them.

"Boarding now."

Theo backs up. "No."

The stairs behind them seal with white tile.

Priya makes a sound somewhere between a laugh and a sob. "Of course."

The train waits.

Inside, there are four empty seats.

Above them, a sign reads:

NOT ONE LESS

Lena understands then, not completely, but enough.

Ashbury doesn't only trap people.

It tests them.

Breaks them.

Sorts them.

The ones who split become the things in the tunnels. The ones who leave someone behind walk behind the living forever. The ones who fail together become the platform crowd, standing with open mouths, speaking in the Conductor's voice.

And the ones who keep surviving?

Maybe they get promoted.

Maybe that's the worst thing here.

The Conductor says, "Please board."

Theo looks at the watching crowd. "And if we don't?"

The music returns, low at first.

The crowd steps forward.

One step.

Then another.

Their mouths hang open, pouring out guitar noise, drum noise, throat-shredded vocals. The sound comes from them now, from the failed passengers, from the dead, from the station's collected choir.

Priya grabs Jalen's sleeve. Lena grabs Priya. Theo stays close.

Together, they back toward the train.

"I don't like this," Jalen says.

"No one likes this," Priya says.

Lena looks into the train car. The seats are plastic blue. The floor is dirty. The route map above the doors shows no stops. Just a black line running in a circle.

The crowd keeps coming.

Theo says, "We get on together. We get off together."

"What if it doesn't stop?" Jalen asks.

Theo looks at him. "Then we make it."

They board.

The doors close.

The crowd stops inches from the glass.

Every face turns toward Lena.

The train starts moving.

It pulls away from Ashbury Station without a sound.

For a moment, there's only the sway of the car, the hum of lights, their own ragged breathing. Lena grips the pole with her wounded hand. Priya sits with her elbows on her knees. Jalen shivers violently. Theo stands by the doors like he can fight the train if it changes its mind.

The route map flickers.

A new station name appears.

WRONG WAY

Priya closes her eyes. "No."

The train slows.

The doors open.

Not onto a platform.

Onto a small room.

White tile.

Two doors.

One says WRONG WAY in red.

One says WRONG WAY in white.

Jalen starts to cry. Quietly. Helplessly.

Theo turns toward the ceiling. "You said final transfer!"

The PA inside the train clicks.

The Conductor's voice is almost gentle.

"Cold."

Lena looks at the room. Then at the doors. Then at the wall between them.

There are no handprints this time.

No seam.

No clue.

The train doors begin to close.

Priya looks up sharply. "Wait."

Too late.

The doors shut.

The train moves again.

The map flickers.

Another station appears.

ASHBURY

Lena's stomach drops.

They haven't escaped.

They haven't even left.

The train glides through darkness. In the window opposite her, Lena sees their reflections.

Four of them.

Then five.

The fifth stands behind Jalen, tall and thin, face blurred by motion. Its head tilts toward Lena's pocket.

The photograph.

Lena reaches into her coat and pulls it out.

The folded picture is wet.

She opens it.

The fifth figure is back. This time it stands between the four of them, one long hand resting on each shoulder at once.

At the bottom, new words appear.

THE ONES WHO STAY ARE TAUGHT TO CONDUCT

Jalen looks at Lena. "What does that mean?"

She doesn't answer.

She's looking at the glass.

At her own reflection.

At Priya's.

At Theo's.

At Jalen's.

Their mouths are closed.

But in the reflection, their mouths begin to open.

Not screaming.

Announcing.

The PA crackles before any of them can speak.

The Conductor says, "Sizzling."

The train plunges into black.

And somewhere ahead, from every speaker in the dark, the music starts again.

The Last Page Changes

Silas Reddy finds the manuscript in a thrift store bin between a stained cookbook and a VHS copy of Sleepless in Seattle with no tape inside.

It has no title.

No author.

Just a stack of cream-colored pages bound with black thread, the kind of thread that looks too deliberate to be homemade and too ugly to be professional. The cover is blank except for a thumbprint near the bottom corner. Brownish. Old. Maybe coffee. Maybe something else.

Silas picks it up because writers are scavengers by nature, even the failed ones. Especially the failed ones. What's unique gives value.

He turns it over. Nothing on the back. No price sticker. No barcode. No charming handwritten note from a dead grandmother. Just paper, thread, and that strange little stain.

"Two dollars," Dottie Murn says from behind the counter.

Silas looks up.

Dottie is tiny and ancient and aggressively floral. Her blouse is pink with yellow flowers. Her lipstick sits slightly outside the lines of her mouth, like it's trying to leave without her. She watches him over a pair of glasses so thick her eyes look underwater.

"There's no tag," Silas says.

"Two dollars," she repeats.

"For blank paper?"

"It's not blank."

He looks at the cover again, then flips it open.

The first page has one sentence typed in the center.

Silas Reddy finds the manuscript in a thrift store bin between a stained cookbook and a VHS copy of Sleepless in Seattle with no tape inside.

His thumb tightens on the page.

For a second, all the noise in the shop drops out. The buzzing fluorescent lights. The rain ticking against the front windows. The distant clatter of someone sorting cheap dishes in the back aisle. Everything goes thin and far away.

Then it all rushes back.

He laughs once.

It comes out wrong.

"Cute," he says.

Dottie smiles at him like she's just watched him step into traffic.

Silas flips to the next page.

It has no title.

He flips again.

No author.

Again.

Just a stack of cream-colored pages bound with black thread, the kind of thread that looks too deliberate to be homemade and too ugly to be professional.

His mouth goes dry.

Someone is screwing with him. That's the obvious answer. The only answer that doesn't require medication, faith, or a complete rethinking of physics.

He looks around the thrift store.

There's an old man trying on a leather jacket near the mirrors. A teenage girl kneels by a crate of records. A woman with wet hair studies chipped mugs like one of them might confess something. Nobody looks at him. Nobody snickers. Nobody holds up a phone.

Silas turns back to Dottie.

"Where did this come from?"

She blinks. "What?"

"This." He lifts the manuscript. "Who donated it?"

Dottie's smile fades into confusion so fast it looks practiced.

"I don't know, honey. People bring things."

"You just priced it."

"Did I?"

Silas stares at her.

Dottie stares back, polite and empty.

Then she leans forward slightly and whispers, "Are you the one it picked?"

The words settle between them like dust.

Silas says, "What?"

Dottie's face clears. "Two dollars."

"You just said something."

"I said two dollars."

"No. Before that."

Her eyes drift to the manuscript. Then to his hands. For one cracked second, fear shows through the powder and lipstick and sweet-old-lady routine.

Then it's gone.

"Cash or card?"

Silas almost leaves it there.

He tells himself that later.

He almost walks out into the rain, gets on the bus, goes home to his lousy apartment and his unpaid electric bill and his laptop full of unfinished documents named things like new book final and new book final final and actually this one and super notes for final final. He almost lets the manuscript stay in the bin where impossible things belong.

Instead, he pays two dollars.

Dottie slides the receipt across the counter without touching his hand.

Outside, rain freckles the sidewalk. Traffic hisses by. The city looks ordinary, gray, bored with itself.

Silas tucks the manuscript under his jacket.

By the time he reaches the bus stop, the last page has changed.

The bus is late.

Of course it is.

The city doesn't care that Silas has a blank, changing manuscript under his jacket. The city has schedules to ignore. Rain to spill. People to disappoint in bulk.

He stands beneath the cracked plexiglass shelter with the book pressed flat against his ribs, feeling ridiculous for protecting it from the rain. A normal person would throw the thing in the gutter. A saner person would march back inside and demand an explanation from Dottie Murn, who probably won't remember him five minutes from now.

Silas does neither.

He waits.

The pages feel warm.

That bothers him more than the first sentence. More than his name appearing in black type. A prank can explain his name. A hidden camera can explain the setup. Someone from the bookstore. Someone who knows he works among used books and dead authors and moldy ambition. Someone who thinks this is funny.

Warm paper is harder.

He pulls the manuscript out just enough to look at it.

Rain taps the shelter roof. A bus growls past on the opposite side of the street, throwing dirty water against the curb. The other person waiting with him, a man in a blue poncho, doesn't look up from his phone.

Silas opens to the back.

The last page is no longer blank.

There's a single typed sentence near the bottom.

By the time he reaches the bus stop, the last page has changed.

Silas closes it so fast the pages slap.

The man in the poncho glances over.

"You good?" he asks.

"Yeah," Silas says.

The man looks at the manuscript. "School?"

"Something like that."

The man nods, because people will accept any answer that doesn't require them to get involved.

Silas opens the manuscript again, slower this time.

The sentence is still there.

He turns to the page before it. Blank. The page before that. Blank. Fifty or sixty blank pages, maybe more. He riffles forward, then backward. Most of it remains empty except for the first few pages describing him finding the thing and the final page describing what just happened.

Not predicting.

Describing.

That distinction matters for exactly three seconds before he hates himself for thinking like a workshop instructor.

The bus pulls up with a wet sigh.

Silas gets on. Pays. Finds a seat near the back, because the back is where you sit when you don't want strangers making decisions about your face. And it limits eye contact.

The bus smells like damp coats, old fries, and somebody's citrus hand sanitizer fighting a losing war. Silas keeps the manuscript on his lap and his hand on the cover.

He shouldn't read more.

So he reads more.

The first pages are the same. The thrift store. Dottie. The line about writers being scavengers. He hates that line. It's the kind of sentence he'd admire if someone else wrote it and resent if someone said it about him.

He flips to the last page again.

There's more now.

Silas Reddy sits near the back of the bus with the manuscript on his lap and his hand on the cover. He tells himself he shouldn't read more. So he reads more.

His stomach drops.

The bus lurches forward.

A woman across the aisle curses under her breath as coffee spills onto her jeans. A baby starts crying near the front. The man in the blue poncho gets on after him and stands by the rear door, dripping.

Silas stares at the page until the letters blur.

Then, beneath the paragraph, a new line appears.

Not suddenly.

Not with a flash or a flourish.

It types itself into existence one letter at a time, black ink pressing up from the fibers of the page like blood rising under skin.

At the next stop, the woman in the yellow coat gets on.

Silas looks up.

The next stop is half a block away.

"No," he whispers.

The bus slows.

Outside, rain turns the windows silver. Shapes wait beneath umbrellas. A man with groceries. A student with a backpack. Someone smoking under the bus sign.

And there, standing perfectly still in the rain, is a woman in a yellow coat.

The bus doors fold open.

The woman in the yellow coat steps inside.

Silas stops breathing for a second. Not dramatically. Not like in movies where someone clutches their throat and stares wild-eyed at God. His body simply forgets the procedure. Air becomes optional. His ribs lock.

She pays in coins.

One after another drops through the slot.

Clink.

Clink.

Clink.

That's what gets him.

Not the coat. Not the timing. Not the sentence sitting black and smug on the last page.

The coins.

One by one, dropped into the slot with soft metallic clicks, as if impossible things still need bus fare.

She's maybe forty. Maybe older. Her hair is tucked beneath a green scarf. Her face is pale and narrow, with rain clinging to the fine lines beside her mouth. The yellow coat isn't bright. It's mustard, worn at the cuffs, belted tight around her waist. Practical. Ugly. Real.

She walks down the aisle.

Silas lowers his head.

Don't sit here.

She sits across from him.

Of course she does.

The bus pulls away from the curb.

Silas stares at the manuscript like he can threaten it by looking hard enough. The page doesn't change. It doesn't need to. It has made its point.

The woman in the yellow coat looks out the window. Her hands rest folded over a black purse. Her fingernails are bitten down too far.

Silas waits for her to speak.

She doesn't.

That almost makes it worse.

He turns back one page. Blank. Another. Blank. He flips forward again, more pages than the manuscript should hold, cream paper slipping beneath his thumb. The last page remains the last page no matter how many pages come before it.

That's a cute trick.

He hates that he thinks that.

The bus hits a pothole. His teeth click together.

The manuscript shifts on his lap and opens itself.

Not much.

Just enough.

A middle page, not the beginning, not the end. Text sits there in neat typed blocks.

Silas hasn't seen this page before.

He doesn't want to read it.

He reads it.

The woman in the yellow coat will not speak first. She has learned not to. She once asked a man whether he liked endings, and he screamed until the driver stopped the bus.

Silas swallows.

She clutches that black purse. Inside the purse is a library card with no name on it, seven expired receipts, a house key that opens no house left standing, and a folded page torn from a manuscript she burned six years ago.

Across the aisle, the woman's fingers tighten on the purse.

Silas looks at her.

She's already looking at him.

Her eyes are gray. Not soft gray. Not poetic gray. Concrete gray. Basement gray. Gray like an overcast winter day.

"You shouldn't have bought it," she says.

His mouth opens, but nothing useful comes out.

The man in the blue poncho glances up from his phone.

Silas leans forward. "What is this?"

The woman's smile is small and sad. "You're still asking the wrong question."

"Great. That's helpful."

"It doesn't like sarcasm."

"The manuscript?"

She flinches.

Silas notices.

So does the page.

A fresh sentence appears beneath the paragraph.

She flinches when he names it because names are handles, and handles are how doors open.

The woman's face changes.

"Close it," she says.

Silas does.

Fast.

The bus keeps moving. The baby keeps crying. Rain keeps smearing the windows. Normal life, stubborn and stupid, refuses to stop for the supernatural.

Silas presses his palm flat against the cover.

"What's your name?" he asks.

She laughs under her breath.

"No," she says. "Absolutely not."

"Why?"

"Because then it gets to use me properly."

"That's insane."

"Yes," she says. "That's usually how people describe insane things."

Silas looks down at the blank cover.

His own reflection shows faintly in the dark wet shine of the thread. Tired eyes. Unshaved jaw. The face of a man trying to decide whether he's terrified or insulted.

The woman stands before the bus reaches the next stop.

"You need to get rid of it before it reaches the ending."

"What ending?"

She grips the pole.

"The one where it doesn't need you anymore."

The bell dings.

The bus sighs against the curb.

She steps toward the rear door, then stops beside him.

Without looking down, she whispers, "Don't take it home."

Then she gets off into the rain.

Silas watches her yellow coat vanish behind a passing truck.

When he opens the manuscript again, the last page has changed.

Silas takes it home anyway.

Silas does take it home.

Not because he's brave.

Not because he's stupid, either, though the distinction feels thinner by the minute.

He takes it home because the bus is already turning onto Marrow Street, because his apartment is three blocks away, because rain leaks through the left shoulder seam of his jacket, because fear doesn't cancel rent, habit, or the gravitational pull of a locked door you pay too much for.

He tells himself he'll put the manuscript in the oven.

Not turn the oven on. That'd be dramatic.

Just put it somewhere contained until he can think.

Maybe call someone.

Maybe not.

Who does a person call for this? Police? Priest? Psychiatrist? Literary agent?

He almost laughs at that, but the sound dies in his throat because the manuscript shifts under his jacket, nudging once against his ribs like a sleeping animal.

"Don't," he mutters.

The bus driver glances at him in the mirror.

Silas gets off at Marrow and Ninth.

Rain hits him sideways. The city is all wet pavement, smeared headlights, brick walls slick as organs. He keeps one hand inside his jacket, gripping the manuscript against his chest. Every step toward his building feels like agreement.

His apartment building waits at the end of the block, six stories of stained beige concrete and balconies nobody uses except to store dead plants. The front door sticks. It always does. Silas yanks it twice before it gives.

Inside, the lobby smells like wet carpet and old onions.

The elevator is broken.

Again.

Of course.

Silas takes the stairs.

By the third floor, he's breathing hard. By the fourth, he's angry at himself for breathing hard. By the fifth, he hears someone crying.

He stops.

The sound comes from above.

Soft. Female. Choked off like someone trying to swallow it.

"Nina?" he calls.

The crying stops.

Silas stands on the landing, rain dripping from his hair onto the floor. His hand tightens around the manuscript.

No answer.

He climbs the last flight slower.

The sixth-floor hallway flickers under weak fluorescent tubes. Apartment doors line both sides, all painted the same depressing brown. His is 6C. Nina Cho lives across from him in 6D.

Her door is cracked open.

That's wrong.

Nina works nights at Saint Orison. She leaves at six-thirty, comes home around seven in the morning, and complains loudly enough for the entire floor to know when the hospital cafeteria runs out of decent coffee.

It's barely five.

"Nina?"

No answer.

Silas steps closer.

The manuscript under his jacket grows hot.

Not warm.

Hot.

He pulls it free with a hiss and nearly drops it. The black thread binding looks damp now. Not from rain. Something darker beads along the spine.

The pages flutter open in his hands.

Not to the last page.

To a new one.

Nina Cho's door is cracked open because Silas needs a witness. A witness makes the scene harder to deny. A witness gives terror another mouth.

"Fuck you," Silas whispers.

From inside Nina's apartment, a voice says, "Silas?"

It's Nina.

He exhales.

Then she says, "Why are you already in here?"

His skin goes cold.

Silas looks at the open door.

"I'm not."

A pause.

Floorboards creak inside Nina's apartment.

Then Nina speaks again, lower now. Closer to the door.

"You're standing in my kitchen."

Silas backs away from the threshold.

"I'm in the hall."

"No," Nina says.

Her voice trembles.

"You're in my kitchen, and you're reading out loud."

Silas doesn't move.

For a second, he can't.

The hallway flickers around him. The manuscript lies open in his hands. Nina's voice hangs between the door and his skull, and somewhere inside her apartment, floorboards creak again.

Not near the kitchen now.

Closer.

Silas looks down at the page.

The manuscript adds a line.

He will want to run. This is natural. This is also useless.

"Silas?" Nina whispers from inside. "Say something."

"I'm in the hall," he says.

"You're not."

"I'm looking at your door."

"You're looking at me."

"No, I'm not."

"Yes, you are." Her breathing turns ragged. "Your mouth is moving, but it's not your voice."

Silas stares at the narrow black gap between Nina's door and frame.

"What's it saying?"

Nina doesn't answer.

"Nina."

"I don't know," she says. "It's… I don't know. It sounds like reading, but the words are wrong."

The page warms beneath his thumb.

A new paragraph appears.

Nina Cho stands barefoot behind her kitchen island with a paring knife in her right hand and her phone in her left. Her scrubs are damp at the collar because she showered ten minutes ago. She smells like hospital soap and panic. She can see Silas Reddy near the sink. He doesn't look wet from the rain. He doesn't blink. He reads from pages that aren't there.

Silas's knees go soft.

Inside Nina's apartment, something laughs.

It's his laugh.

Not perfectly. That makes it worse. It's his laugh with the human part sanded down. His laugh being remembered by someone who doesn't understand humor.

Nina makes a small broken sound.

Silas steps toward the door.

The manuscript snaps shut on his fingers.

Pain bursts through his hand.

"Shit!"

He jerks back, but the pages clamp harder, biting down between his knuckles. Not paper now. Teeth would make more sense than this. Teeth would be honest. This is pressure, intention, a book deciding to hurt him.

Blood beads along the edges of the pages.

The door to Nina's apartment swings open another inch.

Silas sees part of her living room. A gray couch. A standing lamp. A pile of clean laundry in a basket. Normal things, defenseless things.

Then he sees a shadow move across her back wall.

His shadow.

Tall, thin, head bent as if reading.

"Nina," he says carefully, "come to the door."

"I can't."

"Why not?"

"Because you told me not to."

"I didn't."

"The other you did."

The manuscript releases his fingers.

Silas staggers back against the opposite wall. Blood slides down his hand and drips onto the floor.

The page opens again.

He bleeds because symbols require ink.

"Fuck symbols," Silas says.

Inside Nina's apartment, the other Silas says it at the exact same time.

Same words.

Same rhythm.

Same breath.

Nina screams.

Silas kicks the door open.

It bangs against the inside wall, hard enough to rattle the chain lock still hanging loose.

Nina stands in the kitchen exactly as the manuscript described. Bare feet. Dark hair wet and tucked behind one ear. Navy scrubs. Phone. Knife.

And near the sink stands Silas Reddy.

Dry.

Still.

Smiling faintly.

He holds nothing in his hands, but his eyes move left to right, left to right, as if words are passing in front of them.

Nina looks from one Silas to the other.

"Oh, hell no," she says, voice shaking. "No. No, absolutely not."

The dry Silas turns his head.

Too smoothly.

His smile widens by one careful degree.

"You brought it home," he says.

Silas raises the manuscript without meaning to, like it's proof or weapon or confession.

The other Silas looks at it and whispers, "There you are."

Nina throws the paring knife.

It's a terrible throw. Panicked. Wild. Beautiful.

The knife spins once and strikes the dry Silas in the cheek, handle-first.

He doesn't flinch.

He only turns his eyes to Nina.

The lights in her apartment dim.

The manuscript in Silas's hand opens to the last page.

One sentence sits there now.

Nina Cho becomes useful when she stops screaming.

Silas reads the sentence once.

Then again.

His brain does the stupid thing brains do when terror gets too large. It focuses on grammar.

Becomes useful.

Doesn't die.

Doesn't run.

Doesn't scream.

Becomes useful.

That feels worse.

"Nina," he says. "Get behind me."

Nina stares at the other Silas, still holding her phone like customer service might save her if she finds the right extension.

"Which behind you?" she says.

"Fair," Silas says.

The dry Silas smiles.

It looks almost patient.

Almost proud.

"There's no need to make this ugly," it says.

Silas hates hearing his own voice used that way. Calm. Soft. Reasonable. The voice he uses when he's trying to sound smarter than he feels.

Nina backs away from the kitchen island, one careful step at a time.

The dry Silas doesn't follow. His eyes drop to the manuscript in Silas's bleeding hand.

"You haven't even reached the good part yet," it says.

"What are you?"

The dry Silas tilts his head.

"An improvement."

Nina laughs once, sharp and terrified. "Oh, gross."

The lights flicker.

The manuscript's pages flutter even though there's no wind. Silas tightens his grip, and pain flashes through his torn fingers. Blood spots the cream paper. The ink seems darker where it drinks him in.

A new line appears beneath the one about Nina.

She is funny when cornered. The book considers keeping that.

Nina's eyes flick to the page.

"The book considers what?"

Silas closes it before she can read more.

"Don't look at it."

"I already looked at you twice," she says. "I'm pretty sure my night is ruined either way."

The dry Silas takes one step forward.

The apartment changes around him.

Not much.

That's what makes Silas's stomach twist.

The refrigerator hum lowers. The magnets on Nina's fridge rearrange themselves. A photo of Nina and two women at a beach fades, returns, then fades again with one woman missing. A stack of mail on the counter becomes a different stack of mail. Older. Yellowed. Addressed to someone named Anselm Rote.

Silas sees the name and his mouth goes dry.

The dry Silas notices.

"There," it says. "You recognize a clue. Writers love clues."

Nina grabs Silas by the sleeve and yanks him backward into the hall.

He lets her.

The second they cross the threshold, Nina slams her door shut.

Something hits the other side.

Not hard.

Just one soft knock.

Then another.

Then Silas's voice from inside her apartment says, "Nina, open the door."

Nina backs away until she hits the opposite wall beside Silas.

"Not in this lifetime," she says.

The voice behind the door changes.

It becomes smaller.

Younger.

"Nina, please."

Her face drains.

Silas looks at her.

"What?"

She shakes her head. "That's my brother."

The voice behind the door says, "I'm scared."

Nina's eyes shine, but she doesn't move.

Silas understands then. Not fully. Maybe no one fully understands anything like this and gets to remain functional. But he understands enough.

The manuscript doesn't create from nothing.

It revises what's already damaged.

"Nina," Silas says softly. "Is your brother…"

"Dead," she says. "Yeah."

The door handle turns.

Slowly.

Nina makes a sound through her teeth. Then she grabs Silas's wrist and pulls him down the hallway.

They run.

Behind them, Nina's door opens.

Silas doesn't look back.

The manuscript does it for him.

It opens in his hand while they pound toward the stairwell, pages whipping against his wrist, sentence after sentence appearing so fast they blur.

They run because running gives the scene shape.

They run because fear looks better in motion.

They run because the hallway is longer than it was.

Silas looks up.

The stairwell door should be ten feet away.

It's fifty.

Then seventy.

Then farther.

Nina sees it too.

"Oh, come on," she snaps. "That's cheap."

The hallway lights pop one by one behind them.

Darkness follows.

Not like shadow.

Like ink spilling across the world.

Silas shoves the manuscript under his arm, grabs Nina's hand, and runs harder.

A door opens ahead.

Not the stairwell.

6C.

His apartment.

Impossible, because it should be behind them.

His door stands wide open.

Inside, his lamps are on. His desk waits. His laptop glows.

And from the desk, a woman's voice says, "Silas?"

Sabine Wex steps into view, holding a printed page in one hand.

She looks pale.

Angry.

Afraid.

Sabine shouldn't be there.

That's Silas's first thought, stupid and useless as a paper umbrella.

Sabine Wex shouldn't be standing in his apartment at five-something in the evening, holding a printed page like it's a dead thing she found in her food. She shouldn't have a key anymore. She gave it back eight months ago, the night she told him love isn't supposed to feel like managing someone's decline.

She looks exactly like she did when she left, which is to say too composed to be fine.

Short dark hair tucked behind one ear. Black coat still buttoned. Boots wet from rain. Face pale beneath the apartment's yellow lamp light.

Her eyes move from Silas to Nina, then to the manuscript under his arm.

"Tell me," Sabine says, "that isn't what I think it is."

Nina points at her. "Who the hell is this?"

"My ex," Silas says.

"Of course she is."

Sabine looks past them into the hallway.

The dark is still coming.

It doesn't rush. It doesn't need to. It spreads along the carpet, swallowing the flickering ceiling lights one at a time, smooth and black and patient. A voice speaks from somewhere inside it.

Nina's brother.

Small. Pleading.

"Nina, please."

Nina's mouth tightens.

"Not him," she whispers. "Not him."

Sabine grabs Silas by the front of his jacket and yanks him into the apartment. Nina follows. Sabine slams the door, locks it, chains it, then drags a chair beneath the handle.

Silas almost laughs. "You think furniture helps?"

"No," Sabine says. "But it gives my hands something to do."

That's Sabine. Terrified, but still herself.

For one second, Silas loves her so sharply it hurts.

Then she slaps him.

Hard.

His head snaps sideways.

Nina winces. "Actually, I'm okay with that."

Silas touches his cheek. "What was that for?"

Sabine shoves the printed page against his chest. "For sending me this."

"I didn't."

"My printer turned on by itself twenty minutes ago."

Silas looks down.

The page is fresh. Warm. One sheet of white printer paper from Sabine's apartment across town. The text is centered, typed in the same clean black font as the manuscript.

Sabine Wex arrives too late to save him, which means she arrives exactly on time.

Beneath that:

She still loves him. This will make her useful.

Silas's throat closes.

Sabine watches his face. "It knows things, doesn't it?"

Nina laughs without humor. "Oh, it knows dead brothers too. It's very well-rounded."

Something knocks on Silas's door.

Once.

Softly.

Everyone goes still.

Then Silas's own voice says from the hallway, "Open up. You're missing the revision."

Sabine's eyes narrow. "Is that you?"

"No," Silas says.

"Good. I like him less."

The manuscript jerks under Silas's arm.

He drops it.

It hits the floor and opens itself in the middle of his living room.

Pages flip so fast they become a pale blur. The air changes. Pressure builds in Silas's ears. The apartment seems to bend toward the book, walls leaning in, bookshelves stretching taller, shadows sharpening at their corners.

Then the pages stop.

Silas doesn't want to look.

He looks.

Three readers in the room. One writer. One witness. One sacrifice.

Nina says, "Nope."

Sabine reads over his shoulder. Her face doesn't change, but Silas feels the moment she understands.

"It wants a structure," she says.

"What?"

"It's not just hurting people randomly. It's arranging us. Roles. Functions. It thinks like a story."

The other Silas laughs from behind the door.

"Listen to the editor," it says.
Sabine flinches, but only once.
Silas stares at the manuscript. "How do we stop it?"
The pages flutter.
A fresh line appears.
He asks how to stop it because he still believes endings belong to him.
Sabine crouches near the manuscript but doesn't touch it.
"No," she says quietly. "It's defensive."
"What?"
"It comments when you threaten its control. It mocks you when you start thinking in the right direction."
Nina looks at her. "Fantastic. Can we insult it to death?"
"No," Sabine says. "But maybe we can bore it."
The knocking stops.
Silas hears breathing behind the door.
His breathing.
The manuscript writes again.
Sabine thinks she's found the weakness. She has not.
Sabine smiles.
It's small and mean and beautiful.
"There," she says.
Silas looks from her to the page. "There what?"
"It lied too fast."
Nina wipes at her face with the heel of her hand. "Could someone explain before the hallway ink eats us?"
Sabine points at the manuscript. "I edited your drafts for six years. I know when something is trying too hard to look inevitable."
The other Silas whispers from behind the door, "Don't listen to her."
Sabine's smile vanishes.
"That," she says.
The manuscript snaps shut.
Silas takes a step back.
Nina looks at Sabine. "So we just sit here and act normal?"
"No," Sabine says. "Normal is still a scene. We need to do the one thing Silas hates most."
Silas already knows.
He feels it before she says it.

"Don't finish," Sabine says.

The words hit him harder than the slap.

Because he does hate it.

Because all his life is unfinished things. Drafts. Novels. So many novels. Promises. Relationships. Apologies. Everything left open, rotting at the edge of completion. The manuscript knows that. It chose him because he wants an ending so badly he'd mistake doom for purpose.

"No," Silas says.

Sabine's face softens, and that's worse. "Silas."

"No. That can't be the answer."

The book opens again.

He cannot bear incompletion. This is why he was chosen.

Nina stares at him. "You're kidding."

Silas says nothing.

Nina throws both hands up. "You're telling me we're in evil book hell because you've got commitment issues with Microsoft Word?"

The other Silas begins laughing outside the door.

The chain trembles.

The chair scrapes an inch across the floor.

Sabine grabs the manuscript.

"Don't," Silas says.

But she already has it.

The second her fingers touch the cover, her body locks. Her eyes widen. She inhales as if plunged into freezing water.

"Sabine?"

Her lips move.

Not her voice.

His.

"She leaves him in November because she gets tired of being a mirror he resents," Sabine says in Silas's voice. "She says she's saving herself, but part of her hopes he'll become better just to prove she mattered."

Silas reaches for her.

Nina grabs his arm. "Wait."

Sabine's eyes fill with tears. The manuscript trembles in her hands.

"She keeps every draft he ever sent," Sabine says, still in his voice. "Not because they're good. Because she can see the man he might've been if he'd stopped confusing pain with depth."

Silas feels something in him split.
"Stop," he says.
Sabine's voice changes again.
Now it sounds like the dry Silas in the hall.
"She will die believing he finally wrote something true."
Silas rips the manuscript from her hands.
Sabine collapses to her knees, gasping.
The apartment lights go out.
For one breath, there is only black.
Then the laptop on Silas's desk glows brighter.
A document sits open on the screen.
Untitled.
The cursor blinks.
Silas steps toward it.
Sabine catches his ankle.
"Don't."
The door chain snaps.
Nina turns. "Guys."
The knob turns.
Slowly.
Silas looks at the laptop. Then at the manuscript in his hand. Then at Sabine on the floor, breathing hard, angry and alive. Then at Nina, holding a lamp like a club.
The door opens.
The dry Silas stands in the hallway, smiling with Silas's mouth.
Behind him, the corridor is gone. Not dark. Just gone. A flat black nothing presses up to the threshold, and inside it float torn sentences, pale and twitching, like dying fish under ice.
The dry Silas steps in.
"Ending time," he says.
Silas looks down at the manuscript.
The last page is there.
Of course it is.
It's changed again.
Silas Reddy understands at last. To stop the manuscript, he must give it what every story requires. A death with meaning.
Below that, three names appear.
Nina Cho.
Sabine Wex.

Silas Reddy.

The ink waits beside them.

A choice.

A clean shape.

A beautiful little trap.

Silas laughs.

It surprises him. It surprises everyone.

Even the dry Silas stops smiling.

"Oh," Sabine says softly.

Silas wipes blood from his fingers across the page.

"No," he says.

The manuscript burns cold in his hands.

"No meaningful death. No sacrifice. No tragic arc. No final lesson. Nothing."

The dry Silas takes a step forward. "That isn't how this works."

Silas backs toward the laptop. "I know."

The manuscript starts typing on itself, letters appearing in frantic bursts.

He tries defiance. Defiance is still a choice.

Silas nods. "Sure."

He sits at the desk.

The cursor blinks.

The dry Silas lunges.

Nina swings the lamp.

This time, her aim is better.

The lamp smashes across the dry Silas's face. Bullseye. Glass bursts. The bulb pops. The thing staggers, not from pain, but from insult. Its face dents inward, then slowly begins correcting itself, features sliding back into place.

Nina drops the broken lamp stem. "Still cheap."

Sabine crawls up beside Silas. "What are you doing?"

"What I'm best at," Silas says.

"Ruining things?"

"Not finishing them."

He starts typing.

Not a climax.

Not an explanation.

Not a clever reversal.

He types badly on purpose.

He writes a sentence that wanders. Then another. He repeats details. He contradicts himself. He introduces a man named Greg who has nothing to do with anything and then describes Greg's shoes for six lines. He writes about weather, then soup, then a memory he doesn't finish, then a joke with no punchline.

The manuscript shakes in his lap.

The dry Silas screams.

Not loud.

Worse.

It screams in a whisper, like paper being torn one fiber at a time.

The room flickers.

For half a second, Silas sees other rooms layered over his apartment. A motel room. A hospital hallway. A kitchen with a yellow wall. A basement with a typewriter on a crate. Men and women sitting at desks, standing in bathrooms, kneeling beside fires, all holding the same cream-colored pages.

Anselm Rote is among them.

Silas knows him instantly.

Narrow face. Heavy brow. Eyes ruined by sleeplessness. He sits at a table in some older decade, writing with both hands while blood runs from his nose. He looks up through time, straight at Silas.

"Don't end it," Anselm says.

Then he's gone.

The dry Silas crawls toward the desk.

Sabine grabs a bookshelf and pulls.

The whole thing tips over with a cracking groan. Books spill across the floor. The shelf crashes down over the dry Silas's legs, pinning him.

The thing wearing Silas's face looks almost amused.

"You can't bury an author under books," it says.

Sabine picks up the heaviest hardcover she can find and slams it into his mouth.

"Watch me."

Silas keeps typing.

His sentences get worse.

He refuses beauty.

He refuses rhythm.

He refuses meaning.

To hell with pace.

The manuscript flaps open on his lap, pages thrashing. Words appear, vanish, reappear crooked.

Stop.

Silas types Greg's shoe size wrong, then corrects it, then changes his mind and wonders whether Greg even has feet.

The apartment groans.

Nina's front door appears inside Silas's kitchen, then disappears. Dottie Murn's thrift store counter flashes where his couch should be. The woman in the yellow coat stands in the corner for one breath, gray eyes fixed on him.

She smiles.

Just a little.

Then she turns and walks into a tear of darkness that folds shut behind her.

The dry Silas drags himself out from beneath the bookshelf. His legs are crushed flat, but he moves anyway, pulling himself with hands that leave black ink on the floor.

"You'll come back," it says. "You always come back. You need the last page."

Silas stops typing.

For one terrible second, the temptation opens inside him.

Because he does want to know.

He wants to know the ending. His ending. Their ending. The true ending. The page that makes all this chaos into a shape. The page that proves he was chosen for a reason, even a horrific one.

Sabine touches his shoulder.

Not a grab.

Not a plea.

Just contact. Light. Friendly.

"You don't have to make it good," she says.

That breaks him more than anything else.

Silas turns back to the keyboard.

He types one final line.

And then nothing important happens for a very long time.

The manuscript goes still.

The dry Silas opens his mouth.

No sound comes out.

His face caves inward like wet paper. His eyes flatten into black punctuation marks. His skin wrinkles, folds, becomes pages, hundreds of pages, thousands, all collapsing into one another. The body drops to the floor in a soft pile of cream paper and black thread.

Then the pages rot.

Fast.

Deterioration in real time.

They yellow, brown, curl, and crumble into dust.

The laptop screen goes black.

The apartment lights come back on.

Rain taps the windows.

A siren passes somewhere far below.

For a while, nobody moves.

Nina is the first to speak.

"I'm quitting nursing," she says. "I don't know what I'm doing instead. Maybe soap and candles."

Sabine laughs.

It sounds half hysterical. Half alive.

Silas looks down at his lap.

The manuscript is gone.

Not burned. Not torn. Gone.

Only a faint rectangle of dust remains on his jeans, and a thin black thread wrapped around his bleeding finger.

He pulls it loose.

It comes away easily.

Too easily.

Sabine notices. "Silas?"

"I'm okay," he says.

She gives him a look.

He almost smiles. "I'm not okay. But I'm here."

That seems acceptable enough for the moment.

Nina goes to the door and opens it a crack.

The hallway is back. Ugly carpet. Brown doors. Flickering lights. No ink. No dead brother. No other Silas.

Her own apartment door stands closed across the hall.

She stares at it.

Silas stands. "Don't go in alone."

"I wasn't planning to."

They sit in Silas's apartment until the police arrive.

Nobody called them.

Or maybe someone did.

Detective Petra Gann comes in with two officers and a face that suggests she's seen enough ordinary misery to distrust extraordinary explanations on principle. She looks at the broken lamp, the overturned bookshelf, the blood on Silas's hand, the dust on the floor, Sabine's pale face, Nina's shaking hands.

Then she looks at Silas.

"What happened here?"

Silas opens his mouth.

Nothing comes out.

How do you tell the truth when the truth sounds like metaphor?

Sabine answers for him.

"We had a fight," she says.

Petra Gann looks at the three of them. "With a bookshelf?"

Nina nods. "It started it."

The detective doesn't laugh.

She takes statements. Separate ones. Long ones. She asks why Nina's apartment door has damage on the inside. She asks why Silas's printer tray is full of blank cream-colored paper he swears he doesn't own. She asks why all three of them have ink under their fingernails.

No one has good answers.

By dawn, the police leave unsatisfied.

Sabine stays.

Nina refuses to go back into her apartment until the sun is fully up, so she sleeps on Silas's couch with a kitchen knife on the coffee table and one shoe still on.

Silas sits at his desk.

The laptop is dead.

Not asleep. Dead. Kaput. As in, it won't turn on. He should care more than he does. Every unfinished draft he has is on it. Years of them. False starts. Better starts. Bad endings. No endings. Some just a sentence. Others an extended note.

He feels hollowed out.

Not clean.

Just emptied.

Sabine stands beside him with two cups of coffee. "You're thinking too loudly."

"Sorry."

"You always do."

He takes the cup.

For a while, they watch the pale morning press itself against the rain-streaked windows.

"What now?" he asks.

Sabine looks at the dead laptop. "Now you write something else."

He laughs once. "After that?"

"Especially after that."

"I don't know if I can."

"Good," she says. "That's more honest than usual."

He looks at her.

She doesn't soften the sentence. That's why he believes it.

Later, after Sabine leaves to get clean clothes, after Nina wakes and declares she's never forgiving either of them for making her live through literary trauma, after maintenance comes to fix nothing and complain about everything, Silas finds the receipt from Dottie Murn's thrift store in his jacket pocket.

It's damp.

The ink has run.

But he can still read the price.

Two dollars.

Beneath it, where the store name should be, there's a typed sentence.

Not from a register.

From a typewriter.

A story can survive a bad ending.

Silas stares at it for a long time.

Then the sentence fades.

Another appears.

But it prefers a sequel.

The paper warms between his fingers.

Across the hall, Nina laughs at something on her phone. Somewhere downstairs, a door slams. The city wakes itself reluctantly, one ugly noise at a time.

Silas walks to the kitchen.

He turns on the burner.

The flame clicks, catches, and blooms blue.

For one second, he hesitates.

Then he feeds the receipt to the fire.

It curls.

Blackens.

Vanishes.

Behind him, in the dead laptop's dark screen, his reflection watches.

Half a second late.

You

The road has more twists than a corkscrew.

Callum Rook knows this road, even under dim moonlight. He knows where the gravel spills loose near the shoulder. He knows where the second guardrail bends inward from the time Pilcher's logging truck kissed it sideways in the snow. He knows the blind curve locals call Widow's Elbow, even though nobody can agree which widow gave it the name.

The maroon Mustang growls under him, too much engine for a road this narrow, too much speed for rain this fine.

Callum doesn't care.

He downshifts before the next switchback, slowing the car to a crawl for all of three seconds. The engine revs, deep and angry, then he shifts again and powers out of the turn. The rear tires chew at the wet asphalt, spitting road grit and pine needles. The back end fishtails right, just enough to make his pulse kick, just enough to make him grin.

"Still got it," he says.

Nobody's there to hear him.

That's fine. Callum's always preferred an audience, but he can perform for himself when necessary.

Pine trees line both sides of the road, tall and black and crowded close, their needled arms stirring in the night breeze like they're whispering him through. The Mustang rips down a straightaway, tossing leaves into its wake. They flip and twist in the tunnel of wind behind him until the dark swallows them whole.

Something pops under the tires.

A pine cone, maybe.

It bursts with a wet little crack, smearing sap across the road.

Callum glances at the rearview mirror for no reason.

For half a second, he thinks someone's sitting in the back seat.

He jerks his eyes fully to the mirror.

Nothing.

Just black leather seats. The empty back window. The soft pulse of red taillight glow catching the mist behind him.

"Jesus," he mutters, and looks back at the road.

His phone buzzes in the cup holder.

Tamsin again.

The screen lights his hand, his thigh, the underside of the dash.

Don't take that road tonight.

He laughs once, but it comes out flatter than he wants.

The rain thickens, going from mist to steady needles. Windshield wipers drag themselves back and forth, clearing the glass just in time for more water to stipple it. Fog lifts off the pavement. It curls over the hood, silver in the moonlight, then disappears beneath the Mustang's charging nose.

Lightning flashes far beyond the pines.

White light stutters through the woods.

For one clean instant, the whole road ahead appears.

Wet asphalt. Yellow center lines. Sagging telephone wires.

And a human shape standing in the lane.

Callum's breath punches out of him.

He slams both feet onto the brake pedal.

The Mustang screams.

Tires slide uselessly over the wet road. The steering wheel bucks in his grip, hard enough to burn his palms. The car spins half sideways. Pine trunks flick past the windshield like bars. The back end swings toward the ditch, catches a dry patch, straightens too fast, then rockets forward with brutal stupidity.

"No, no, no…"

The passenger side smashes into a telephone pole.

The sound is enormous.

Metal folds.

Glass bursts.

The world kicks sideways.

Then there's only ringing.

Callum sits there, both hands locked on the wheel. Smoke leaks from under the hood. Rain taps through a spiderweb crack in the windshield and lands cold on his cheek.

He blinks.

Again.

His forehead is wet.

At first, he thinks it's rain.

Then it slides into his eye, hot and thick.

"Shit."

He touches his brow and his fingers come away black in the dashboard glow.

Outside, something moves.

Callum turns his head slowly.

The driver's door sticks when he shoves it. He throws his shoulder into it once, twice, then the hinges squeal and the door gives. He spills out into the rain, boots skidding on wet leaves, one hand catching the roof before he goes down.

The Mustang hisses behind him. Steam rises from the crushed hood.

Callum wipes blood from his eye and stumbles toward the road.

"Hey!" he yells.

No answer.

There are people standing ahead of him.

Not one.

Not two.

A crowd.

They gather in the rain just beyond the reach of his headlights, black shapes on shining asphalt.

Callum plants his hands on his knees, breathing hard.

"Hey, what the hell?"

The people don't move.

Rainwater runs down his face, pulling blood with it. His curls hang heavy and dark against his cheeks. There's pressure inside his skull now, swelling behind his eyes, pushing against his teeth.

He straightens.

"I'm talking to you."

Still nothing.

Callum takes a step forward.

The headlights flicker.

The crowd becomes faces.

His stomach drops before his brain understands why.

He takes another step.

Lightning flashes.

Twenty Callums stare back at him.

Callum stops breathing.

The rain doesn't.

It drums on the road, on the ruined Mustang, on twenty identical heads of dark curls. It beads on twenty versions of his leather jacket. It runs down twenty copies of his face.

Except they're not identical.

Not exactly.

One has blood drying under both nostrils. One smiles with a split lower lip. One stands crooked, left shoulder higher than the right. One has eyes so wide Callum can see the white all the way around the irises.

One looks seventeen, maybe eighteen, thinner through the cheeks, cockier around the mouth.

That one is the worst.

That one is wearing the red flannel Callum burned in a barrel behind Lenny Brusk's garage.

"No," Callum says.

The word falls out weak.

The Callum closest to him steps forward. He's clean. Too clean. The rain touches him, but doesn't soak in. His hair stays loose and dry. His jacket looks fresh from the closet. His face is Callum's face on its best day, charming and rested and cruelly awake.

Callum backs up a step.

The clean one smiles.

"Don't run."

Callum's laugh comes out broken.

"What the hell is this?"

"You know."

"No, I don't."

"You always say that."

The crowd shifts.

Twenty boots scrape wet asphalt.

Callum looks over his shoulder at the Mustang. It's dead. The front end is folded around the pole. The passenger door is crushed inward like something took a bite out of it. Smoke rolls low, mixing with fog. The airbag hangs from the driver's door.

His phone buzzes again inside the car.

The clean Callum tilts his head.

"You gonna answer her?"

Callum turns back fast.

"Who are you?"

The clean one's smile widens.

"You."

"Bullshit."

One of the others laughs. It's Callum's laugh, but younger. Meaner. The sound shoots cold straight through him.

The teenage version steps out from behind the others, hands tucked in the pockets of that old red flannel. His hair is shorter. His skin is clearer. His mouth has the old smug hook Callum hasn't seen in years except in drunk bathroom mirrors.

"Still saying bullshit when you're scared," Young Callum says. "That's cute."

Callum's stomach clenches.

"You're not real."

Young Callum shrugs.

"Corbin said that too."

The name hits harder than the crash.

Callum's mouth opens.

Nothing comes out.

The rain pours heavier now, loud enough to flatten the world. Trees sway on both sides of the road, black needles shivering. Somewhere far down the mountain, thunder rolls through the valley like something huge clearing its throat.

Clean Callum steps closer.

Callum raises one hand.

"Stay back."

"Or what?"

"I mean it."

"You usually don't."

Callum looks from face to face. His face. His eyes. His mouth. His old sneer. His tired jaw. His bleeding forehead. His lies, worn in different ways.

"What do you want?"

Clean Callum's smile disappears.

All twenty answer together.

"You."

Callum flinches from the force of it.

The sound isn't loud. It's intimate, almost whispered, like every version of him is speaking from inside his own skull.

He backs away, boots slipping in the leaves.

"No. No, screw this."

He turns and runs for the Mustang.

The crowd moves behind him.

Not fast.

Not yet.

More like they know running would cheapen it.

Callum yanks open the driver's door and dives inside. Pain detonates in his ribs. He grabs his phone from the cup holder, blood smearing across the screen.

Three missed calls from Tamsin.

One text.

Please tell me you didn't.

Clean Callum appears in the cracked windshield, standing on the hood like he weighs nothing.

Callum screams and drops the phone.

The thing crouches slowly, face inches from the broken glass.

"You did," it says.

Callum throws the Mustang into reverse.

The engine gives him a single ugly cough.

Then nothing.

"No, no, come on." He twists the key again. "Come on, you bastard."

The starter clicks. The dash lights flutter. Somewhere under the hood, something pops and lets out a fresh ribbon of smoke.

Clean Callum stays crouched on the hood, one hand pressed flat to the cracked windshield. His fingers look real. The half-moons of his nails. The tiny scar across the knuckle from when Callum punched a mailbox at nineteen because a girl laughed at him.

"You always think machines are gonna save you," Clean Callum says.

Callum grabs the gearshift and slams it into park.

"Get off my car."

"Our car."

"Get off."

The windshield caves inward with a soft, icy crunch.

Callum jerks back as Clean Callum pushes his fingers through the glass like it's thin paper. Cracks spread from his hand. Rainwater leaks through in crooked lines.

Callum fumbles for anything, anything, and his hand closes around the tire iron wedged beneath the passenger seat.

He swings.

The iron catches Clean Callum across the cheek.

The impact sounds wet and satisfying.

Clean Callum's head snaps sideways. For a second, Callum sees torn skin, white teeth, the dark meat inside the cheek.

Then the wound puckers shut.

Knits itself right up.

Clean Callum slowly turns back.

"That's new," he says.

Callum swings again, but this time the tire iron stops midair.

Another hand has it.

Broken Callum leans in through the smashed passenger window. The right side of him is crushed flat. His shoulder caves toward his chest. His jaw hangs off-center, clicking as he grins.

"Seat belt," Broken Callum says. "Should've worn it."

Callum kicks at him, heel smashing into that ruined face. Bone gives under his boot. Broken Callum laughs anyway, a gargling, bubbly sound.

Outside, the others gather around the car.

Palms slap the roof.

Fingers squeal down the windows.

One of them crawls over the trunk on all fours, his neck twisted backward so his face watches Callum through the rear glass.

Callum screams and swings the tire iron again, smashing the cracked windshield wider. Clean Callum drops from the hood, graceful as a cat.

Callum doesn't wait.

He crawls through the broken windshield.

Glass slices his palms. It opens his forearm in a hot red grin. He lands badly on the hood, slips in rain and engine smoke, then tumbles off the front of the car into the mud.

His left knee hits a rock.

Pain flashes white.

"Goddamn it."

He shoves himself up, limping, and runs toward the trees.

The road vanishes behind him fast. Rain turns the pine slope slick and treacherous. Branches slap his face. Needles cling to his hair and jacket. He can hear them coming now, not running exactly, but following.

Walking.

Laughing.

Whispering.

"You remember the ditch?"

"You remember his teeth?"

"You remember how he sounded?"

Callum stumbles over a root and catches himself on a pine trunk. Bark bites into his shredded palm. He looks back.

Headlights glow through the trees below, cut into strips by trunks and rain.

Between those strips, the Callums move.

One drags his leg.

One crawls.

One walks with his head cocked too far sideways.

Young Callum steps into a pale band of light and looks up the slope.

He cups his hands around his mouth.

"Hey, Cal."

Callum freezes.

Nobody calls him Cal anymore.

Nobody living.

Young Callum smiles.

"Corbin's waiting."

Callum turns and climbs.

He doesn't think. Thinking has sharp teeth now. Thinking has Corbin's name in it, and the red flannel, and Lenny's garage, and the sour stink of beer on a summer night too warm for the mountains.

So he climbs.

Rain slicks the pine needles under his boots. Mud sucks at his soles. His knee pulses with each step, hot and loose, like something inside it's come unhooked. He grabs roots, branches, stones, anything that'll hold his weight for half a second.

Behind him, Young Callum keeps calling.

"Cal."

Then closer.

"Cal."

Then from his left.

"Cal."

Callum whips around.

Nothing there but trees.

He hurries on, breath tearing up his throat. His phone's still in his hand, somehow. The screen is cracked now, but alive. Tamsin's name sits there in the recent calls like a dare.

He jabs it with his thumb.

It rings once.

Twice.

The woods answer.

Not the phone.

The woods.

Tamsin's ringtone floats through the pines somewhere ahead of him, tinny and cheerful and wrong. Callum stops so suddenly his boots slide. He grabs a branch to steady himself.

The ring comes again, farther up the slope.

His phone against his ear keeps ringing.

"What the hell?" he whispers.

Tamsin picks up.

"Callum?"

Relief almost knocks him down.

"Tam. Jesus. Listen to me."

"Where are you?"

"I wrecked. I'm on Pitch Hook Road. Near Widow's Elbow, I think. There are people here."

Silence.

Rain patters through the connection.

Then Tamsin says, very softly, "What people?"

Callum looks down the slope. Shapes move between trees.

"I don't know."

"You do know."

His blood chills.

"Tamsin?"

The line crackles.

When her voice comes again, it's closer.

Not in the phone.

In the woods ahead.

"You always know."

Callum lowers the phone.

Between two black pines stands Tamsin.

Or something wearing her.

Same chopped black hair. Same pale eyes. Same old army jacket she stole from her brother and never gave back. Rain runs over her face, but her expression doesn't change.

Callum's voice breaks.

"No."

The phone still whispers against his ear.

"You should've listened."

He backs away from her and bumps into someone.

A wet hand slides around his throat.

Callum drives his elbow back. It hits ribs. The grip loosens. He spins and comes face-to-face with Empty Callum.

No eyes.

Just smooth skin stretched tight over both sockets.

Callum makes a sound he doesn't recognize.

Empty Callum smiles with his mouth closed.

"I didn't see him," it says.

Callum shoves him hard. Empty Callum drops backward onto the slope, boneless and laughing. His head hits a rock with a hollow crack, but the laugh keeps going.

Callum bolts sideways, no longer climbing, no longer choosing a direction. He crashes through brush until the ground suddenly disappears beneath him.

He falls.

The slope becomes sky, mud, pine, sky again. His shoulder slams something. His teeth clip together. He tumbles through bracken and dead leaves, then lands hard in a shallow creek bed.

Cold water rushes around his ribs.

For a moment, he can't move.

He lies there staring up at the pines while rain falls through them.

Then something brushes his cheek.

Not water.

Fingers.

Callum turns his head.

A bloated version of himself lies beside him in the creek, blue-lipped and swollen, pine needles tangled in his curls.

Wet Callum opens his mouth.

Black water spills out.

"Found him," he gurgles.

Callum scrambles backward on his elbows.

Creek stones grind into his spine. Water slaps cold against his ears. Wet Callum rolls toward him with a heavy, soft splash, one bloated hand dragging through the current. His fingers are pale and fat like sausages, the nails packed with black mud.

"Don't touch me," Callum says.

Wet Callum's swollen lips peel apart.

"You touched him."

Callum kicks.

His boot sinks into Wet Callum's chest with a sound like stepping into rotten fruit. The body folds around his foot, soft ribs collapsing inward, and something dark squirms beneath the waterlogged shirt.

Callum yanks his leg free and crab-walks away, gagging.

"No. No, I didn't."

The woods go quiet.

Even the rain seems to pause.

Then all around him, from the banks, from the trees, from the creek itself, his own voices whisper back.

"No, I didn't."

"No, I didn't."

"No, I didn't."

Callum gets to his feet. His knee almost buckles. He grabs a slick boulder and hauls himself upright, panting, shivering, bleeding from too many places now.

A flashlight beam cuts through the trees above.

"Callum?"

Real voice.

Human voice.

Lenny.

Callum sucks in a breath so hard it hurts.

"Lenny!"

The beam jerks toward him.

Lenny Brusk appears on the creek bank in a yellow rain slicker stretched tight over his belly. His face is ghost-white beneath his ball cap. One hand holds the flashlight. The other holds a hunting rifle.

"What the hell happened to your car?" Lenny calls.

"Help me."

Lenny starts down the bank, then stops.

His flashlight sweeps across the creek bed.

Wet Callum is gone.

Callum looks around fast. Nothing but rushing water and stones and dark leaves.

Lenny's mouth hangs open.

"Who else is out here?"

Callum limps toward him.

"Nobody. Just help me up."

"That ain't what I asked."

"Lenny."

The name comes out sharp enough to cut.

Lenny flinches.

Good.

That still works.

Callum reaches up. Lenny hesitates, then grips his wrist and pulls. Callum climbs the bank, slipping twice, nearly taking them both down.

When he reaches the top, he grabs Lenny's slicker with both hands.

"We gotta go."

Lenny stares at Callum's face.

"You're bleeding bad."

"We gotta go now."

"Did you hit somebody?"

Callum freezes.

Lenny's eyes change.

There it is.

That old night.

The shape of it rising between them.

"Don't," Callum says.

Lenny swallows.

"I saw your car from the lower bend. Then I saw people in the road."

Callum tightens his grip.

"What people?"

Lenny looks past him into the trees.

"You," he whispers.

A twig snaps behind them.

Both men turn.

Young Callum stands at the edge of the creek, red flannel soaked dark, hands in his pockets. Rain drips from his chin. He grins at Lenny.

"Hey, Len."

Lenny raises the rifle.

Young Callum's grin widens.

"You still got the shovel?"

Lenny fires.

The rifle blast cracks the night open.

Young Callum jerks backward, red flannel kicking in the rain. A dark hole appears under his collarbone. For one bright, stupid second, Callum thinks that's it.

Good.

Done.

Real things die when you shoot them.

Then Young Callum looks down at the wound.

He puts one finger into it.

Wiggles it.

Pulls out something pale and small.

A tooth.

Lenny makes a choking sound.

"No."

Young Callum holds the tooth up between thumb and forefinger.

"Not yours," he says.

Callum backs away.

The tooth is too familiar.

Not because he remembers the exact shape. He doesn't. That'd be insane. Nobody remembers a tooth from sixteen years ago.

But he remembers the sound.

Corbin's mouth hitting the rock.

The small click.

The wet gasp after.

Callum presses both hands to his ears, but it doesn't help. The memory isn't outside him.

Lenny chambers another round. His hands shake so badly the rifle barrel wobbles.

Young Callum smiles at him.

"Do it again."

"Run," Callum says.

Lenny doesn't move.

"Lenny, run."

From the trees behind Young Callum, more figures step into view.

Clean Callum.

Broken Callum.

Empty Callum, head tilted toward their voices.

Burned Callum, steaming in the rain, skin splitting pink over black.

Wet Callum crawling from the creek on his stomach, water pouring from his mouth.

And others.

More than twenty now.

Too many.

Some wear Callum's face old and sagging. Some wear it bruised. One has a plastic bag twisted around his neck, his mouth opening and closing against it. One is naked except for mud, with pine roots growing through the meat of his thighs. One carries his own severed hand and waves with it.

Lenny turns in a slow circle, rifle raised.

"Oh God," he says. "Oh God, oh God."

Clean Callum steps forward.

"Not Him," he says. "Just us."

Lenny fires again.

The bullet punches into Clean Callum's chest. He rocks back a half step, looks irritated, then smooths the hole shut with his palm.

Callum grabs Lenny by the collar and yanks him backward.

"Move!"

This time, Lenny moves.

They run uphill, crashing through brush, slipping in mud. Lenny breathes in hoarse little sobs. Callum's knee screams with every step, but fear keeps him upright. Behind them, the crowd doesn't chase hard.

It doesn't need to.

Their voices come through the rain.

"Remember the party?"

"Remember the dare?"

"Remember how he cried?"

"Remember the trunk?"

Lenny trips and goes down face-first.

Callum almost keeps running.

He really does.

For half a second, his body chooses survival. It always does. His legs pump twice before he stops and looks back.

Lenny claws at the mud, rifle gone, ball cap knocked loose. His yellow slicker glows faintly in the dark.

"Callum!" he screams.

Wet Callum has his ankle.

The bloated thing lies half-submerged in a puddle that wasn't there a moment ago. Its fingers sink into Lenny's boot leather like dough. Lenny kicks, heel smashing Wet Callum's cheek. The cheek caves, fills with creek water, and bulges back out.

Callum grabs a fallen branch and swings it down.

The branch breaks across Wet Callum's arm.

Wet Callum looks at him.

His blue lips open.

"Two against one," he gurgles. "That's how you liked it."

Lenny screams again, higher this time, as the hand tightens.

His ankle twists the wrong way.

The crack is sharp.

Callum drives the jagged end of the branch into Wet Callum's mouth. It punches through the back of his head and pins him to the mud.

For a second, Wet Callum stops moving.

Callum grabs Lenny under the arms and hauls.

"Get up."

"My ankle. Jesus, my ankle."

"Get up or they'll take both of us."

Lenny looks past Callum and starts crying.

Callum turns.

The doubles stand in a half circle between the trees.

Young Callum steps forward, still holding Corbin's tooth.

"You didn't take him with you either," he says.

Callum pulls Lenny up anyway.

Lenny's broken ankle folds under him. He screams through clenched teeth and grabs Callum's jacket so hard the leather creaks.

"Shut up," Callum hisses.

"I can't walk."

"Then hop."

"They're right there."

"I know they're right there."

The doubles watch them from the trees. Nobody rushes. Nobody lunges. That's the worst part. They don't have the frantic hunger of animals or the twitchy violence of lunatics. They have patience.

They have all night.

Maybe more than all night.

Young Callum tosses Corbin's tooth into his mouth like candy and swallows it.

Lenny sobs.

Callum gets an arm around him and drags him uphill. Every step is ugly. Lenny's boot scrapes mud. His bad ankle hangs loose. Rain slicks both of them until they're sliding more than walking.

"We gotta get to the fire road," Lenny says.

"Where?"

"Above the ridge. Half mile, maybe."

"Maybe?"

"I'm turned around."

"You live here."

"So did Corbin."

Callum shoves him against a tree.

Lenny cries out and grabs at the bark.

"Don't say his name."

Lenny stares at him, rain running down his round, terrified face.

"They're already saying it."

Behind them, the doubles start whispering.

"Corbin."

"Corbin."

"Corbin."

The name moves through the woods like insects under leaves.

Callum's throat tightens.

"We didn't kill him."

Lenny's face crumples.

"Oh, Callum."

"What?"

Lenny looks past him, then back.

"You really made yourself believe that."

Callum punches him.

It isn't planned. His fist just goes. It catches Lenny high on the cheek and snaps his head sideways against the trunk.

For one second, the woods go still.

Then the doubles laugh.

Not all at once. One starts. Then another. Then another. Twenty, thirty, maybe fifty versions of Callum laugh in the rainy dark.

Lenny slowly touches his cheek.

"You haven't changed," he whispers.

Callum breathes hard. His knuckles sting. Shame tries to rise in him, but anger gets there first and shoves it down.

"I came back for you."

"Yeah," Lenny says. "After you took two running steps."

Callum grabs him again.

"Keep moving."

They push on.

The ground steepens. The pines thin just enough for the sky to show between their crowns. Lightning flashes above, turning every needle silver. Callum sees a rusted hunting blind ahead, half-collapsed between three trees. Beside it, a narrow trail cuts sideways across the slope.

Lenny points with a shaking hand.

"There. That trail hits the fire road."

A voice answers from the hunting blind.

"No, it doesn't."

Callum and Lenny stop.

Something shifts inside the blind. Wood creaks. A pale face appears between broken slats.

Smiling Callum.

Clean. Handsome. Dry.

He looks almost bored.

"That trail goes where we left him," Smiling Callum says.

Lenny whimpers.

Callum backs away.

Smiling Callum leans closer, eyes bright through the rotten wood.

"You remember now, don't you?"

Callum shakes his head.

But he does.

Not all of it.

Enough.

The party at Sutter's quarry. Warm beer. Lenny laughing too loud. Corbin standing near the fire alone, holding a paper cup with both hands like he's afraid someone will take it. Callum saying something. The others laughing. Corbin trying to leave.

The dare.

The trunk.

The road.

Corbin's muffled voice begging through carpet and steel.

Callum whispers, "No."

Smiling Callum's grin spreads.

"Yes."

Lenny starts crying harder.

Not loud. Not dramatic. Just broken little sounds squeezed through his teeth as rain runs down his face.

Callum hates him for it.

He hates the sound. Hates the weakness. Hates that Lenny remembers more clearly. Hates that the doubles seem to enjoy it, standing in the trees with Callum's face and Callum's mouth and Callum's old cruelty.

"We didn't put him in the trunk," Callum says.

Lenny turns his head slowly.

"What?"

Callum's voice shakes.

"It was a joke."

Smiling Callum laughs from the hunting blind.

"That's what you called it."

"It was a joke," Callum says again, louder now, like volume can change history. "He was running his mouth. He was acting weird. Everybody was laughing."

"Everybody wasn't laughing," Lenny says.

Callum glares at him.

Lenny wipes his nose with the back of his hand, shuddering.

"Corbin wasn't."

Lightning flares.

For a second, the woods aren't woods.

They're that old quarry.

Firelight. Beer cans. Muddy boots. A girl named Kitra Dallow with silver glitter around her eyes. Truck beds lined up in a semicircle. Music thumping from somebody's speakers. A couple making out in a back seat.

Corbin Thatch stands at the edge of it all in a blue windbreaker, eyes down, mouth tight.

Callum sees his own young hand shove Corbin's shoulder.

Not hard at first.

Just enough to make him stumble.

Then harder.

The memory snaps away with the thunder.

Callum staggers backward.

"No."

The doubles whisper it with him.

"No."

"No."

"No."

Smiling Callum climbs out of the hunting blind. His boots touch mud, but they don't sink.

"You were so funny that night," he says.

"Shut up."

"You had everyone watching."

"I said shut up."

"You couldn't stop once they were watching."

Callum lunges at him.

Lenny grabs his sleeve.

"Don't."

Too late.

Callum swings at Smiling Callum's face. His fist passes through cold wet air and hits one of the hunting blind's support posts instead. Rotten wood splinters. Pain bursts through his hand, shooting straight to his wrist.

Smiling Callum stands behind him now.

"That's the thing about you," he says near Callum's ear. "You always hit the wrong thing."

Callum spins, but Smiling Callum is already gone.

Lenny whispers, "We gotta go."

From below, the others begin climbing again.

Callum hears branches snap. Hears bodies dragging through brush. Hears wet laughter.

He hooks his arm around Lenny and forces him onto the trail.

The path is narrow, cut into the slope by deer and hunters and years of runoff. One side rises steep with roots and stone. The other drops into black pine. Lenny hops, curses, almost falls, and Callum yanks him upright each time.

"You're hurting me," Lenny gasps.

"Good. Means you're alive."

"For now."

"Don't start that."

"They're not after me."

Callum doesn't answer.

Lenny grips him tighter.

"Callum."

"Keep moving."

"They're not after me."

"You were there."

"I didn't touch him like you did."

Callum shoves him forward, too hard. Lenny stumbles and slams into the uphill bank with a grunt.

"You helped," Callum says.

Lenny looks at him.

"I was scared of you."

The words land clean.

Callum opens his mouth, but nothing comes.

Ahead, the trail bends around a boulder slick with moss. Beyond it, a faint orange light flickers through the rain.

A cabin.

Small. Old. Half-hidden between pines.

Smoke curls from its chimney.

Callum blinks at it.

"That wasn't here," Lenny whispers.

The cabin door opens.

Warm light spills out.

An old woman stands in the doorway, thin as a nail, white hair braided over one shoulder. She holds a lantern in one hand and a long skinning knife in the other.

Nessa Quill looks at Callum like she's been expecting him to arrive bleeding.

"Well," she says. "Took you long enough."

Nessa steps aside.

Callum doesn't move.

Neither does Lenny.

The cabin glows behind her with firelight and old yellow lamps. It should look safe. It should look like rescue. Instead, it looks baited and waiting, a warm mouth in the mountain dark.

Nessa lifts the knife slightly.

"Inside, unless you boys wanna keep bleeding in my doorway."

Lenny makes a weak sound.

"Miss Quill?"

She looks at him.

"Lenox Brusk. You got fat."

"Ma'am?"

"You heard me."

Callum stares at the knife.

"What is this place?"

"A cabin."

"It wasn't here."

"It was when it needed to be."

"That doesn't mean anything."

Nessa gives him a sour smile.

"Sure it does. You're just too scared to understand plain English."

Behind them, a twig breaks.

Callum turns.

The doubles stand at the edge of the lantern light.

Not advancing.

Just waiting.

Rain runs over their faces. Over Callum's face. Some grin. Some stare. Empty Callum tilts his smooth, eyeless head toward the cabin and sniffs like a dog catching scent.

Nessa's expression hardens.

"You don't get to cross my threshold," she calls.

Young Callum smiles in his red flannel.

"Not yet."

Callum shoves Lenny through the door.

Nessa backs up and lets them in, then shuts the door and drops a thick wooden bar across it. The bar is carved with symbols. Not fancy ones. Just rough cuts and gouges, like somebody made them in a hurry with a pocketknife and a little hatred.

The cabin smells of woodsmoke, kerosene, dried herbs, wet wool, and something coppery underneath.

Blood.

Callum sees why a second later.

Things hang from the rafters.

Not bodies.

Not exactly.

Masks.

Dozens of them.

Faces made of bark, bone, stitched hide, roadkill leather, rusted license plates, cracked mirrors, and teeth wired into smiling arcs. Some look human. Some don't. One looks too much like Callum for comfort, though its eyes are made from two black buttons and its mouth is sewn shut with fishing line.

Lenny sinks into a chair near the stove and clutches his ankle. His face has gone gray.

Nessa limps to a cabinet, grabs a bottle without looking, and tosses it to Callum.

He catches it against his chest.

Whiskey.

"Drink or pour it on your cuts," she says. "I don't care which."

Callum unscrews the cap with shaking fingers and drinks.

Fire hits his throat. For a moment, the pain is simple.

Then the cabin windows darken.

Faces press against the glass.

Callum chokes on the whiskey.

Nessa doesn't even look.

"They'll watch. Let 'em."

Lenny's voice cracks.

"What are they?"

Nessa pulls a stool over, kneels in front of his broken ankle, and slices his boot laces with the skinning knife.

"He knows."

Callum wipes his mouth.

"I don't."

"You do."

"I'm getting real sick of people saying that."

"Then stop being stupid on purpose."

Lenny lets out a wet laugh that turns into a sob when Nessa pulls the boot free. His ankle is purple already, swollen huge, bent wrong.

"Sorry," Nessa says, not sounding sorry at all.

Callum moves to the nearest window.

The faces outside follow him.

Clean Callum stands closest. Beautiful. Dry. Patient.

Callum pulls the curtain shut.

Nessa says, "That won't help."

"Then why have curtains?"

"Because I like curtains."

Callum turns on her.

"You know something. So talk."

Nessa wraps Lenny's ankle with a strip of torn sheet.

"That road's old. Older than asphalt. Older than the county. Things got buried up there before men had last names to lie with."

"Great. Folklore."

"You want simple? Fine." Nessa ties the splint tight. Lenny groans. "The road gives back what's owed."

Callum laughs once.

"That's insane."

"So's a crowd of your ugly ass standing in the rain, but here we are."

Something taps the window.

One soft knock.

Then another.

Then twenty.

Callum's shoulders climb toward his ears.

Nessa stands and points the bloody knife at him.

"You left a boy up here."

Callum's face goes numb.

Lenny whispers, "Nessa."

She ignores him.

"You left him in the dark, and the road's been chewing on that night ever since. Chewing and chewing and chewing. But it can't swallow what ain't been confessed."

"I didn't kill him," Callum says.

The cabin goes cold.

The fire dims.

Every mask hanging from the rafters turns slightly, creaking on its wire.

Nessa looks at him with something close to pity.

"You still think this is only about killing him?"

Callum can't answer.

Outside, Young Callum begins to sing.

A stupid song from the quarry party.

Low and soft.

Then the others join in.

Lenny covers his face.

Nessa leans close to Callum and lowers her voice.

"You wanna live till morning, boy?"

Callum nods before he can stop himself.

"Then you're gonna take me to where you put him."

The floorboards under Callum's feet thump once.

From beneath the cabin, someone whispers in his voice.

"He's still cold."

Callum stares at the floorboards.

The whisper comes again from underneath the cabin, muffled by wood and earth.

"He's still cold."

Lenny starts shaking his head.

"No. No, no, no."

Nessa looks down at the floor like she's annoyed at a rat in the walls.

"Quiet," she snaps.

The floorboards go still.

Callum's mouth is dry. Whiskey burns in his empty stomach. His cuts pulse. His knee throbs. Every part of him wants to say this isn't happening, but that's getting harder to sell when the windows are full of his own face and the cabin floor is talking.

"What's under there?" he asks.

Nessa wipes Lenny's blood off her knife with a rag.

"Same thing that's everywhere tonight. What you brought with you."

"I didn't bring anything."

"You drove it right up the mountain in that pretty little car."

Callum laughs, but it comes out thin.

"You people are crazy."

Nessa points the knife at the window.

"Those people are you."

Outside, the singing stops.

That's worse.

The silence has meaty weight.

Callum backs away from the center of the room. His boot heel bumps something. He looks down and sees a trapdoor cut into the floor beside the woodstove. It's small, square, iron-ringed, and sealed with a rusty latch wrapped in black cord.

Something scratches beneath it.

Once.

Twice.

Lenny whimpers.

"Don't open that."

"I wasn't going to."

Nessa steps between them and the trapdoor.

"Good. Because what's under my cabin ain't for you…yet."

"Yet?" Callum says.

Nessa looks at him.

"You catch on when you're scared. That's nice."

A fist hits the front door.

The whole cabin jumps.

Lenny yells. Callum staggers backward, grabbing the whiskey bottle by the neck like it's a weapon.

Another fist hits.

Then another.

Not a mob pounding all at once. One knock at a time. Calm. Measured.

Nessa walks to the door and lifts a finger to her lips.

The cabin holds its breath.

From the other side, Clean Callum says, "We know he's in there."

Nessa rolls her eyes.

"No shit."

Callum whispers, "Don't talk to it."

Clean Callum chuckles outside.

"It?"

The word crawls through the cracks around the door.

"You hear that, boys? We're an it now."

A murmur rolls around the cabin. Faces shift at the windows. Fingers drag down the glass, leaving trails of blood, mud, sap, ash.

Nessa doesn't flinch.

"You can't have him in here," she says.

"Then send Lenny out."

Lenny looks up sharply.

Callum looks at Nessa.

Nessa says nothing.

Clean Callum's voice softens.

"Len knows the way. Len remembers the hole. Len remembers how deep."

Lenny's lips tremble.

"I don't."

Young Callum appears at the side window, red flannel plastered to his chest. His grin is gone now. Without it, he looks almost sad.

"You held the flashlight," he says.

Lenny squeezes his eyes shut.

"You held it steady."

"Stop," Lenny whispers.

Young Callum presses both palms to the glass.

"You cried then too."

Callum snaps, "Leave him alone."

Every face turns toward him.

Nessa does too.

Callum feels the mistake immediately.

Clean Callum says from the door, "There he is."

The windows fog from the outside, not with breath but with heat, as if the things beyond the glass are burning through their patience.

Nessa grabs Callum by the jacket and drags him close. For an old woman, she's stronger than she looks.

"You don't defend him because you're good," she says.

"Get off me."

"You defend him because if he breaks first, he'll tell it wrong."

Callum shoves her hand away, but the words stick.

Lenny stares at him from the chair.

For a moment, all Callum hears is rain, fire, and the slow scrape under the trapdoor.

Then Lenny says, "We didn't bury him."

Callum turns on him.

"Shut up."

Nessa's eyes sharpen.

Lenny's face collapses into something worse than fear.

"We didn't bury him," he says again. "That's the thing."

The cabin lights flicker.

Outside, every Callum smiles.

Lenny looks at the floor, at the trapdoor, then at Callum.

"We heard him breathing when we drove away."

Callum doesn't move.

For once, he doesn't have a comeback. Doesn't have anger ready. Doesn't have that sharp little knife of a smile he uses when someone gets too close to something true.

Lenny's words hang there.

"We heard him breathing when we drove away."

The cabin seems to lean in around them.

The masks creak overhead. The fire pops once, sending sparks up the chimney. Rain ticks at the windows like fingernails impatiently waiting their turn.

Nessa's face goes hard and flat.

"You left him alive?"

Lenny covers his mouth with one hand.

Callum looks at him like he can kill him with a stare alone.

"You don't know that."

"I know what I heard."

"You were drunk."

"So were you."

"You were crying. You were panicking. You don't remember shit."

Lenny laughs. It's small and ugly and full of snot.

"I remember him making that sound."

Callum steps toward him.

Nessa puts the knife between them.

"Touch him and I'll open you from belt to beard."

Callum stops.

He's breathing too fast now. He knows it. He hears himself. Hears the wet rattle in his chest. The same rattle under the floorboards. The same rattle coming from the road outside.

Clean Callum's voice slides through the door.

"Tell her where."

Callum closes his eyes.

He's back there.

Not all the way. Not enough to drown in it. Just flashes.

Corbin's sneaker sticking out of the open trunk before Callum shoves it in. Lenny saying, "Man, this is enough, okay? This is enough." Callum laughing because everybody has laughed all night and he needs the laugh to keep going or else the whole thing becomes something else.

The trunk slamming.

Dark road.

Corbin kicking from inside.

Thump.

Thump.

Thump.

Then not kicking.

Lenny crying in the passenger seat. Callum screaming at him to shut up.

A narrow turnout near the old culvert.

Rain that night too.

Of course rain.

There's always rain in the parts of his life he can't scrub clean.

Callum opens his eyes.

Nessa is watching him.

"You know," she says.

Callum swallows.

"No."

The word comes out by itself.

Weak.

Reflexive.

Useless.

Nessa nods toward the windows.

"Then they'll come in."

As if the cabin understands her, the walls groan.

The wooden bar across the front door bends inward. Not much. Just enough to show strain. The carved symbols glow a dull red along the gouged lines.

Lenny whispers, "Please, Cal."

Callum hates that name.

He hates how Corbin said it. Softly. Like they were almost friends once. Like the world might be gentle if Callum gave it half a chance.

"He was nobody," Callum says.

The room goes silent.

Even Nessa looks surprised.

Outside, the doubles stop smiling.

Callum hears himself. Hears the sentence. Hears how naked it is.

Lenny stares at him with wet, ruined eyes.

"He was seventeen."

Callum turns away, but there's nowhere safe to look. Every wall has a hanging face. Every window has his own. Every shadow has the shape of something waiting.

The trapdoor scratches again.

This time, the latch jumps.

Nessa steps back.
Callum's voice drops.
"What happens if that opens?"
Nessa grips the knife tighter.
"You stop getting asked nicely."
The front door thuds.
The bar cracks.
Lenny sobs.
Callum looks at the whiskey bottle in his hand. At the fire. At the curtains. At the black cord around the trapdoor latch.
A stupid thought comes to him.
Then a worse one.
He moves before either can turn into fear.
Callum throws the whiskey bottle at the front window.
Glass explodes outward. Whiskey sprays across the nearest doubles. He grabs a burning log from the stove with both hands, screaming as heat bites into his palms, and hurls it after.
Flame blooms blue-white in the rain.
The Callums outside shriek.
Not in pain.
In laughter.
Callum grabs Lenny by the back of the slicker.
"We're leaving."
Nessa blocks him.
"Not through them."
"Then through the floor."
Her eyes widen.
"No, you dumb son of a bitch."
Too late.
Callum kicks the trapdoor latch.
Once.
Twice.
The black cord snaps.
The trapdoor blows open.
Cold breath rushes up from below, stinking of mud, pine rot, and an old, terrified mouth.
From the dark beneath the cabin, Corbin Thatch whispers, "Callum."
Callum can't move.

The hole in the floor exhales again, colder this time, and the fire gutters low in the stove. The masks hanging overhead swing gently, all those false faces turning toward the open trapdoor like flowers turning toward sun.

Only this is no sun.

This is a throat.

This is a grave learning how to speak.

"Callum," the voice whispers again.

It's thin. Scraped raw. Not a ghostly moan. Not some theatrical sound from a movie. It's worse because it's human.

A boy's voice, dried out by years underground.

Lenny starts sobbing so hard he can't breathe.

Nessa grabs Callum by the back of the jacket and yanks him away from the opening.

"You stupid little bastard."

The front window burns with blue-white flame. Outside, the doubles stand in the rain with fire crawling over their clothes and skin. They don't burn down. They don't run. They laugh and laugh, mouths open, teeth shining wet, while their faces bubble and mend and bubble again.

Clean Callum steps through the flame.

His jacket burns from the shoulders. His hair catches, curls blackening and shrinking tight to his skull. He smiles anyway.

"You opened it," he says.

The door's wooden bar cracks again.

Nessa shoves Lenny's rifle into Callum's chest.

"You wanna live? Start being useful."

Callum grabs it with shaking hands.

"You said guns don't work."

"I didn't say shoot them."

"What?"

"Shoot the hinges."

The door jumps inward. The bar splinters.

Callum swings the rifle toward the back door.

"What hinges?"

Nessa points with the knife.

"The cellar hatch outside, you idiot. This cabin's got a root cellar. That hole doesn't go to dirt. It goes under."

Lenny looks up, face ruined.

"Under where?"

Nessa's gaze never leaves Callum.

"Where the road keeps what it can't swallow."

The floorboards around the trapdoor blacken with frost.

From below, fingers appear.

Not Corbin's.

Callum knows that at once.

They're his fingers.

Ten of them. Then twenty. Then too many, pale and dirty and clawing at the boards from underneath. They hook into the wood and pull.

The trapdoor opening widens with a wet crack, as if the cabin's bones are breaking.

Callum fires at the back door hinges.

The first shot blows wood chips into the room. The second snaps iron. The third punches the door half off its frame.

Nessa kicks it open.

Rain bursts in.

"Move!"

Callum grabs Lenny under one arm. Nessa gets the other. Together, they drag him toward the back door as the front door explodes inward.

The Callums come in.

Not all of them.

Enough.

Burned Callum squeezes through first, smoking and grinning, skin falling off his jaw in cooked strips. Empty Callum follows, smooth eye sockets twitching as if he can smell them. Broken Callum crawls over the threshold, his crushed side dragging wetly across the floor.

Young Callum steps in last, red flannel dark as liver.

He looks at Lenny.

Then Callum.

Then the open hole in the floor.

"You let him out before," Young Callum says. "Then you put him somewhere worse."

Callum doesn't answer.

Because the memory hits him clean now.

Not flashes.

Not pieces.

The whole rotten thing.

The old culvert. The drainage pipe below Pitch Hook Road, choked with weeds and beer cans and runoff from the mountain. Corbin isn't dead when they pull him from the trunk. His face is swollen. One eye is sealed. Blood bubbles from his mouth when he tries to talk.

Lenny keeps saying they should call someone.

Callum keeps saying his father will ruin them both if this gets out.

Corbin looks up at Callum and whispers that name.

Cal.

Not angry.

Begging.

Callum kicks him.

Once.

In the ribs.

Not hard enough to kill him.

Just hard enough to stop the sound.

That's what he tells himself.

Then they shove Corbin into the culvert.

Not bury.

Not kill.

Worse.

They hide him alive in a concrete throat under the road while the rain comes down and the water rises.

Callum stumbles through the back door into the rain, dragging Lenny with him. Nessa comes after them and slams the broken door shut behind her, though it won't hold for more than a breath.

The back of the cabin drops into a narrow clearing crowded by pines. Beside the wall, half-buried under weeds and a sheet of rusted tin, is the root cellar hatch.

Nessa points.

"There."

Callum fires once.

The lock jumps but doesn't break.

He fires again.

This time the latch blows apart.

The cabin door behind them crashes open.

Nessa hauls the cellar hatch up.

"Down."

Lenny stares into the dark.

"I can't."

"You can or you can die up here."

Callum shoves him.

Lenny screams as he drops down the short ladder, his broken ankle banging every rung. Nessa follows. Callum turns back.

The doubles stand in the rain.

All of them now.

More than all of them.

The clearing fills with Callum Rooks. Burned. Broken. Smiling. Drowned. Eyeless. Young. Old. Mangled. Beautiful. Dead. Not dead enough.

Clean Callum stands at the center.

The fire's gone out on him. His face is perfect again.

"We're not trying to scare you," he says.

Callum laughs. It sounds insane even to him.

"Could've fooled me."

"We're trying to bring you home."

"I'm not going with you."

Clean Callum's eyes soften.

That's the most frightening expression yet.

"You already did."

Hands grab Callum's ankle from below.

Real hands.

Nessa's.

"Down, dumbass."

Callum drops into the root cellar and slams the hatch as fingers scrape across the top.

Darkness swallows him.

For three seconds, there's nothing.

Then Nessa strikes a match.

Yellow light blooms.

The root cellar isn't a root cellar.

It's a tunnel.

Stone walls. Low ceiling. Mud floor. Roots hang down like veins. Old mason jars line shelves along one side, but what floats inside them isn't preserves.

Teeth.

Fingernails.

Clumps of hair.

Tiny scraps of cloth.

A toy car.

A silver lighter.

A cracked black button.

Callum's stomach folds.

Lenny sees the jars and starts praying under his breath.

Nessa lights a lantern hanging on a nail.

"This way."

"Where does this go?" Callum asks.

Nessa starts walking.

"You know where."

"No, I don't."

She doesn't even turn around.

"You're still doing it."

Above them, footsteps move across the hatch.

Too many feet.

The tunnel slopes downward. Mud sucks at their boots. The air gets colder with every step. Lenny limps between them, one arm around Callum, one around Nessa, and his breath comes in torn little whistles.

The walls start changing.

At first, Callum thinks it's just shadows. Then he sees the marks.

Names scratched into stone.

Not one or two.

Hundreds.

Some old enough that the letters have softened with damp. Some fresh, sharp, white against black stone.

Callum sees Pilcher.

The logging truck driver.

He sees Dallow.

Kitra's family name.

He sees Brusk, scratched three times.

He sees Rook so many times he stops counting.

Then he sees Corbin Thatch.

The letters are carved deeper than the rest.

Lenny stops walking.

"Oh God."

Nessa lifts the lantern.

The tunnel opens into a wide concrete chamber.

A culvert.

Not the one under the road.

All of them.

Every drainage pipe, every ditch, every runoff channel on the mountain seems to meet here in a place that shouldn't fit beneath the cabin. Water trickles from round black mouths set into the walls. Rainwater. Road water. Grave water.

And in the center of the chamber sits Corbin Thatch.

Or what's left of him.

He's seventeen forever and not seventeen at all. His blue windbreaker clings to bones and blackened skin. His head tilts too far to one side. Mud packs one eye socket. His hair hangs in strings over his forehead. Pine roots weave through his ribs and into the concrete beneath him, pinning him upright like the mountain has grown through him.

But his mouth moves.

Callum makes a small sound.

Corbin lifts his face.

"Cal," he says.

Lenny collapses to his knees.

"I'm sorry. I'm sorry. I'm so sorry."

The chamber trembles.

Water runs faster from the pipes.

Nessa steps back, giving the dead boy room.

Callum wants to run. There's nowhere to run to. Behind him are the doubles. Ahead is Corbin. Inside him is the truth, finally loose and clawing.

Corbin looks at Lenny first.

"You held the light."

Lenny nods, weeping.

"I did. I'm sorry."

"You heard me."

"Yes."

"You left."

"Yes."

Corbin's jaw works. Mud slides from his cheek.

The water around Lenny's knees darkens.

Then Corbin looks at Callum.

Callum shakes his head.

Not in denial now.

In plea.

"Don't."

Corbin's ruined mouth almost smiles.

"You said I was nobody."

Callum can't speak.

The doubles arrive behind them.

They fill the tunnel mouth, shoulder to shoulder, face upon face, all of them watching. Silent now. No laughter. No whispers.

The show is over.

This is the part they came for.

Nessa speaks softly.

"Say it."

Callum turns on her.

"Say what?"

"The thing you've been swallowing for sixteen years."

"I was a kid."

"So was he," she snaps.

Callum looks at Corbin.

At the roots in his ribs.

At the windbreaker.

At the mouth that begged through carpet and steel.

His throat closes.

"I didn't mean for it to go that far."

The chamber groans.

The doubles hiss.

Nessa's eyes flash.

"That ain't it."

Callum's anger rises because anger is easier than horror. Easier than grief. Easier than anything.

"What do you want from me?"

Corbin answers.

"You."

The word isn't monstrous now.

It's tired.

Callum laughs once, shattered.

"Everybody keeps saying that."

Corbin lifts one hand. It shouldn't move. It does. Roots snap softly as his fingers rise and point toward the water.

Callum looks down.

His reflection stares back from the black puddle.

Then another reflection.

And another.

All the Callums crowd around him in the water, their faces layered under his skin.

Clean Callum speaks from behind him.

"We're the parts that got made when you wouldn't become one whole thing."

Broken Callum clicks his jaw.

"The crash."

Burned Callum peels black skin from his cheek.

"The rage."

Empty Callum touches his smooth eye sockets.

"The not seeing."

Wet Callum coughs creek water.

"The leaving."

Young Callum steps beside Corbin and looks smaller now. Less cruel. More scared.

"The first choice," he says.

Callum's legs weaken.

Lenny reaches for him.

"Callum."

Callum jerks away.

"Don't."

Corbin watches him.

The dead boy waits.

The mountain waits.

Every version of Callum waits.

And for the first time in his life, Callum understands there's no sentence clever enough to save him. No father. No money. No beautiful car. No grin. No lie polished smooth enough.

Only the thing.

The true thing.

He drops the rifle.

It lands in the water with a dull splash.

"I killed you," Callum says.

The chamber shivers.

Lenny bows his head.

Nessa closes her eyes.

Callum's voice breaks, but he keeps going because if he stops now, he'll never start again.

"I put you in the trunk. I hit you. I laughed. I drove you up here. I shoved you into that pipe while you were still breathing."

Corbin's face doesn't change.

Callum presses both hands to his mouth, but the words force themselves through.

"You begged me. You called me Cal. You asked me not to leave you. And I left you."

The doubles begin to breathe.

All of them at once.

One inhale.

Deep.

Endless.

Callum looks at Lenny.

"We left him."

Lenny nods, crying.

"Yes."

"No," Callum says. "I did."

The chamber goes silent.

Even the water stops.

Nessa opens her eyes.

Callum turns back to Corbin. His voice is barely there now.

"He wanted to call someone. I wouldn't let him."

Lenny looks up sharply, stunned.

Callum doesn't look away from Corbin.

"I told him my father would crush us. I told him you were probably dead anyway. I told him nobody would believe your family over mine. I told him you were nobody."

The truth strips him down to meat.

"I was wrong."

For a moment, nothing happens.

Then Corbin exhales.

It's small.

Almost peaceful.

The roots in his ribs loosen.

The pipes around the chamber begin to roar.

Water surges in from every opening, black and cold, rising fast around their ankles, their calves, their knees.

Lenny screams.

Nessa grabs him.

"Up. Now."

The doubles part around the tunnel mouth.

All except Clean Callum.

He stands between Callum and the way out.

"You confessed," Clean Callum says.

Callum nods, shaking.

"Yeah."

Clean Callum smiles sadly.

"That doesn't mean you leave."

Behind Callum, Corbin stands.

Bones crack. Roots tear. Mud falls from him in chunks. The dead boy steps out of the concrete and into the water.

He's small.

God, he's so small.

Seventeen.

Just seventeen.

Callum backs away until Clean Callum's hand settles on his shoulder.

There's no force in it.

There doesn't need to be.

Lenny is sobbing in the tunnel.

"Callum! Come on!"

Callum looks at him.

For once, he could ask for help.

For once, someone might even try.

But the water is at his waist now, and Corbin is in front of him, and every version of himself is behind him.

Callum thinks of the Mustang wrapped around the pole. The road. Tamsin's text. Lenny's flashlight. Nessa's knife. Corbin's voice in the dark.

You should've listened.

He laughs softly.

Not because anything is funny.

Because he finally hears it.

"Go," he tells Lenny.

Lenny shakes his head.

"No."

"Go."

Nessa grabs Lenny by the collar and drags him hard.

"Don't waste it."

The doubles close in around Callum.

Hands touch him. Burned hands. Broken hands. Young hands. Wet hands. His hands.

They don't rip him apart.

Not yet.

They guide him.

Corbin turns toward the largest pipe, the one at the far end of the chamber. Black water pours from it, rushing backward somehow, flowing uphill into darkness.

Callum understands.

The pipe.

The road.

The place they left him.

"No," Callum whispers.

Corbin looks back.

Callum starts crying then. Real crying. Ugly and useless and too late.

"I'm sorry."

Corbin studies him with his one mud-dark eye.

Then he says, "I know."

That's worse than hate.

The hands push Callum forward.

Water closes over his thighs. His chest. His throat.

He fights at the last second because of course he does. Because truth doesn't make him brave. Confession doesn't make him noble. He thrashes and screams and grabs at the concrete lip as the doubles shove him into the pipe.

His nails tear.

His knee strikes stone.

His head hits the low ceiling.

Darkness swallows him feetfirst.

Corbin crawls in after him.

So do the others.

Every version.

All of him.

The pipe is too narrow. It crushes his shoulders. Water fills his mouth. Pine needles scrape his face. Somewhere ahead, he hears his own old laughter from the night at the quarry. Somewhere behind, Corbin breathes wetly.

Thump.

Callum kicks.

Thump.

His heel hits concrete.

Thump.

Nobody opens the trunk.

Nobody comes back.

The mountain takes him deeper.

Above, Lenny and Nessa burst out through the root cellar hatch into rain just as the cabin collapses inward.

It doesn't burn.

Doesn't explode.

It just collapses like a wet cardboard box.

Like it's been hollow for a hundred years and only now remembers.

The doubles are gone.

The Mustang's headlights still glow through the trees below, weak and yellow, pointed at the empty road.

Nessa drags Lenny through the mud until they reach the trail. He's half-conscious, mumbling prayers, apologies, names. She doesn't comfort him. She doesn't tell him it's over.

Because it isn't.

Not for him.

Not exactly.

Dawn comes thin and gray over Pitch Hook Road.

Deputy Orla Senn finds the Mustang first. Passenger side crushed around the telephone pole. Driver's door open. Blood on the seat. Phone cracked in the mud outside, still lit somehow, though the battery should've died hours ago.

One message sits unsent on the screen.

Tamsin, I need to tell you what I did.

They find Lenny near the lower trail, shivering under Nessa Quill's old coat, his ankle broken, his hair gone white at the temples. He tells them everything.

Not at once.
Not cleanly.
But enough.
By noon, men with ropes and lights pry open the culvert below Widow's Elbow.
They find Corbin Thatch's remains wedged deep inside, tangled in roots and silt and sixteen years of runoff.
They don't find Callum.
Not then.
Not ever.
The official story becomes simple because people need simple stories. Callum Rook crashes his car, wanders into the woods, and falls somewhere no one can reach. Maybe a sinkhole. Maybe the creek. Maybe animals.
Lenny tells the truth until people stop inviting him into rooms.
Nessa Quill closes her bait shop for three days, then opens again like nothing happened.
Tamsin comes once, standing at the edge of the road in a black coat while rain taps the hood of her car. She reads the police report. She listens to Lenny's confession. She doesn't cry where anyone can see.
Before she leaves, she walks to the bend near the culvert.
The road is quiet.
Pines stir in the wind.
Water trickles through the pipe below.
Then something thumps from inside.
Once.
Tamsin freezes.
Another thump.
Soft.
Far away.
Like a fist against carpet.
She steps closer, breath caught in her chest.
From deep inside the culvert, a man's voice whispers her name.
Not Callum's voice.
Not exactly.
Too many voices underneath it.
Too many mouths trying to use one throat.
"Tamsin."

She backs away.

The whisper follows.

"I'm sorry."

For a moment, she almost answers.

Then she remembers every warning he ignored. Every lie he dressed up as charm. Every time he made someone else carry the cost of his survival.

Tamsin turns and walks back to her car.

Behind her, the pipe thumps again.

Harder this time.

Then harder.

Then many fists beat from inside the mountain.

Tamsin gets in, locks the doors, and drives away slowly, carefully, both hands steady on the wheel.

In the rearview mirror, the road behind her twists like a corkscrew.

For one pale second, lightning flashes without thunder.

The pavement gleams.

And in that brief white shine, twenty Callum Rooks stand at the bend, watching her go.

One of them raises a hand.

Not waving.

Knocking.

The road waits.

Then the rain starts again.

Blood Bus

The sky turns the color of old bruises before the tornado siren starts screaming.

Rafe Bellamy stands beside a clogged drainage culvert on County Road 6, one boot sunk ankle-deep in mud, one hand gripping a shovel, and watches the clouds fold over themselves above Harker's Mill.

Green sky.

Not green like grass. Not green like money. Green like sickness under skin.

"Shit," he says.

The siren kicks up from town a second later, long and hungry, rising over the wheat fields. It makes the hairs on Rafe's arms stand up. He hates that sound. Everybody in Kansas hates that sound, even the ones who pretend they don't. It's the sound of roofs leaving houses. Cows flying sideways. Power lines snapping in wet blue sparks. People praying to a God they haven't bothered with since Easter.

His county truck sits behind him with its amber light spinning uselessly. Rain ticks against the windshield. Soft at first.

Then harder.

Rafe pulls his phone from his pocket. One bar. Enough to show him a missed text from Junie.

Mom says I don't have to stay if weather gets bad.

He reads it twice, jaw tightening.

Junie's supposed to be at his place. Summer custody. Two weeks, starting yesterday. Not that either of them calls it custody out loud. She's fourteen now, which means every legal arrangement sounds stupid and every adult sounds worse.

He types back with his thumb.

You at the house?

Three dots appear.

Disappear.

Appear again.

At Lottie's. Mom dropped me here because your house smells like mouse death.

Rafe almost smiles.

Almost.

Stay there. Basement if sirens keep going. I'm heading in.

This time she answers fast.

Don't die. I still need rides.

That gets the smile.

"Love you too, gremlin," he mutters, and pockets the phone.

The wind shifts.

That's the thing people who don't live here never understand. Tornado weather doesn't just get windy. It changes its mind. It's finicky like a cat. The air goes hot, then cold, then weirdly still, like the whole world is holding its breath with its mouth open.

Rafe looks west.

The wheat field beyond the road bends flat in one long wave. A flock of blackbirds lifts from the ditch all at once, hundreds of them, a ragged black sheet thrown into the sky. They don't call. They don't scatter.

They just leave.

"Yeah," Rafe says. "Good idea."

He tosses the shovel into the truck bed, climbs behind the wheel, and throws the truck into drive.

By the time he reaches Main Street, the rain is coming sideways.

Harker's Mill is five blocks of stubbornness surrounded by farmland. A diner. A church. A pharmacy with more greeting cards than medicine. A Dollar General that kills local businesses while pretending to be one. The old movie theater, closed since 2009. The high school mascot painted on the grain elevator, sun-faded and peeling, one eye missing so the wildcat looks drunk.

The tornado siren keeps howling.

People move fast but not panicked. Not yet. This town has done this dance before. Men pull flags down. Mothers drag children by the wrists. Old folks stand on porches pretending they're checking the sky, when really, they're daring it.

Rafe parks crooked outside Lottie Crane's diner.

The sign over the door reads LOTTIE'S EAT because the S burned out years ago and Lottie says signs, like people, have a right to age ugly.

Inside, the diner smells like coffee, fryer grease, wet denim, and fear.

Half the town is packed in there.

Lottie stands behind the counter with a cigarette tucked unlit behind one ear, her dyed-red hair piled high, one hand on the radio like she might slap better news out of it.

"Basement," Rafe says as he steps in, dripping water onto the black-and-white tile.

Lottie looks at him. "Well, hell, Rafe, I thought we'd all go stand on the roof and wave."

"I'm serious."

"So am I. People get dumb when weather gets biblical."

At the back booth, Junie sits curled in an oversized gray sweater, sketchbook open, pencil moving. She doesn't look up at first. She's drawing something with wings and too many teeth.

Rafe walks over.

"You okay?"

"Define okay."

"Alive and not currently inside a tornado."

"Then I'm crushing it."

He glances at the page. "That's cheerful."

"It's a bird."

"It's got human hands."

"Evolution."

Before he can answer, the front door bangs open so hard the bell above it snaps off and skitters across the floor.

Everyone jumps.

Deputy Amos Greel stumbles in, soaked to the skin, hat gone, mustache dripping.

"Funnel touched down west of Miller's place," he says. "Power's out past the co-op. Sheriff's moving people to the church basement."

Lottie reaches for the radio volume.

Then the siren cuts off.

It doesn't fade.

It just stops.

The diner drops into a silence so sudden it feels physical.

Every face turns toward the windows.

Outside, through the sheeted rain and low green light, something rolls slowly onto Main Street.

At first Rafe thinks it's an ambulance.

Then he sees the red cross painted on the side. The clean white body. The dark tinted windows. The cheerful letters across the flank.

HARKER'S MILL COMMUNITY BLOOD DRIVE

The bus hisses to a stop in front of the diner.

Its door folds open.

A young woman in red scrubs steps out smiling, untouched by the rain.

The woman stands there like the storm has decided to go around her.

Rain lashes the street. It bounces off truck hoods, turns gutters into fast brown ropes, drums on the diner windows hard enough to make them tremble. But not one drop touches her hair. Not one dark spot blooms on her red scrubs. Her glossy black bob stays sharp against her jaw. Her lipstick is too red for the weather, too fresh for a day like this.

Junie stops drawing.

Rafe feels her go still beside him.

"Who the hell is that?" Amos asks.

Nobody answers.

The woman lifts one pale hand and waves through the diner window.

Not frantic.

Friendly.

Like she's arrived for a bake sale.

Lottie squints. "I didn't hear about any blood drive."

"Because there isn't one," Dr. Camber Holt says from the counter.

He's been sitting there since before Rafe came in, coffee untouched, collar damp, wire-rimmed glasses fogged at the edges. He stands slowly now, thin hands smoothing the front of his shirt. "The county canceled mobile services this week because of the weather. I got the email."

Outside, the woman in red scrubs turns her smile toward him.

The diner seems to take one small breath.

Then the lights flicker.

Every bulb buzzes, dims, flares bright.

When they steady, the woman is already at the door.

The bell doesn't jingle because it's lying dead on the floor. She steps around it with small, neat grace and comes inside carrying a clipboard against her chest.

"Afternoon," she says.

Her voice is warm. Soft. A little amused. The kind of voice that makes people lean in before they know they're doing it.

Lottie points at the windows. "Honey, it's the end of days out there. Afternoon packed its bags an hour ago."

The woman smiles wider. "Weather does make time feel unreliable."

Rafe doesn't like that answer.

He doesn't like the way people seem to relax when she talks. Shoulders lowering. Mouths unclenching. Even Amos lets out a breath, though his hand stays near his belt.

Dr. Holt steps forward. "I'm Camber Holt. I run the clinic here."

"I know," she says.

A pause.

Dr. Holt blinks. "You know?"

"I was hoping you'd be here."

That lands strange.

Rafe sees it land on Holt, too.

The woman looks around the diner at all the wet, frightened, crowded people. Her expression softens into something almost tender.

"My name's Sable," she says. "We're with a regional emergency blood collection program. Storm systems like this cause shortages fast. Wrecks, injuries, displaced patients. Hospitals burn through supply quicker than folks realize."

"Which hospitals?" Dr. Holt asks.

Sable turns those dark eyes back to him. "All of them, eventually."

Another bad answer.

Rafe shifts his weight.

Junie murmurs, "Dad."

It's quiet, but he hears it.

He looks down. Her pencil is still in her hand, but the tip has snapped against the paper. Her face has lost its bored teenage armor.

"What?" he asks.

She doesn't look at him. She looks at Sable.

"Her badge," Junie whispers.

Rafe follows her stare.

Sable wears a white plastic name badge clipped to her scrub top.

It doesn't have a hospital logo.

It doesn't have a last name.

It doesn't have a photo.

Just one word in block letters.

SABLE

Below that, in smaller type:

YOU'RE GIVING MORE THAN YOU KNOW

Rafe's stomach tightens.

Lottie snorts. "Cute slogan."

"It's true," Sable says.

Nobody laughs.

Outside, thunder rolls low enough to rattle the coffee cups.

Sable moves farther into the diner, and people part without thinking. She touches Mrs. Danner's shoulder as she passes. Squeezes Reverend Pike Talmadge's wrist. Brushes two fingers across Marnie Vetch's knuckles where the girl sits at the counter chewing gum too fast.

Every person she touches goes quiet.

Not scared, exactly.

Listening quiet.

Like something under the floor has begun humming a song only they recognize.

"We're set up for quick donations," Sable says. "Ten minutes per person. Juice and crackers afterward. Fully sterile. Fully safe."

"During a tornado warning?" Rafe says.

Sable looks at him for the first time.

Her eyes are so dark he can't tell where the pupils end.

"And you are?"

"Not interested."

A few people chuckle. Small. Nervous.

Sable's smile doesn't change, but something behind it adjusts.

"Needles bother you, Rafe?"

The diner goes cold around him.

Junie turns her head slowly.

Rafe hears his own heartbeat once, hard and stupid.

"I didn't tell you my name," he says.

"No," Sable says. "You didn't."

Amos steps between them then, not fast, but firm. "Ma'am, I think we need to see some identification beyond a plastic badge."

"Of course."

Sable opens the clipboard.

There's no paper on it.

Just a sign-up sheet printed directly onto the board, names already written in neat blue ink.

Lottie Crane.

Dr. Camber Holt.

Pike Talmadge.

Marnie Vetch.

Sheriff Nadine Crosswell.

A dozen more.

Half the people in the diner.

Lottie leans over, face twisting. "Now wait a goddamn minute."

At the bottom of the list, one blank line waits.

Sable taps it with one red fingernail.

"Looks like we still need one more."

Rafe stares at the blank line.

Outside, the wind presses its whole body against the diner. The front windows bow inward, just a little, and every pane gives a faint complaint. Somewhere down the block, metal tears loose with a shriek and goes tumbling into the street.

Nobody moves toward the basement.

That's the first thing that scares him.

These people know storms. They know when to run low and hunker down. But right now they're all staring at Sable's clipboard like the tornado's been postponed.

Dr. Holt reaches for the sign-up board.

Sable lets him take it.

He studies the names, jaw tight, glasses slipping down his nose.

"This is impossible," he says.

"Is it?" Sable asks.

Holt looks up. "Yes."

"Then it must be something else."

Smooth as cream.

Rotten underneath.

Lottie snatches the clipboard from Holt. "I didn't sign shit."

"No," Sable says. "Not yet."

"Then why's my name on it?"

"Because you're generous."

Lottie gives a harsh laugh. "Lady, I'm mean as a snake and everybody here knows it."

"Mean people can still bleed beautifully."

That shuts her up.

Junie slides out of the booth and steps behind Rafe. She's trying not to make it obvious. He feels her fingers pinch the wet back of his work shirt anyway.

"Basement," Rafe says again, louder this time. "Everybody. Now."

A few heads turn toward him. Mrs. Danner looks confused, like she's waking up in a room she doesn't remember entering. Marnie Vetch stops chewing her gum. Reverend Pike Talmadge puts one hand over his chest.

Then Sable claps once.

Soft.

Barely louder than a moth hitting glass.

Everyone looks back at her.

"Before anyone shelters," she says, "we really should begin. Emergency supply matters most during emergency conditions. That's when good people show what's inside them."

Pike gives a little nod.

Rafe sees it and wants to shake him.

The reverend rises from his booth. He's broad-shouldered, handsome in that polished church-sign way, with damp blond hair combed back from his forehead. He looks at the others as if there's already a congregation seated before him.

"She's right," Pike says. "There's life in the blood."

Sable's smile turns private.

Dr. Holt frowns. "Pike, maybe we should wait until after the warning."

"People may need help now."

"You don't even know who she works for."

"I know need when I hear it."

"No," Rafe says. "You know a pretty voice when it flatters you."

That gets Pike's eyes on him.

For one second, the old football player shows under the preacher. The man who likes being followed. The man who likes standing tallest in a room.

"Careful, Rafe."

"Been careful all day. It's overrated."

Amos clears his throat. "Let's not make this worse."

The lights flicker again.

This time they go out.

The diner drops into a murky green dimness, lit only by the storm outside and the red emergency sign over the back hallway.

Someone gasps.

A child starts crying.

Then the blood bus lights up.

Through the front windows, its interior glows warm and golden. Too warm. Too steady. The white bus sits in the chaos of the storm like a clean tooth in a smashed mouth.

Its door waits open.

Sable gestures toward it.

"We can take six at a time."

"No," Rafe says.

But Lottie is already moving.

Not like she wants to. Not exactly. Her face is twisted with anger, but her feet carry her anyway. She comes around the counter, wiping her hands on her apron, cigarette still behind her ear.

"Lottie," Rafe says.

She looks at him, and for a moment he sees real fear in her eyes.

"I don't know why I'm walking," she whispers.

Then Sable touches her elbow.

Lottie's face eases.

"Oh," she says softly. "Well, hell."

Pike follows. Then Marnie. Then Mrs. Danner's husband, Bill, who's got liver spots on both hands and a tremor that suddenly looks less shaky. Two more rise from separate tables.

Dr. Holt reaches for Lottie, but Sable steps in front of him.

"Doctor," she says. "You'll be needed inside."

Holt's expression changes.

Grief crosses it so fast Rafe almost misses it.

His dead wife. Leukemia. Years of blood bags and hospital nights. Rafe remembers the whole town collecting money in coffee cans.

Sable knows too.

Somehow.

"You understand better than most," she tells him.

Holt swallows.

Then he walks toward the door.

Junie grips Rafe's shirt harder.

"Dad," she says.

This time there's no sarcasm in it.

Rafe grabs her hand.

Amos moves with them, one hand on his holster, eyes wet and angry.

"Everybody else," Amos barks, "basement. Right now. Move."

The remaining people flinch into motion.

Sable glances back once from the doorway.

Her eyes settle on Rafe, then Junie.

"Don't worry," she says. "We won't forget you."

Then she steps into the rain that still doesn't touch her.

And the donors follow her into the bus.

The bus door folds shut behind the last donor.

The sound is soft, almost polite.

Inside the diner, people start moving again as if someone's untied invisible strings from their wrists and ankles. Chairs scrape. Coffee cups rattle. A little boy sobs into his mother's coat. Amos keeps waving folks toward the back hallway, his voice getting rougher every time he says basement.

"Move it. Come on. Don't stand there gawking. You wanna meet Jesus, do it someplace less stupid."

Rafe pulls Junie with him, but she twists hard enough to make him stop.

"What?" he says.

She points at the window.

The bus is full of light now.

Not fluorescent hospital white.

Gold.

Thick.

Honeyed.

It leaks around the dark window seams and glows through the rain, making every drop look briefly alive before it hits the pavement.

Junie's voice comes out small. "You hear that?"

Rafe listens.

At first, he only hears the storm. The wind. The diner sign clacking on its rusted hooks. The wet slap of something loose hitting brick down the street.

Then he catches it.

A slow thump.

Not from the sky.

From the bus.

Thump.

Pause.

Thump.

"Generator," Amos says from behind them, but he doesn't sound like he believes it.

The rhythm comes again. Deeper now.

Thump.

The diner windows tremble.

Junie presses both palms over her ears. "That's not a generator."

Rafe looks toward the back hallway. The last of the customers are disappearing down the stairs. Lottie's place has an old cellar under it, low ceiling, concrete floor, canned tomatoes on metal shelves, enough spiders to start a government. Right now it sounds pretty damn good.

But the bus keeps thumping.

He sees movement behind one tinted window.

A hand presses against the glass.

Lottie's hand.

He knows it by the wedding ring she still wears from husband number two, a fat turquoise stone she says is ugly enough to keep thieves away.

Her fingers spread.

Then curl.

Then slide down, leaving no streak.

"Rafe," Junie says.

"I see it."

"No. Her hand."

"I said I see it."

"No, look at her hand."

He does.

At first, it's just a palm against black glass.

Then it changes.

The knuckles smooth. The swollen joints narrow. The crooked middle finger, bent for years from arthritis and old diner work, straightens itself with a delicate little twitch.

Rafe feels his mouth go dry.

Lottie's hand presses harder.

Younger.

That's the only word his brain gives him.

Then it drops out of sight.

Dr. Holt's voice comes muffled from inside the bus.

It's not a scream.

Worse.

A sob.

Amos draws his gun.

"Deputy," Rafe says.

"Don't tell me not to."

"I wasn't."

The bus rocks once on its shocks.

The thump changes.

Now it's faster.

Thump-thump.

Pause.

Thump-thump.

Like two hearts trying to learn each other.

Junie steps backward and bumps into a table. Her sketchbook falls from under her arm. It hits the tile open-faced.

Rafe looks down despite himself.

The page isn't the bird with human hands anymore.

It's the bus.

She's drawn it without remembering, maybe without knowing. A long white bus with a red cross, parked under a black sky. But in the drawing, the wheels aren't wheels.

They're mouths.

Each tire is a ring of lips puckered around dark holes.

Rafe bends, grabs the sketchbook, and shoves it against her chest.

"Basement," he says.

This time she doesn't argue.

They run for the hallway.

Behind them, someone knocks on the diner window.

Three neat taps.

Rafe turns.

Sable stands outside, smiling through the glass.

Still dry.

Still perfect.

The wind whips debris past her. Paper. Leaves. A strip of tin. None of it touches her. It curves away at the last second like she's got her own little pocket of calm carved out of the world.

She raises the clipboard.

The blank line isn't blank anymore.

Through rain and glass and green light, Rafe can read the name written there now.

Juniper Bellamy.

Junie makes a sound like she's been punched.

Rafe's anger comes so hot it feels clean.

"No," he says.

Sable can't hear him.

Or maybe she can.

Her red smile widens.

Then something big slams into the diner roof.

The whole building jumps.

The front windows burst inward.

Glass flies across the booths in a glittering spray. Wind invades the diner with a roar. Plates lift off tables. Napkins explode into the air. The old pie case tips over and shatters. Somewhere in the back, pipes groan like they're trying to speak.

Amos fires once.

The shot vanishes into the storm.

Sable is gone.

Rafe grabs Junie and throws himself over her as the world comes apart in green light and screaming wood.

For a second, there is no town.

There is only sound.

Then the floor drops beneath them.

They don't fall far.

Three steps, maybe four.

Rafe lands hard on his hip, shoulder cracking against a concrete wall, one arm still locked around Junie. Something sharp bites into his palm. Glass, probably. He doesn't know or care yet.

The cellar door slams shut above them.

The diner screams overhead.

Wood tears. Metal pops. Plates break in bright little deaths. Then something much larger groans, deep and slow, and the ceiling rains dust onto them.

Junie coughs against his chest.

"Dad?"

That one word does more damage to him than the fall.

"I'm here," he says. "I've got you."

"I think you broke my skeleton."

"Your skeleton's dramatic."

She gives a shaky little laugh that almost turns into a sob.

"Everybody okay?" Amos shouts from somewhere below.

A dozen voices answer in pieces. Yes. Here. I'm bleeding. Where's my mom? Somebody's crying. Somebody's praying. Somebody keeps saying no, no, no like it's the only word left in their head.

Rafe helps Junie sit up. Emergency lights glow red along the basement wall, making everyone look boiled. The cellar smells like damp concrete, old grease, mouse poison, and canned peaches.

Mrs. Danner clutches her little boy under one arm. The boy's cheek is cut. Two teenage dishwashers crouch by the shelves. The town pharmacist sits on a sack of flour, pressing a napkin to his forehead. Amos stands at the foot of the stairs with his gun in one hand and a flashlight in the other, breathing hard.

The stairs above them are half-blocked by splintered wood.

Not completely.

Not yet.

Rafe looks around.

"Where's Lottie?"

No one answers.

Of course no one answers.

Lottie's on the bus.

So are Holt, Pike, Marnie, and the others.

Junie hugs her sketchbook against her stomach. "She wrote my name."

"I know."

"That means something."

"Not if we don't let it."

She looks at him with fourteen-year-old contempt trying hard to cover terror. "That sounded better in your head, didn't it?"

"Most things do."

Amos limps over. Blood runs from a shallow cut above his eyebrow into his mustache. "We need to stay down here till the storm passes."

"That wasn't just storm," Rafe says.

"No shit."

The lights flicker.

The little boy starts crying harder.

Then every phone in the basement buzzes at once.

Not rings.

Buzzes.

A low, angry vibration from pockets, purses, tabletops, hands. Everyone freezes. For a second the cellar sounds full of insects.

Rafe pulls his phone out.

No bars.

No signal.

Still, there's a notification glowing on the cracked screen.

THANK YOU FOR DONATING

Under it, a red droplet icon pulses.

Junie holds up her phone with trembling fingers.

Same message.

Mrs. Danner whimpers. "I didn't donate."

The pharmacist says, "None of us did."

The droplet pulses faster.

Then a second line appears.

SUPPLY LOW

A third.

PLEASE REMAIN AVAILABLE

From above, the thumping starts again.

But it's not outside now.

It's inside the building.

Slow.

Wet.

Heavy.

Thump.

Dust jumps from the basement ceiling.

Thump.

A jar of peaches rattles on a shelf.

Thump.

Amos raises the flashlight toward the stairs. "Who's up there?"

Nobody answers.

Then Lottie Crane's voice drifts down through the broken wood.

"Rafe?"

It's weak.

It's scared.

It's Lottie.

Junie grips his wrist. "Don't."

Rafe doesn't move.

The voice comes again.

"Rafe, honey, help me."

Honey.

Lottie has called him dumbass, road boy, handsome-if-you-squint, and once, during a particularly nasty ice storm, a mule-brained son of a bastard.

Never honey.

Amos hears it too. His gun hand tightens.

"Lottie?" he calls.

A pause.

Then laughter.

Soft at first.

Then higher.

Then too many voices laugh with her. Men. Women. Children. All of them pressed behind Lottie's throat.

The basement goes silent except for that horrible blended giggle.

Then something pushes into the gap at the top of the stairs.

A hand appears.

Lottie's hand.

Smooth now. Pale. Young. The turquoise ring hangs loose around one finger.

Her nails have gone red without polish.

They dig into the wood.

Another hand joins it.

Not hers.

Longer. Bonier. With translucent skin and veins moving underneath like worms learning directions.

Rafe steps in front of Junie.

The hands pull.

The blocked cellar door lifts an inch.

Two.

Amos fires.

The muzzle flash fills the basement white.

The bullet hits the hand that isn't Lottie's.

It bursts open.

Something dark and glossy spatters the stairs, steaming where it lands. It smells sweet. Coppery. Like hot pennies dropped into molasses.

The thing above them shrieks.

Then Lottie speaks again, voice suddenly calm.

"Oh, Amos," she says. "You shouldn't waste what's inside you."

Amos backs down one step.

Just one.

But in that cellar, with everyone pressed together under the ruined diner, it feels like surrender.

The dark stuff on the stairs bubbles.

Junie whispers, "That's not blood."

"No," Rafe says. "No it isn't."

The thing above the stairs breathes.

Not Lottie.

Not any one person.

It breathes through gaps in the broken wood, through cracks in the doorframe, through the old bones of the building. The sound is sloppy and crowded. Like a dozen mouths tasting the same air.

Then Sable speaks from above.

"She's improving."

Rafe looks up.

Through a jagged slit between two planks, he sees one dark eye.

Not pressed to the hole.

Waiting inside it.

"Come down here," Amos says, gun raised.

Sable laughs softly. "Deputy, that's so brave. It's almost nutritional."

The word slides into the cellar and sits there.

Nutritional.

Mrs. Danner starts crying without sound. Her little boy stops. His eyes are fixed on the stairs.

Rafe doesn't like that either.

He kneels in front of Junie. Keeps his voice low.

"Back corner. Behind the shelves."

"I'm not leaving you."

"Didn't ask for a debate."

"You never ask. You just grunt and expect people to listen."

"This isn't the time to discover communication."

"It kind of is."

Despite everything, he almost smiles. Then something slams against the cellar door hard enough to shake dust loose in gray sheets.

Everybody screams.

The broken boards jump.

A gap opens wider.

Lottie's face appears upside down at the top of the stairs.

At least, it used to be Lottie's.

Her dyed-red hair hangs in damp ropes around a face twenty years younger and wrong as hell. The deep lines beside her mouth are gone. The sag in her jaw tightened. Her eyes shine black, not brown, and her smile spreads too wide, stretching the skin until tiny red cracks open at the corners.

The cigarette still sits behind her ear.

That tiny detail is somehow worse than everything else.

"Basement's no place for children," she says.

Junie makes a small choking sound.

Rafe stands.

"Lottie," he says.

Her shiny eyes roll toward him. For a second, her smile flickers. Something like the old woman comes up through the new face, kicking and furious.

"Rafe," she says, and now it really is her. "Don't let me in."

Then her mouth snaps shut.

Her head jerks back so hard the neck cracks.

Another voice comes out of her.

Sable's voice.

"But she's so hungry."

Amos fires again.

The bullet takes Lottie in the cheek.

Her head snaps sideways. Black-red fluid spatters the doorframe. The little boy shrieks. Mrs. Danner grabs him and pulls him against her chest.

Lottie's face slides out of sight.

For one heartbeat, there's silence.

Then something drops down the stairs.

It lands on all fours halfway down, too fast for a woman her age, too loose for a human being. Her cheek hangs open where the bullet tore through, but underneath there isn't bone.

There are teeth.

Small ones.

Dozens.

Packed beneath the skin in a wet white cluster, chattering against each other.

Amos says, "Jesus Christ."

Lottie launches herself at him.

Rafe hits her first.

He doesn't think. He just swings the emergency shovel he'd grabbed from the truck, the short one still clipped to his belt by a loop. The metal blade catches Lottie across the temple with a flat, ugly crack.

She hits the wall, bounces, and drops onto the stairs.

For half a second, she looks dead.

Then the wound in her cheek grins.

Junie screams, "Dad!"

Rafe turns as the other hand, the long bony one, snakes through the gap above and grabs Amos by the shoulder.

The deputy fires straight up.

Once.

Twice.

The hand doesn't let go.

Its fingers sink into him like hooks into wet bread.

Amos gasps.

His face changes instantly.

Not pain.

Wonder.

"Oh," he whispers.

Rafe grabs his belt and pulls.

Too late.

The skin around Amos's neck tightens. Veins rise black under his cheeks. His eyes fill with red, not bloodshot, but red all the way through, as if someone's poured sunset behind them.

"Rafe," Amos says.

Then his mouth opens.

A thin red tube slides out from under his tongue.

Living.

Searching.

It trembles in the air between them, smelling.

Junie backs into the shelves. Jars crash around her feet.

Rafe raises the shovel again.

Amos looks horrified.

He knows.

For one second, he's still in there.

"Do it," Amos whispers.

Rafe swings.

The shovel blade takes Amos under the jaw.

It isn't clean.

Nothing about it is clean.

The metal bites through skin, cracks teeth, and knocks him sideways into the cellar wall. The red tube whipping from his mouth snaps against Rafe's wrist, hot and slick. It leaves a burning line across his skin.

Amos drops to one knee.

Not dead.

Not even close.

His gun clatters down the steps, bouncing once, twice, then skidding across the concrete toward Junie.

"Get it!" Rafe shouts.

Junie stares at the gun like it's a snake.

"Junie!"

She moves.

Good girl, he thinks, and hates that the thought sounds like something from when she was five, when she'd climb jungle gyms too high and look back to see if he was watching.

She dives for the gun.

Amos makes a wet clicking sound.

His head snaps toward her.

The thing inside him smells the motion.

Rafe swings again, this time with both hands and every bit of fear in his body. The shovel caves in the side of Amos's face. Bone gives. The red tube lashes out, catches the shovel handle, coils around it, and yanks.

Rafe loses his grip.

Amos rises.

Behind him, Lottie starts crawling down the stairs again, cheek full of teeth chattering like dentures in a jar.

The people in the cellar finally break.

They rush toward the far wall, toward old shelves and stacked flour sacks, toward nowhere. Mrs. Danner trips. Her little boy slips out of her arms and falls hard on the concrete.

Lottie's head snaps toward him.

"Oh, shit," Rafe says.

He slams into her before she can leap.

They go down together on the stairs. Her body feels too strong, too warm, packed with a terrible new life. She claws at his face. Her red nails open his cheek, his neck. The teeth inside her torn face chatter inches from his eye.

"Sweet," she hisses.

"Still mean as a snake," he grunts.

He drives his elbow into her throat.

Something pops.

Lottie laughs through the hole in her cheek.

Then Junie fires the gun.

The shot is huge in the cellar.

Lottie jerks.

A black hole opens in her forehead. For a second, Rafe sees the old woman underneath again. Her eyes clear. Her mouth trembles.

"Burn the bus," she whispers. "Burn that fucker to ash."

Then the teeth in her cheek scream.

Not her mouth.

The teeth.

Rafe shoves her off him and scrambles backward down the stairs as Junie fires again. The second shot catches Lottie in the chest and knocks her into the broken boards. The whole mess above shifts with a heavy groan.

"Dad!" Junie yells.

Amos is coming for her.

He moves badly now, one side of his skull crushed, jaw hanging, but the red thing under his tongue has grown longer. It drags along the floor in front of him, tasting concrete, tasting spilled peach juice, tasting blood.

Junie backs up, gun raised in both hands.

Her arms shake.

"Shoot him," Rafe says.

"I can't."

"He's not Amos anymore."

Amos stops.

His red eyes flick toward Rafe.

Then, somehow, Amos speaks.

"Not… all… gone."

The words come around the tube. Broken. Slippery. Human enough to hurt.

Junie starts crying. Silent tears. Furious tears.

Rafe gets to his feet, but his leg buckles. Pain shoots through his hip. His whole right side feels loose and wrong.

Above them, Sable hums.

The tune slides down through the broken diner, sweet as a lullaby.

Amos turns his ruined face up toward it.

So does the little boy.

So does Mrs. Danner.

So do half the people in the cellar.

Their phones begin buzzing again.

One after another.

Rafe's cracked screen lights up on the floor.

SUPPLY CRITICAL

The cellar door tears wider.

Hands reach through.

Pike's big preacher hands.

Marnie's thin fingers with mint-green nail polish.

Dr. Holt's precise hands, clean and careful as ever.

All of them reaching down into the red emergency glow.

Sable's voice follows.

"Please remain available."

Junie raises the gun at the ceiling.

Rafe sees what she's aiming for before she fires.

The old gas line.

He doesn't know if there's enough pressure left. Doesn't know if sparks will catch. Doesn't know if they'll all burn before the bus does.

Junie looks at him.

This time she doesn't ask permission.

Rafe smiles with blood in his teeth.

"Evolution," he says.

Junie fires.

The bullet punches through the pipe.

For one second, nothing happens.

Just a sharp metallic ping.

Just Junie standing there with the gun bucking in her small hands.

Just Rafe tasting blood, dust, and old grease while the cellar waits to become either miracle or grave.

Then the gas begins to hiss.

Thin at first.

Almost polite.

Then louder.

A dry serpent sound.

Everyone hears it.

Even the things wearing people hear it.

The reaching hands stop.

Amos freezes on all fours, the red tube under his tongue lifting toward the pipe like a blind worm smelling weather.

Above them, Sable stops humming.

"Oh," she says.

That one little word is the first thing Rafe has heard from her that isn't smooth.

Junie looks at him, eyes huge.

"Now what?"

Rafe looks around for anything, anything at all. Matches. Lighter. Pilot light. Stove flame. But they're in a basement full of canned peaches, mouse traps, flour sacks, broken glass, and terrified people.

Lottie would've had a lighter.

Of course she would.

The cigarette behind her ear.

Rafe turns toward the stairs.

Lottie lies twisted near the bottom, twitching, not dead, trying to remember how limbs work. Her cigarette is still tucked in her hair, but her lighter isn't visible.

Then he sees it.

A small chrome rectangle clipped inside the front pocket of her apron.

"Junie," he says. "Stay behind me."

She gives a broken laugh. "That's becoming a pretty tired plan."

"Still my favorite."

He lunges.

Amos moves at the same time.

The red tube snaps around Rafe's ankle and pulls. He hits the concrete chin-first. Pain flashes white through his skull. His teeth click together. Something in his mouth goes loose.

Junie screams his name.

Rafe grabs at the floor, fingers scraping through broken glass and peach syrup. The tube tightens around his ankle. Hot acid bites through his sock and into skin.

Amos crawls backward, dragging him closer.

The deputy's ruined face watches him with red eyes.

Human eyes are gone now.

Mostly.

"Hungry," Amos whispers.

"No, you're not," Rafe grunts. "You hate diner meatloaf. Remember?"

The tube squeezes harder.

Rafe kicks with his free foot and catches Amos in the side of the head. Once. Twice. The second kick makes the crushed part of his skull sag inward. Amos shudders, but doesn't let go.

Then Junie comes up behind him with a jar of peaches held over her head.

She brings it down fast and hard on Amos's skull.

The jar explodes.

Glass, syrup, peaches, and black-red fluid splash everywhere.

Amos drops.

The tube loosens.

Rafe tears his ankle free, skin coming with it, and crawls for Lottie.

The gas hiss grows louder.

The air turns sharp. Chemical. Dangerous.

People start coughing.

Mrs. Danner pulls her boy's sweater over his nose. The pharmacist shouts something about sparks, but nobody listens because the things above are tearing the cellar door open now.

Pike's face appears through the gap.

He looks beautiful.

That's the horror of it.

The years have fallen off him. His eyes shine. His skin glows with health. His preacher smile is wide, weird, and wet, and behind him stand Marnie, Dr. Holt, and three others from town, all fresh-faced, all ravenous, all breathing together.

Pike's voice rolls down like Sunday morning.

"Don't be afraid," he says. "We're all one body."

Rafe reaches Lottie.

Her black eyes roll toward him.

"Still in there?" he asks.

Her fingers twitch.

For a second, one hand closes around his wrist. Too strong. He thinks she's going to pull him close and bite his face off.

Instead she shoves him toward her apron pocket.

"Take it," she rasps.

He grabs the lighter.

Her cheek-teeth chatter angrily.

The thing inside her doesn't like that.

Lottie's real mouth twists.

"Tell folks," she whispers, "my pie was better than Nadine's bake-sale garbage."

Rafe almost laughs.

Almost cries.

No time for either.

He flicks the lighter.

Nothing.

Again.

Nothing.

"Come on," he says.

Above, the cellar door finally gives.

Boards split.

Pike drops down the stairs with his arms spread wide.

Behind him, Marnie crawls along the ceiling.

Not the stairs.

The ceiling.

Her mint-green nails dig into concrete as if it's soft mud. Her hair hangs down. Her mouth opens too far, jaw unhinging with a wet click. Her acne is gone. Her skin is perfect.

Her teeth aren't.

They've sharpened into little white needles.

"Rafe," Junie says.

He flicks the lighter again.

A spark spits.

Dies.

Pike lands on the cellar floor.

The red tube slides from under his tongue, thicker than Amos's, pulsing with borrowed heartbeats.

Junie raises the gun.

Click.

Nothing.

Click.

Empty.

Shit.

Pike smiles at her.

"Juniper," he says. "You're needed."

Rafe flicks the lighter one last time.

Flame blooms.

Small.

Blue-orange.

Perfect.

Sable screams from above.

Not angry.

Afraid.

Rafe looks at Junie.

She looks back.

Everything he's failed to say for years crowds up his throat at once. Sorry I got quiet. Sorry I let your mother do the talking because I thought silence was safer. Sorry I didn't know how to be sad without disappearing. Sorry this is the moment I finally figure out what matters.

What comes out is smaller.

"Love you, gremlin."

Junie's face crumples.

"Dad."

Rafe throws the lighter at the broken gas pipe.

The world opens its mouth.

And fire answers.

The basement becomes sun.

Heat punches Rafe flat before sound catches up. For one impossible instant, everything is white and clean, burned free of shape.

Then the roar comes.

It lifts him.

Throws him.

Turns the world into brick, flame, smoke, and screaming.

He hits something hard with his back and slides down through a rain of burning splinters. His ears ring so loud he can't hear his own breath. The right side of his face feels cooked. His hands are empty. His mouth is full of grit.

Junie.

The name doesn't come out.

It only tears through him.

Rafe rolls onto his stomach. Pain blooms everywhere at once, too big to sort. He sees the cellar in shattered pieces. The shelves are down. The stairs are gone. The old freezer tipped onto its side. Peach jars burst and bleed syrup across the concrete, bubbling where embers land.

Bodies move in the smoke.

Some human.

Some not.

Pike stands in the middle of the wreckage, on fire from the waist down.

He doesn't scream.

He laughs.

His preacher suit burns black around him. His skin blisters, splits, then tightens again, healing even as the flames eat it. The red tube from under his tongue thrashes in the air like a hose with pressure behind it.

"We're not dying," Pike says.

His voice isn't just his anymore. It's Lottie's. Amos's. Marnie's. Holt's. A choir crammed into one throat.

"We're becoming."

Then Lottie slams into him from the side.

Rafe stares, stunned.

She's burning too. Her apron is on fire. Her red hair crackles and curls down to the scalp. The thing in her cheek shrieks through its little teeth, but Lottie's real mouth is smiling.

"Not in my goddamn diner," she says.

She drives Pike backward into the remains of the stairs.

Above them, through the blown-open ceiling, the bus glows.

The explosion has ripped the diner's front half apart. Rain pours through broken roof beams. Main Street looks like a war photograph. A parked truck lies upside down against the pharmacy. Power lines whip and spark in the road. The blood bus still sits where it was, white sides scorched, windows cracked, red cross shining through smoke.

Its door is open.

Sable stands inside it.

Her perfect hair is mussed now. One side of her face has peeled loose, showing something underneath that isn't bone. Something smooth and red and threaded with tiny pulsing veins.

She's looking at the diner.

No.

At Junie.

Rafe follows her gaze.

Junie lies near the overturned freezer, half-covered by flour sacks. She's moving. Barely. Her sweater smokes at one sleeve. Blood runs from her nose. Her eyes flutter open, unfocused.

Sable steps down from the bus.

The rain touches her now.

Where it hits, her skin steams.

Rafe tries to stand. His left leg refuses. He crawls instead, dragging himself over glass and hot debris.

"Junie," he rasps.

She hears him. Her head turns.

Sable crosses the broken sidewalk with calm, careful steps. Around her, the storm rages, but the tornado has passed or moved on to ruin some other part of the world. Behind the bus, the clouds churn purple-black, lit from within by silent lightning.

Dr. Holt crawls out behind Sable.

Half his body is burned. His glasses are melted into the skin beside one eye. But his hands are steady, careful, doctor hands still.

"She's compatible," he says.

Sable smiles through her torn face. "Yes. Warm blood. Frightened blood. Loved blood."

Rafe pulls himself faster.

A hand grabs his boot.

Amos.

What's left of him.

The deputy lies under a fallen beam, blackened and broken. One red eye stares from a face that barely holds together.

"Go," Amos whispers.

Then he uses both hands to pull the beam harder against himself, pinning the red thing trying to crawl out of his mouth.

Rafe kicks free and keeps crawling.

Sable reaches Junie first.

Junie tries to scoot back. Her body doesn't obey.

"Don't touch her," Rafe says.

It comes out thin.

Almost nothing.

Sable hears it anyway.

She crouches beside Junie and strokes ash from her cheek with one long finger.

"Your father's blood is stubborn," she says softly. "Yours is *sweeter.*"

Junie spits in her face.

For one second, Sable looks confused.

Then Junie jams something into Sable's torn cheek.

A pencil.

Her sketching pencil, snapped and dirty, driven straight into the wet red meat beneath the peeled skin.

Sable shrieks.

Junie rolls away as Sable claws at her own face. Rafe reaches his daughter, grabs the back of her sweater, and hauls her against him.

"Nice," he gasps.

Junie coughs blood and smiles. "Art school."

Behind Sable, the bus begins to thump again.

Faster.

Louder.

The cracked windows pulse gold.

The tires flex against the pavement.

Not rubber.

Lips.

Just like Junie drew.

They open all at once and scream.

The sound comes from under the bus, from inside the bus, from every window and seam and red-painted letter on its shining white skin.

It's not mechanical.

It's hunger.

The tires open wider, black rubber splitting into wet red mouths. Each mouth is rimmed with flat human teeth. Not fangs. Not monster teeth. Ordinary teeth. The kind that smile for school pictures, bite toast, chatter in cold weather, click together during prayer.

The bus screams with all of them.

Main Street answers.

From the broken pharmacy, someone moans.

From the church basement down the block, people start shouting.

From somewhere beyond the grain elevator, a dog howls once and then stops.

Rafe wraps both arms around Junie and drags her backward through the rain and debris. Every part of him wants to stop. His leg burns. His ankle feels chewed down to wire. His face is wet with blood. His lungs scrape against smoke.

But Junie's alive.

So he moves.

Sable staggers near the curb, both hands pressed to her ruined cheek. The pencil sticks out between her fingers. Black fluid drips from her chin and steams on the pavement.

"You little bitch," she says.

Junie coughs. "Wow. Bedside manner."

Rafe almost laughs again, but the laugh gets stuck because Sable lowers her hands.

The pencil slides out of her face on its own.

The wound closes around the hole.

The red meat pulls together in tiny muscular knots. Her pale skin creeps over it like wax softening near flame.

Dr. Holt stands behind her, twitching, one melted eye fixed on Junie. The rest of his face looks almost peaceful.

"She needs collection," he says.

"Doctor," Rafe says, "you're having a real shitty day."

Holt turns toward him.

For one second, something human flickers there. Some memory of Camber Holt in his little clinic, checking lungs, prescribing antibiotics, telling old farmers to take their damn pills.

Then the thing in him smiles with his mouth.

"All wounds close," Holt says. "Eventually."

The blood bus lurches forward.

Not drives.

Lurches like a cough.

Its front wheels lift, mouths snapping at the pavement, and the whole vehicle shudders like an animal trying to crawl out of its own disguise. The windshield bows outward. A crack branches across it in the shape of veins. Inside, gold light pulses in rhythm with the thumping.

Thump-thump.

Thump-thump.

Thump-thump.

Rafe understands then.

The bus isn't carrying the thing.

The bus is the thing.

Or part of it.

A shell. A stomach. A bright white lure with a clean red cross painted on its side because people trust symbols when they're scared.

The red cross splits down the middle.

Something underneath pushes out.

A slick length of tissue, thick as a man's torso, presses against the white metal from inside, stretching it until rivets pop and steam hisses from the seams. It pulses once.

Twice.

Then the side of the bus tears open.

Blood pours out.

Not gallons.

A river.

It washes across Main Street in a dark red sheet, carrying juice boxes, cotton balls, tubing, plastic donor bags, and things that look like fingers until Rafe sees they're not severed.

They're growing.

Little fingers budding from clots. Tiny hands opening and closing in the flood.

Junie screams.

Rafe hauls her onto the hood of an overturned sedan as the blood river rushes around them. It steams in the rain. It smells sweet and coppery, like hot pennies and spoiled cherries.

Sable wades through it.

The blood climbs her legs like it loves her.

"You can't burn us out," she says. Her voice starts changing. It doubles, triples, deepens. "Fire purifies. Fire prepares. Storm opens. Blood receives."

Rafe looks around for another weapon.

The gun is empty.

The shovel is gone.

The diner is burning.

The gas explosion didn't kill it. It hurt it, sure. It broke the mask. But now the thing is showing its real face, and real faces are always worse.

Junie tugs weakly at his sleeve.

"Dad."

"What?"

She points to the grain elevator.

At first, Rafe doesn't understand. The tall concrete structure stands at the end of Main Street, scarred by years of weather, the faded wildcat mascot glaring down with its one drunk eye. The storm knocked one of its loading chutes loose. It hangs over the street like a broken arm.

Then Rafe sees what's behind it.

The county fuel truck.

His county fuel truck.

He left it by Lottie's diner, but the storm shoved it halfway down the block, spinning it sideways until it wedged against the elevator's lower supports. The tank is dented. One rear tire is gone. Diesel leaks in a shining black puddle beneath it, spreading toward the gutters, mixing with the red flood.

Rafe stares.

Junie's voice is hoarse. "That enough fire?"

"Maybe."

"That's a yes in emotionally constipated dad language."

He presses his forehead against hers for half a second.

Then he says, "I need you to run."

"No."

"Junie."

"No."

The red water slaps against the car hood. One of the tiny hands in the blood grabs at Junie's shoe. She kicks it loose with a strangled cry.

Rafe grips her shoulders.

"Listen to me. You're faster than I am right now. You get to the church. You get anybody left out of the basement. You tell them to run east, away from Main. Don't let anybody touch the blood. Don't let anybody who donated near them."

"And you?"

"I'm going to move the truck."

"You can barely move you."

"Yeah. Well. Trucks are easier. Less mouthy."

Her face twists.

He knows that look.

She knows, too.

This is the moment stories lie about. The noble moment. The music-swelling moment. But there's no music. Just rain, screaming tires, burning diner, and the sound of a monster wearing half their town.

Junie grabs his shirt.

"No. You don't get to disappear now. That's bullshit."

"I know."

"You don't get to finally say things and then leave."

"I know."

"You don't."

"I know."

For once, he doesn't argue. Doesn't joke. Doesn't hide inside quiet. He puts his bloody hand against her cheek.

"I'm sorry," he says.

Her eyes flood.

"That's not enough."

"No," he says. "It isn't."

Sable turns toward them. She has reached the sedan. Blood swirls around her waist. Behind her, the bus unfolds another few inches, white panels peeling back to reveal wet red chambers inside. People are in there. Not whole. Not dead. Donor bodies hang in loops of tubing, suspended like fruit in a butcher's window. Pike's torso pulses near the front. Marnie's face presses against an inner membrane, eyes open, mouth working silently.

Dr. Holt stands beside the torn bus, feeding tubing into his own arm with calm precision.

The doctor is still helping.

That's the worst of it.

Rafe shoves Junie toward the far side of the car.

"Run."

She shakes her head.

"Run, Juniper."

Her mouth opens.

Then something slams into Sable from behind.

Old Cal Bratcher comes out of the smoke in his bathrobe, rubber boots, and an old army helmet sitting crooked on his bald head. He carries a twelve-gauge shotgun almost as long as he is, and the left lens of his thick glasses is cracked.

"Get away from them, you bloodsucking bus whore," Cal says.

He fires into Sable's back.

The blast throws her against the sedan. Black-red meat explodes out of her chest and splatters across the hood. Sable shrieks, folding around the wound.

Cal pumps the shotgun with shaking hands.

"Bellamy," he shouts. "You planning on dying slow or doing something useful?"

Rafe grins despite everything.

"Useful."

"Then do it."

Junie looks at Cal, then at Rafe.

The old man jerks his chin at her. "Girl, if your daddy says run, run. You can hate him later. That's how surviving works."

Junie's face breaks wide open, but she moves.

She slides off the sedan into shallow blood, yelps as it splashes her jeans, then bolts toward the alley beside the pharmacy.

Sable twists to follow.

Cal fires again.

This time the blast takes her lower jaw clean off.

It hits the pavement and keeps moving, crawling on its teeth toward the blood flood.

Rafe drops from the sedan, nearly collapses, catches himself on the car door, and limps toward the fuel truck.

Every step is pain.

Every breath is smoke.

The blood on the street tries to hold him. Not like mud. Like hands. Soft little grips forming around his boots, tugging, pleading. He feels pulses through the soles of his feet. Human pulses. Hundreds of them.

Names whisper from the blood.

Lottie.

Amos.

Pike.

Marnie.

Nadine.

People he knows. People he's seen buying coffee, pumping gas, arguing over scratchers, laughing outside church, smoking behind the diner.

Help us, some whisper.

Join us, others whisper.

One voice says, Rafe, honey.

He doesn't look down.

At the truck, the driver's side door is jammed. He grabs the handle and pulls. Nothing. He pulls again and feels something tear in his shoulder.

"Come on!"

The bus thumps behind him.

The sound grows enormous.

Thump-thump.

Thump-thump.

The whole street pulses with it. The blood river surges higher, climbing curbs, swallowing tires, pouring into storm drains that choke and cough red foam back up.

Rafe slams his elbow through the truck window.

Glass punches into his arm. He reaches inside, unlocks the door, and hauls himself into the cab.

The keys are still in the ignition.

For one perfect second, luck exists.

Then Dr. Holt appears at the passenger window.

His burned face presses to the glass.

"Rafe," he says. "You don't have to lose her."

Rafe freezes.

Holt smiles gently. Sadly.

That's the hook.

Not hunger.

Not threat.

Mercy.

"We preserve what love wastes," Holt says. "We keep the body from betrayal. We keep the heart from stopping. We keep daughters. We keep wives. We keep every precious thing blood abandons."

Rafe's hand tightens on the key.

Holt's one good eye shines.

"I heard my wife again," he whispers. "Inside it. I heard Evelyn singing. Do you understand? She's not gone. No one's gone. Not if enough of us carry them."

For the first time, Rafe sees the grief inside the monster.

It doesn't erase the horror.

It sharpens it.

This thing doesn't just feed on blood. It feeds on the part of people that can't let go.

Rafe thinks of his silent house after the divorce. Junie's empty room. The untouched cereal bowl she'd left in his sink one weekend and how he hadn't washed it for three days because it proved she'd been there.

He understands wanting preservation.

He understands rot pretending to be love.

"No," Rafe says.

He turns the key.

The engine coughs.

Holt's face changes.

"Rafe."

The engine coughs again.

The bus screams.

The fuel truck roars alive.

Rafe slams it into gear.

The truck lurches forward, scraping against the grain elevator support. Metal shrieks. The tank bangs hard behind him. Diesel sloshes.

Holt clings to the passenger side, fingers punching through the cracked window, red tube sliding from his mouth, seeking Rafe's throat.

Rafe stomps the gas.

The truck breaks free.

Holt loses his grip and drops under the rear wheels.

The bump is sickening.

Rafe doesn't stop.

He aims at the bus.

Through the cracked windshield, he sees Sable standing in the street, jaw gone, face split, hair plastered wet to her skull. The blood flood gathers around her, lifting her, rebuilding her. Cal fires from somewhere behind her until the shotgun clicks dry.

She points at Rafe.

The bus turns toward him.

Its front grill opens.

A mouth stretches across the entire front end, chrome bending into lips, headlights rolling like eyes in sockets of meat. Inside that mouth, Rafe sees seats. Donor chairs. IV poles. Children's stickers. Lottie's turquoise ring stuck between two teeth.

He presses the gas harder.

The fuel truck hits the bus at forty miles an hour.

The impact folds the world in half.

Rafe goes through the windshield.

For a moment, he flies.

Rain touches his face.

Fire follows behind him.

The tanker ruptures as it slams into the bus's open mouth. Diesel sprays everywhere, a black shining fan. Sparks from the downed power lines leap across the flood. The blood catches first, not burning red but blue, then green, then a hungry white that races across Main Street faster than thought.

The bus tries to scream.

Fire pours down its throat.

The explosion lifts it off the ground.

Windows burst outward. White metal peels back. The red cross flares bright enough to burn itself into Rafe's eyes. Inside the bus, all the borrowed bodies ignite at once, and the choir inside them becomes a sound too large for one town.

Sable burns standing up.

For a second, through the fire, her face is almost human.

Almost sad.

Then she comes apart.

The shock wave throws Rafe into the side of the grain elevator. Something breaks inside him. Maybe several things.

He drops into the mud and burning rain.

And there, under the fading roar, he hears a normal sound.

A girl screaming.

"Dad!"

Junie runs toward him through smoke, coughing, limping, alive. Cal hobbles behind her with the empty shotgun in both hands. Behind them, a few others spill from the church basement and alleyways, faces gray with ash, eyes huge and shining.

Junie falls to her knees beside Rafe.

"Don't you dare," she says. "Don't. Don't. Don't."

He wants to answer.

His mouth fills with blood instead.

She grabs his hand and squeezes. Her face swims above him, rain streaking clean lines through soot.

"Rafe Bellamy, you do not get to make me feel feelings in public and then die in the street."

That should make him laugh.

It comes out as a wet cough.

Cal kneels with a grunt on Rafe's other side. "Boy's stubborn. Might live just to irritate everybody."

Junie looks at him. "Can you help him?"

"I'm an old crank with a shotgun, not a hospital."

"That's not helpful."

"I'm aware."

Rafe squeezes Junie's hand.

Barely.

Her eyes snap back to him.

"Dad?"

He forces the words up through blood and smoke.

"Church," he whispers. "Get… east."

"No."

"Still… coming."

She looks over her shoulder.

Main Street burns.

The bus is gone.

Not destroyed exactly. Nothing that old dies clean. But its body is scattered across the road in flaming sheets of metal and meat. The blood flood blackens and curls in the fire, shrinking from the rain. The mouths in the tires shrivel into smoking rubber.

Then something moves in the gutter.

A clot the size of a fist pulses once.

Junie sees it.

So does Cal.

The clot splits.

A tiny red hand emerges.

Cal lifts his boot and stomps it flat.

"East," he says.

Junie looks back at Rafe, torn in half.

He squeezes her hand again, stronger this time.

"Go," he says.

"No."

"Gremlin."

Her face crumples.

"Don't call me that like it's goodbye."

He tries to smile.

"Then don't make it one."

That gets her.

She nods hard, tears cutting through soot. Then she turns to Cal.

"We're carrying him."

Cal opens his mouth.

Junie points one shaking finger at him. "Do not argue with a traumatized teenage girl holding an empty gun."

Cal closes his mouth.

"Fair."

They carry him.

Not well.

Not gracefully.

It's bumpy and ugly.

Cal takes his shoulders. Junie takes one arm and half his weight, cursing at him every time he slips. Other survivors help once they understand. Mrs. Danner. The pharmacist. One of the dishwashers. Together they drag Rafe away from Main Street as the town burns behind them.

They move east, toward the wheat fields, under a sky still bruised green at the edges.

No one speaks much.

The ones who donated are either burning, dead, missing, or worse.

Nobody says that out loud.

At the edge of town, Junie looks back.

Harker's Mill is a black wound in the rain. The diner is gone. The blood bus is gone. The church bell rings once, though no one is pulling it.

Maybe heat.

Maybe wind.

Maybe something saying it isn't finished.

Then the bell rings again.

Cal flinches.

Junie hears it and looks at him.

"What?"

The old man's face has gone slack with fear.

"Cal?"

He swallows.

"After the wagon burned in '51," he says, "my granddad heard bells."

Rafe tries to lift his head.

Can't.

Junie's voice goes flat. "What does that mean?"

Cal stares back at town.

"It means the thing doesn't die where it feeds," he says. "It dies where it's remembered."

The rain softens.

Far behind them, in the ruined center of Harker's Mill, something under the street gives one slow thump.

Junie hears it.

Everyone hears it.

Thump.

Then nothing.

For a while.

They keep walking.

By dawn, the storm has passed, leaving the world washed pale and steaming. Emergency lights flicker on the horizon. Sirens approach from the highway. Real ambulances this time. Real uniforms. Real people carrying real bandages, shouting real questions.

Junie sits in a ditch with Rafe's head in her lap and refuses to let anyone take him until she sees their badges, their vehicle markings, their faces in the rising light.

A paramedic says, "Honey, we're here to help."

Junie looks at the red cross on the side of the ambulance.

Her hands tighten in Rafe's hair.

The paramedic follows her stare, confused.

Rafe opens one swollen eye.

The ambulance waits on the road, white and clean.

Too clean.

For a second, nobody moves.

Then the ambulance engine idles.

Normal.

Just an engine.

No thump underneath it.

No gold light behind the windows.

Junie lets out a breath that breaks halfway through.

"Okay," she says. "But nobody takes blood from anybody."

The paramedic blinks. "What?"

Junie points toward the smoking town.

"Nobody," she says.

Three days later, the news calls it a tornado-related chemical fire.

A tragic chain reaction.

Fuel truck. Gas leak. Local diner destroyed. Multiple casualties. Survivors in shock, offering inconsistent accounts due to trauma.

That's what the news calls it.

Rafe survives.

Barely.

He wakes in a hospital bed in Wichita with tubes in both arms and Junie asleep in a chair beside him, curled under a blanket two sizes too small. Her sketchbook lies open on her lap.

He turns his head, slow and painful.

The page shows a road.

A long road through wheat fields.

At the far end sits a wagon.

Not a bus.

A wagon.

Wooden wheels. Red canvas. A painted symbol on the side that isn't quite a cross and isn't quite a mouth. Beside it stands a woman in red, her face left blank.

Rafe's heart monitor beeps faster.

Junie wakes instantly.

"What?" she says.

He can't speak yet.

His throat is raw from smoke and tubes and all the things he almost didn't get to say.

So he points.

Junie looks at the drawing.

All color leaves her face.

"I drew that in my sleep," she whispers.

From the hallway comes the sound of hospital wheels.

A cart rolling past.

Normal sound.

Rubber on tile.

Rafe and Junie both listen until it fades.

Neither of them relaxes.

On the windowsill, in the hard white morning light, a small plastic blood donation sticker sits where no sticker had been before.

It's bright red.

Cheerful.

Shaped like a drop.

Printed across it in tiny white letters are six words.

YOU'RE GIVING MORE THAN YOU KNOW

Junie takes Rafe's hand.

This time, neither of them lets go.

The Missing Girl

Nolan Vey sees the poster at dusk, when the whole town looks bruised, broken, and ashamed.

The sky above Brindle Creek is purple at the edges and yellow near the sawmill, where the sun hangs low behind the dead stacks and rusted conveyor belts. The air smells like cut grass, hot tar, and the creek mud that never quite dries. Somewhere down the street, somebody's burning leaves even though the town council sends out little reminder cards twice a year telling people not to burn leaves.

Nobody listens.

Cricket stops first.

She's got her leash stretched out in front of Nolan, her old gray muzzle lifted, her cloudy eyes fixed on the telephone pole near the corner of Tulip and Carr. Her back legs tremble the way they do when she's tired or when rain is coming. Nolan waits for her to sniff, pee, change her mind, do one of the thousand mysterious dog things that make a ten-minute walk take half an hour.

But Cricket doesn't move.

"What?" Nolan asks.

Cricket gives a low sound in her throat.

Not a bark.

Not a growl.

Something smaller. Almost embarrassed.

Nolan follows her stare to the pole.

There are the usual layers of small-town paper grief stapled into the wood. A yard sale from three Saturdays ago. A lost orange cat named Pickles. A church fish fry with the date bleached pale by weather. A handwritten note offering lawn care, no job too big, no job too small, call Dale.

And over all of them, fresh and bright and wrong, is a missing child poster.

MISSING

LISSY BELL

AGE 9

LAST SEEN WEARING PINK SWEATSHIRT, JEAN SHORTS, WHITE SNEAKERS

The girl's school photo sits in the center. Dark hair. Narrow chin. One front tooth a little crooked. A pale scrape on her right cheek. She should look awkward and stiff the way kids look in school pictures, trapped between the command to smile and the terror of doing it wrong.

But she doesn't.

She looks scared.

Real scared.

Not camera-shy scared. Not my-mom-cut-my-bangs scared. Her eyes are wide enough that Nolan can see too much white around the irises. Her mouth is parted slightly. Her shoulders are raised, like something behind the photographer just touched the back of her neck.

Nolan steps closer.

Cricket whines and pulls back.

"Easy," he says, but his own voice comes out thin.

The poster is stapled at all four corners. Clean paper. Fresh ink. There's a phone number at the bottom for the sheriff's department, plus a smaller one that says CALL MOTHER ANYTIME. A cash reward is listed in bold black type.

Five thousand dollars.

Nolan looks back at the photo.

The girl's eyes aren't pointed at the camera.

That's the first thing his mind refuses to understand.

He blinks and tries to put the image where it belongs. Maybe the school photographer is standing to one side. Maybe the printer warped the photo. Maybe the girl's got a lazy eye. Maybe it's just the angle, just the evening light, just the fact that Nolan has slept like garbage for three nights because the neighbor's new security light clicks on whenever a moth farts within six feet of it.

But no.

The girl's looking to her left.

His right.

Down.

At him.

Nolan takes one step sideways.

The eyes follow.

His skin tightens from his scalp to the backs of his hands.

Cricket yanks the leash hard enough that the nylon cuts into his palm.

"Okay," he says. "Okay, I see it."

He doesn't know who he's talking to. The dog, probably. Himself, maybe.

The girl, not a chance.

He backs away from the pole.

The eyes don't blink.

A car rolls past, a dented green Subaru with two kids in the back seat. The driver, a woman in scrubs, glances at Nolan like he's the strange part of the picture. Man standing on the sidewalk, staring at a missing girl poster with his dog trying to drag him into traffic.

Nolan lifts one hand, pretending everything's normal.

The woman doesn't wave back.

Cricket pulls again, and this time Nolan lets her lead him across the street. She doesn't stop tugging until they're half a block away. Even then, she keeps looking back over her shoulder, lips drawn tight from her teeth.

"You're acting weird," Nolan tells her.

Cricket glances up at him.

Her expression says, You're one to talk.

They walk home under the maples, past houses with blue porch lights and dead flowerpots and tricycles tipped sideways in yards. Nolan tries not to think about the poster. He tries very hard, which means he thinks about nothing else.

Lissy Bell.

He knows the name, kind of. Everybody does by now. Brindle Creek isn't big enough for a missing child to belong only to one family. She vanished five days ago from the strip of woods behind Bircher Elementary. Last bell at 3:10. Seen by two girls near the monkey bars at 3:18. Gone by 3:22. Her backpack found hanging on the chain-link fence like somebody lifted it off her shoulders and set it there carefully.

Not tossed.

Not dropped.

Set there.

Placed gently.

That detail bothers Nolan. It bothered him when he heard it from Mrs. Weikel at the library circulation desk, and it bothers him worse now. Careful things are worse than violent things. Violence can be stupid. Careful means somebody is thinking.

He knows something about missing girls.

That thought comes uninvited, a cold finger tapping the inside of his skull.

Nolan pushes it away.

His sister's name is Tessa, not Lissy. Was Tessa. Is Tessa. He hates that grammar changes when people die, as if language gets to help shovel dirt over them.

Tessa vanished when she was eleven and Nolan was sixteen. County fair. September heat. Ferris wheel lights. Fried dough. The stink of livestock and diesel generators. Nolan let go of her hand for one minute because some girl from school smiled at him from the ring toss booth.

One minute.

Three days later, Tessa came back.

People call that a miracle.

Nolan knows better.

Miracles don't leave rope burns around a child's wrists. Miracles don't make a girl scream when a Polaroid flashes. Miracles don't teach her to sleep under the bed instead of on it.

Cricket stops beside their mailbox.

Nolan realizes his hand is shaking.

"Come on," he says.

Inside, the house is dark and stale. Nolan flicks on the kitchen light, feeds Cricket half a scoop of senior dog food with a spoonful of canned chicken on top, then stands at the sink and drinks water straight from the tap. He doesn't bother with a glass. Glasses are for people who plan on sitting down like humans afterward.

He looks out the kitchen window.

The street behind his house is empty.

The maple leaves shift in the evening wind.

For one ugly second, he expects to see a telephone pole at the edge of his yard where no telephone pole belongs. A fresh white rectangle nailed to it. A little girl's terrified face turned toward his window.

There's nothing there.

Of course there's nothing there.

He shuts the blinds anyway.

Cricket eats three mouthfuls, then leaves the rest. That's how Nolan knows she's really bothered. Cricket never believed in moderation. Cricket once ate a whole stick of butter, paper and all, then looked offended when gravity and biology teamed up against her.

Now she walks into the living room and lies with her chin on her paws, staring at the front door.

Nolan sits in his recliner with the television off.

The house makes its usual nighttime sounds. Refrigerator hum. Floorboards cooling. Pipes clinking inside the wall. A truck coughs past outside, then fades. Somewhere a dog barks twice and quits.

His phone buzzes.

Nolan flinches.

He digs it from his pocket.

Unknown number.

He stares at it until the call dies.

A voicemail pops up immediately.

No.

Absolutely not.

He sets the phone on the side table.

Cricket raises her head.

The phone buzzes again.

Voicemail transcription appears in gray text across the screen.

Nolan doesn't touch it.

He only reads because it's already there, because his eyes betray him before his hand can turn the phone facedown.

Static fills most of the transcription. Nonsense words. Broken syllables. The phone guesses badly.

Then one sentence appears.

don't let them find me

Nolan stops breathing.

The screen brightens in his hand.

Another line crawls into place beneath the first.

please Mr. Vey

His phone slips from his fingers and lands on the carpet.

Cricket stands.

The house is silent now.

Too silent.

The refrigerator stops humming. The pipes stop clicking. Even the night bugs outside seem to have pressed themselves flat against the dark.

Nolan bends slowly and picks up the phone.

The voicemail is gone.

No missed call.

No unknown number.

No transcription.

Nothing.

He checks recent calls with clumsy fingers. Checks messages. Checks deleted voicemails. Checks everything twice because panic makes him stupid and methodical at the same time.

Nothing.

Cricket growls.

Nolan looks up.

The front door is closed. Locked. The deadbolt sits turned in its brass slot.

But something comes through the mail slot.

A rectangle of white paper lies facedown on the entry rug.

Nolan doesn't move.

Cricket growls again, deeper now, her old lips peeling back from yellow teeth.

The paper shifts.

Just a little.

Like something underneath it has taken a breath.

Nolan stands so fast his knee knocks the side table. His phone clatters down again. He doesn't care.

"Who's there?" he calls.

Nobody answers.

The entryway light flickers once.

The paper shifts again.

This time it turns itself over.

Nolan sees the word first.

MISSING

Then the photo.

Lissy Bell is closer than she was on the telephone pole. Her face fills more of the frame now. Her eyes still look at him, but they aren't just scared anymore.

They're desperate.

Her right hand presses against the inside of the paper, flattening small pale fingers against the surface. The ink puckers around them like skin.

Her mouth opens.

No sound comes out.

But Nolan can read lips.

He learned after Tessa came back, because for almost a year his sister couldn't speak above a whisper.

Lissy Bell shapes three words.

It found you.

Nolan doesn't scream.

He wants to. His body has the shape of a scream inside it, all ribs and throat and animal panic, but nothing comes out. He stands in his living room with his hands half-raised, like maybe he's about to surrender to a sheet of printer paper.

Cricket barks once.

The sound cracks the room open.

Nolan jerks backward, hits the edge of the recliner, and nearly falls over it. The poster stays on the rug. Lissy Bell's face stares up at him from the paper, eyes huge, mouth moving without sound.

It found you.

No.

No, that isn't real.

That's a thought. That's trauma putting a mask on coincidence. That's his stupid brain dragging Tessa out of the grave because another little girl is gone and Nolan still can't walk past a carnival flyer without tasting bile.

The paper buckles.

Lissy's fingers press harder from the other side.

Not printed fingers.

Real ones.

The nails are dirty. One is cracked down the middle. The pads of her fingertips blanch white against whatever thin membrane separates her from his living room.

Nolan takes another step back.

Cricket doesn't.

"Cricket," he says, and his voice barely exists. "Come here."

She stands between him and the poster, her legs stiff, her tail low, her gray hackles raised in a crooked ridge down her back.

The poster slides an inch across the rug.

Toward the dog.

Nolan moves then.

He grabs Cricket's collar and hauls her back. She yelps, more surprised than hurt, and snaps at the air near his wrist. Nolan doesn't let go. He drags her into the kitchen, gets the baby gate out from beside the refrigerator, and jams it into the doorway even though Cricket hasn't needed it in years.

She barks at him. Then at the hall. Then at the thing on the rug.

"Stay," he says.

She doesn't care for that.

"Stay."

The second one comes out sharper, meaner, scared enough to sound cruel.

Cricket stops barking. She looks at him with wounded confusion.

That almost breaks him.

"I'm sorry," he whispers.

Then he goes back into the living room.

The poster hasn't moved.

It lies there under the flickering entryway light. The paper is cheap, the kind people buy in bulk for school newsletters and church bake sales. It should be harmless. It should crumple if he steps on it. It should tear if he grabs one corner.

It shouldn't breathe.

But it does.

The surface lifts and settles around Lissy's open mouth.

Nolan circles it, keeping his back close to the wall. The room seems longer than it was before. His front door looks too far away. His own furniture becomes unfamiliar, crouched in shadow like witnesses pretending not to see.

The television screen reflects him.

That's bad enough.

Then it reflects something behind him.

Nolan whirls.

Nothing.

No one.

The kitchen light buzzes. Cricket whines from behind the gate.

Nolan looks back at the poster.

Lissy is turned toward the television reflection now.

Her mouth forms one word.

Behind.

Nolan doesn't turn this time.

He runs.

He bolts into the kitchen, grabs Cricket's leash from the hook, and knocks the baby gate loose with his shin. It clatters against the tile.

Cricket lunges through before it even lands. Nolan gets the leash clipped on wrong the first time, clips it right the second, and yanks open the back door.

Cold air rushes in.

Too cold for September.

His backyard is narrow, fenced with old cedar boards going soft at the bottoms. Beyond it sits the alley, then the backs of other houses, their porch lights glowing in yellow squares. Normal houses. Normal garbage cans. Normal patches of dead lawn and lawn chairs and kids' bicycles left sideways against sheds.

Nolan runs anyway.

Cricket limps as fast as she can. Her hips don't like it. Her breath rasps hard in her throat. Nolan hates himself for making her hurry, but he doesn't slow down.

He gets the gate open and stumbles into the alley.

A raccoon knocks over a trash can two houses down and freezes with its paws on the lid. It looks at Nolan. Nolan looks at it.

The raccoon makes a chittering sound and flees.

Smart animal.

Nolan keeps moving until he reaches the next street over. He doesn't know where he's going until he sees the blue-white glow of the 24-hour laundromat at the corner.

Brindle Creek Suds.

The place is nearly empty. It smells like detergent, wet lint, and old coffee. Three dryers tumble unattended. A teenage boy in a red hoodie sits on a folding table, scrolling through his phone with earbuds in. An elderly man sleeps in a plastic chair with a newspaper folded over his stomach.

Nolan enters too fast.

The bell above the door jingles violently.

The teenager looks up.

Nolan tries to seem normal and fails immediately.

He's barefoot.

He's still holding his phone in one hand. Cricket's leash is wrapped around his wrist. His T-shirt is stuck to his chest with sweat.

"Bathroom?" Nolan asks.

The teenager points without removing an earbud.

Nolan nods too many times. "Thanks."

He doesn't go to the bathroom.

He goes to the pay phone mounted beside it.

It's mostly there as a joke now, a beige relic with a cracked receiver and graffiti scratched into the metal shelf. OUT OF ORDER is written on a piece of tape, but the tape looks older than some of the kids in town.

Nolan lifts the receiver.

No dial tone.

Of course not.

His phone still works. He knows it does. But using it feels wrong now. The impossible thing got in once. It knew his name. It spoke through dead air and vanished from his call log like a hand slipping back under dark water.

Still, the sheriff's department is a phone call away.

A real one.

With real people and fluorescent lights and guns in lockboxes and forms on clipboards.

Nolan unlocks his phone.

The screen shows his reflection for one second before the keypad opens.

His reflection isn't alone.

A pale blur stands behind him, tall and narrow, face lost in a smear of movement.

Nolan drops the phone.

It hits the tile and skids beneath a rolling laundry cart.

Cricket goes insane.

She barks so hard the old man wakes with a snort and flings the newspaper off his lap.

"What the hell?" the man snaps.

The teenager pulls out one earbud. "Yo, control your dog."

Nolan turns around slowly.

There's nobody behind him.

Not in the laundromat. Not by the soda machine. Not near the long row of washers. Just spinning clothes, buzzing lights, a sleeping man no longer sleeping, and a teenager looking annoyed because terror is less interesting than whatever is happening on his phone.

Cricket keeps barking at the blank wall beside the pay phone.

Then Nolan sees it.

Not a person.

A poster.

It's taped beside the bathroom door, half over an old notice about not washing horse blankets in the machines.

MISSING

LISSY BELL

The photo's changed again.

Her face is even closer now. One cheek is flattened sideways as if shoved hard against glass. Her eye on that side looks painfully compressed. Her fingers press near her mouth, five little white shapes bending the paper outward.

And behind her, in the black blur at the back of the photo, something stands.

Nolan can't see its face.

Maybe it doesn't have one.

Maybe it has too many and none of them settle long enough to be called a face.

The teenager follows Nolan's stare.

"Yeah," he says. "Sad, right? My mom made me put one up yesterday."

"Don't look at it," Nolan says.

The teenager laughs once. "What?"

"Don't look at it."

Now the old man looks too.

So does the teenager.

So does Nolan, because trying not to look at something terrible only puts a hook in your eyes and pulls harder.

The poster crinkles.

Lissy's mouth opens wider.

The teenager slides off the table. "Dude. Is it moving? It's moving."

Nolan lunges and slaps his hand over the boy's eyes.

The boy shouts, "Get off me!"

Cricket barks.

The old man curses.

The dryers keep turning. Clothes tumble away.

In the poster, Lissy screams without sound.

Behind her, the blurred shape tilts toward the new attention like a dog hearing its name.

The teenager shoves Nolan back. "You psycho!"

Nolan hits the rolling cart and almost falls. His bare foot lands on something wet. He doesn't look down. He can't afford to look at anything else.

"We have to take it down," Nolan says.

The teenager backs away from him. "I'm calling the cops."

"Good. Call them. But don't look at the poster."

"Why?"

"Because that's what it wants."

The boy stares at him.

Nolan hears himself. He hears every insane word. If he were the teenager, he'd call the cops too. He'd call them and say some barefoot middle-aged guy with a limping dog is losing his goddamn mind in the laundromat.

Then the old man says, quietly, "The girl blinked."

Nobody moves.

The lights hum.

Cricket stops barking and starts whining.

The old man stands from his chair. He's thin and bent, with liver spots on both hands and suspenders over a plaid shirt. His mouth hangs slightly open. "I saw it. She…oh hell, she blinked."

"Sir," Nolan says, "please step away from it."

The old man doesn't.

He takes one slow step closer.

The poster rustles.

Lissy's eyes snap toward him.

"No," Nolan says.

The old man lifts a trembling hand. Not to tear it down. Not to help. To touch it.

The paper bows outward to meet him.

Nolan rushes forward, but he's too late.

The old man's fingertip touches Lissy's printed cheek.

The laundromat goes black.

Not dark.

Black.

Like ink.

The kind of black that fills the mouth first.

For half a second, Nolan is nowhere. There's no floor under him, no air around him, no Cricket pulling on the leash. There's only cold and the stink of wet paper.

Then the lights blast back on.

The old man is gone.

His shoes remain in front of the poster.

His socks too.

Empty.

Flat.

The teenager makes a sound like he's trying to swallow his own tongue.

The poster hangs on the wall, smooth again.

Lissy's face has changed.

Now she's crying.

And behind her, the shape is closer.

Much closer.

Something black and long presses one hand against the inside of the paper beside hers.

The fingers are too many.

The old man's voice comes from inside the poster.

Far away.

Small.

"Oh," he says. "Oh, God. Oh, somebody help me."

The teenager bolts for the door.

Nolan doesn't stop him.

He grabs Cricket's leash with both hands and backs away, but the poster's surface ripples.

The old man screams once.

Then not again.

A thin red line appears at the bottom edge of the paper.

It runs down the wall like spilled ink.

Nolan stares at it.

The red line thickens.

It isn't ink.

The laundromat door bangs open behind him.

The teenager is outside, yelling into his phone, voice cracking, pacing under the streetlight.

Nolan should leave.

He knows that.

He knows it the way animals know fire is hot and cliffs are not suggestions.

But Lissy's mouth moves again.

Slow.

Careful.

She knows he can read her lips.

Burn them.

Nolan swallows.

"What?"

Her small hand slides against the paper. The impossible black hand beside hers twitches closer, fingers spreading like roots.

Burn every door.

There it is.

Not every poster.

Every door.

Every printed cry for help. Every copied face. Every screen, flyer, notice, and page made by desperate people trying to find what's gone. The thing doesn't use paper because paper matters.

It uses searching.

The poster bulges again.

Not where Lissy is.

Behind her.

The thing in the dark leans forward, and for the first time Nolan sees one detail clearly.

A smile.

Not a human smile.

Not even close.

A split in the dark where teeth should be, except there are no teeth. Just a pale wet opening made for saying names.

The lights flicker.

The poster whispers.

Not in Lissy's voice.

Not in the old man's.

In Tessa's.

"Nolie?"

Nolan freezes.

His sister is dead seven years.

She's been dead seven years, four months, and nine days, and nobody has called him Nolie since the county fair, since the Ferris wheel lights, since that one minute he let go.

"Nolie," the poster whispers again. "I'm scared."

His knees go weak.

Cricket growls at him now, not the poster.

At him.

Like she knows the hook has gone in. Like she knows he's leaning toward it.

The thing behind the paper keeps smiling.

"Nolie," Tessa says from the wall. "Come find me."

Nolan almost does.

That's the worst part.

Not the poster. Not the old man's empty shoes sitting on the laundromat floor like a magic trick performed by a drunk devil. Not the blood crawling down the wall in a thin red ribbon. Not even the shape behind Lissy Bell, grinning with a mouth that doesn't belong on anything living.

It's the way Nolan's body betrays him.

His foot slides forward.

One inch.

Then another.

Cricket lunges and sinks her teeth into his calf.

Pain blows the spell apart.

Nolan shouts and stumbles backward, jerking the leash so hard Cricket yelps. He hits a washer with his hip. The machine rocks. Quarters rattle somewhere inside it like teeth in a cup.

The poster whispers in Tessa's voice.

"Nolie, don't leave me."

He clamps both hands over his ears.

It doesn't help.

The voice is inside the room, inside the lights, inside the wet blink of his own eyes.

"Nolie, please."

"Shut up," he says.

The shape behind Lissy presses closer to the paper.

The old man's blood drips faster.

Lissy's face twists, her mouth forming words she can't make him hear over the thing using his sister's voice.

Don't listen.

Nolan sees it that time.

Don't listen.

He grabs the rolling laundry cart and shoves it at the wall.

It crashes beneath the poster. The metal frame catches one corner and tears it loose with a papery shriek that sounds too much like a child. The lights pop bright, then dim. The poster flaps from two strips of tape, curling outward.

From the gap between paper and wall comes a smell like old rainwater trapped in a basement.

Then fingers slide around the torn edge.

Black fingers.

Too long.

Too jointed.

They pinch the paper from the inside and start pulling it flat again.

Nolan doesn't wait.

He runs for the exit, dragging Cricket with him because her old legs can't keep up. She tries. God help her, she tries, claws skidding on the tile, back hips wobbling, breath coming hard and wet.

The teenager stands under the streetlight, phone to his ear, crying now.

"I'm telling you, he disappeared," the boy says. "His clothes are there. His shoes are there. He's gone."

Nolan slams through the door.

The teenager sees him and backs away.

"You did something," he says.

"No," Nolan says. "Listen to me."

"You did something to him."

"No."

The boy points at Nolan's leg. Blood runs down his calf from Cricket's bite. "You're bleeding."

"Yeah, that's the least insane thing that's happened tonight."

Sirens sound in the distance.

The boy hears them and looks relieved, which makes Nolan feel worse. The cops are coming. Real authority. Real radios. Real forms. Real questions.

And there's a door inside the laundromat.

A thing leaning closer.

Nolan grabs the boy by both shoulders. "Do you have a lighter?"

The boy recoils. "What?"

"A lighter. Matches. Anything."

"No."

"Do you smoke?"

"No."

"You smell like weed and mints."

"Okay, yeah, I smoke. But I'm not giving you fire, man. You're crazy."

Nolan shakes him once. Not hard. Hard enough. "That thing took him."

The boy starts crying harder. "I know."

"No, you don't. You saw it, but you don't know. It's not just him. It's the posters. All of them. Every time people look, every time they print more, every time they search harder, it gets closer."

The boy's face pinches with terror and disbelief.

"Who is she?" he asks.

"Lissy Bell."

"I know her name. I mean what is she?"

Nolan glances back through the laundromat window.

Inside, the poster is visible beside the bathroom door.

For a second it looks ordinary.

Then the paper twitches.

Something on the other side taps one black finger against it.

Once.

Twice.

Like it's knocking.

Nolan turns back to the boy. "She's holding it back."

The first sheriff's cruiser turns the corner fast, lights strobing blue across the laundromat glass. Then another comes behind it.

Deputy Alva Rinn steps out of the first one before it fully stops.

Nolan knows her. Everybody knows her. Brindle Creek doesn't have enough law enforcement for strangers. Rinn is broad-shouldered, gray-haired, and allergic to bullshit. She handled the noise complaint when Nolan's ex-wife threw a flowerpot through his porch window. She was there when Tessa's body was found in the rented room above Harker's Pharmacy seven years ago, cold in the tub, wrists opened neatly, face peaceful in a way Nolan still hates.

Rinn sees Nolan barefoot and bleeding, sees Cricket panting beside him, sees the teenager sobbing into the phone.

Her hand rests on her sidearm.

"Nolan," she says. "What happened?"

He's got one second to decide how much sanity to pretend.

Not enough.

"There's a poster inside," he says.

Rinn stares at him.

The second deputy, a young guy named Ellis Pratt, moves toward the laundromat door.

"Don't go in," Nolan says.

Pratt pauses.

Rinn's eyes narrow. "Where's Howard Timple?"

Nolan looks at the old man's empty shoes through the glass.

"Inside," he says. "Kind of."

The teenager makes a strangled sound. "It ate him."

Pratt glances at Rinn.

Rinn doesn't move.

Good.

For one fragile moment, Nolan thinks maybe experience helps. Maybe Rinn's spent enough years pulling bodies from creek beds and breaking up Christmas fights and telling parents bad news to recognize when fear has a shape too specific to be fake.

Then the laundromat door creaks open by itself.

Nobody touches it.

It just opens.

The bell above it gives one cheerful little jingle.

Everyone freezes.

From inside, Howard Timple's voice calls out, "Alva?"

Rinn's face changes.

Only a little.

Enough.

"Howard?" she says.

Nolan grabs her arm. "No."

She twists free. "Take your hand off me."

"It's not him."

"Howard?" she calls again, louder.

Inside the laundromat, the lights flicker.

Howard's voice comes closer to the doorway.

"I fell," he says. "I'm hurt."

Pratt steps forward. "Deputy?"

Rinn raises a hand to hold him back, but her eyes stay fixed on the open door.

Nolan sees the trap and knows she does too. That's the sick part. She knows something is wrong. Her body knows. Her cop brain knows. But the voice belongs to a man she's probably known since high school, a man who buys coffee at the same diner and complains about property taxes and calls her by her first name because small towns blur lines until they become rope.

"Alva," Howard says. "Please."

Rinn takes one step.

Nolan does the only thing he can think to do.

He punches her.

Not well. Not clean. His knuckles catch more cheekbone than jaw. Pain flashes up his wrist. Rinn staggers back, shocked more than injured.

Pratt shouts and draws his weapon.

The teenager screams.

Cricket barks.

Nolan raises both hands. "Don't go in!"

Rinn touches her cheek, then looks at him with cold murder in her eyes.

"You better have a damn good reason," she says.

The laundromat door slams shut.

All the lights inside go out.

For three seconds, the building is a black rectangle with glass windows.

Then every dryer starts at once.

No clothes tumble now.

Something else.

Wet impacts thump inside the machines. Slow at first. Then faster. Heavy shapes rolling, striking metal, smearing the round windows from within.

The teenager bends over and vomits on the curb.

Pratt keeps his gun raised, but his hands are shaking.

Rinn lowers hers from her cheek.

Nobody speaks.

In the dark glass of the laundromat window, white rectangles begin to appear.

One at a time.

Posters.

Not taped.

Not stapled.

Blooming against the inside of the glass like fungus.

MISSING
LISSY BELL
MISSING
LISSY BELL
MISSING
LISSY BELL

Her face fills every one.

In some, she's crying.

In some, she's screaming.

In one, she's turned almost completely away, both hands braced against something Nolan can't see.

In all of them, the dark behind her moves.

Rinn whispers, "Jesus."

"Now do you believe me?" Nolan asks.

Rinn doesn't answer.

From down the street, porch lights flick on. Front doors open. People step outside in bathrobes, pajama pants, work boots. Small-town curiosity rises faster than smoke. A man across the street lifts his phone to record.

"No," Nolan says.

The phone flash pops.

Every poster in the laundromat turns toward it.

Not Lissy.

The darkness behind her.

The man filming screams and drops his phone.

The screen lands face-up on the sidewalk, still recording, its little white light aimed at the laundromat.

The posters ripple.

A crack opens in the glass.

Rinn snaps out of it. "Pratt, get people back. Now."

Pratt runs into the street, shouting, voice cracking but loud. "Back inside! Everybody inside!"

Nobody listens at first. They ask questions. They point. They say Howard's name. They say Lissy's name. They say, Is that blood? They say, Is this some kind of joke?

Then the crack in the laundromat window spreads.

A black fingertip pushes through.

Not brown.

Black.

Black like India ink.

The crowd finally understands enough to move.

Not fast enough.

The glass bows outward.

Nolan looks at Rinn. "I need fire."

Rinn stares at the window.

The fingertip becomes two fingers.

Then three.

But they're wrong. The hand is wrong in every direction. Too many knuckles. Too smooth. Too hungry.

"I need fire," Nolan says again.

Rinn reaches into her pocket with a shaking hand and tosses him a lighter.

Nolan catches it.

It's silver, heavy, engraved with initials worn almost smooth.

He doesn't ask why a deputy carries a lighter.

People carry grief in all kinds of shapes.

The window bursts.

Glass sprays across the sidewalk.

The posters don't fall.

They hang in the empty frame, fluttering in a wind that blows from inside the laundromat out into the world. Cold air slams Nolan's face. It smells like wet paper, old blood, and the underside of a rotten log.

The black hand grips the window frame.

Then another hand appears beside it.

Lissy's face in the posters twists with effort.

Her mouth forms one word.

Run.

But Nolan doesn't.

He flicks the lighter.

Nothing.

He flicks it again.

A tiny flame jumps up, weak and gold and ridiculous against all that dark.

Cricket presses against his leg.

Rinn says, "Nolan."

He steps toward the broken window.

The thing inside whispers in Tessa's voice.

"Nolie, don't."

Nolan keeps walking.

His eyes burn. His leg hurts. His heart feels like it's trying to punch through his ribs and leave without him. Blood trickles down his calf.

"I'm sorry," he says.

He doesn't know if he means Tessa, Lissy, Howard, Cricket, himself, or every lost thing that's ever learned the hard way that being found can be worse.

He touches the flame to the first poster.

For one second, nothing happens.

Then the paper catches.

Lissy Bell screams.

This time everybody hears her.

The scream rips through Brindle Creek like a siren made of bone.

People drop to their knees in the street. Windows crack in their frames. Somewhere nearby, a baby starts crying and then stops so suddenly Nolan's stomach twists. Cricket collapses against his shin, legs folding, but she doesn't run. She stays there trembling, her old body pressed to him as if she's the only thing keeping him nailed to the world.

The burning poster curls from the bottom up.

Lissy's face blackens.

For one terrible second, Nolan sees her through the flames, not as ink, not as a photograph, but as a real girl pressed behind a thin white skin. Her mouth is open. Her eyes find his.

She isn't accusing him.

That's worse.

She's grateful.

The thing behind her isn't.

The black hands jerk back from the window frame. The shape inside the laundromat thrashes, and every machine in the place starts banging at once. Washers buck against the floor. Dryers vomit socks, underwear, blue work shirts, a child's pajama top, then clumps of wet hair and something pale Nolan refuses to name.

The flames crawl across the first poster and jump to the next.

Then the next.

For half a breath, Nolan thinks it might work.

Then the posters peel themselves away from the broken window.

Not falling.

Fleeing.

They flap into the air like panicked birds, burning edges smoking, Lissy's face screaming from every sheet. Some fly up into the night. Some slap onto cars. One lands against Deputy Pratt's back.

He screams and spins, clawing at it.

Rinn tackles him into the street and rips it free. The paper stretches between her hands like rubbery skin. Something on the other side grabs back. Her arms jerk forward.

Nolan runs to her and presses the lighter to the poster.

It catches fast.

The thing inside lets go.

Rinn falls backward on top of Pratt, both of them breathing hard, both of them wide-eyed with the stupid fresh horror of still being alive.

Nolan doesn't wait to thank anyone.

"Every poster," he says.

Rinn looks up at him.

"Every one of them," Nolan says. "Burn them. All of them. Now."

From inside the laundromat, Tessa's voice says, "That won't bring me back."

Nolan turns.

The flames have eaten half the posters in the window, but the dark behind them remains. It pools in the broken frame, thick and restless. Not smoke. Not shadow. Something deeper. Something that hates being given a shape but uses one anyway because people are easier to hurt when they think they understand what's hurting them.

Lissy stands in front of it now.

Not in a poster.

In the broken window.

She's small. Barefoot. Her pink sweatshirt is dirty and torn at one shoulder. Her hair hangs in damp strings around her face. She looks exhausted beyond childhood, like the last few days have lasted years where she is.

Behind her, the Finder unfolds.

Nolan's mind stutters trying to make sense of it. It's tall, then wide, then low to the floor. It has arms where arms should be, then doesn't. It has a head only when Nolan expects one. Its face is a suggestion written in wet blackness.

The mouth stays.

A pale split.

A hungry comma in the dark.

Lissy braces both hands backward, as if holding a door shut with her spine.

"Go," Nolan says to her.

She shakes her head.

"Go!" he shouts.

Her lips move.

Can't.

The Finder's mouth opens.

It speaks with Tessa's voice again, but not sweet now. Not frightened. It wears her like an old coat.

"He left me," it says. "One minute. That's all it took."

Nolan's hand tightens around the lighter.

Rinn gets up beside him, gun drawn again though her face says she understands how useless that is.

"Nolan," she says quietly.

"Get people burning posters," he says.

"Nolan."

"Do it."

Rinn looks at him, then at Lissy, then at the thing behind her. Whatever she sees there wipes twenty years of law and procedure from her face.

She turns and shouts, "Pratt! Move! Get everyone out here. Trash cans, grills, burn barrels, anything. Every poster with her face goes in the fire. Nobody looks at them longer than they have to. Nobody takes pictures. You hear me? No pictures!"

Pratt staggers up, still shaking. "What about the station?"

"All of them," Rinn snaps. "The station, the school, the market, the church, every damn pole in town."

People hesitate.

Of course they do.

There's a missing girl standing in a broken laundromat window and a deputy telling them to burn her face.

That's not a thing people understand quickly.

Probably not at all.

Nadine Bell's voice cuts through the crowd.

"No."

Nolan turns.

Lissy's mother stands barefoot in the street, wrapped in a robe, hair tangled around her pale face. Her eyes are fixed on the laundromat window.

On her daughter.

Everything in her breaks open at once.

"Lissy," she whispers.

The girl in the window flinches.

"Mama," Lissy mouths.

Nadine runs.

Nolan catches her around the waist before she reaches the sidewalk. She fights him with a grief-strength that almost knocks them both down.

"Let go of me!" she screams. "That's my baby!"

"It's using her."

"That's my baby!"

"She's holding it back."

Nadine elbows him in the ribs. Nolan loses air but not his grip.

"You don't get to tell me not to find my child!" she shrieks. "You don't get to stand here and tell me to burn her!"

Nolan understands her so well it nearly kills him.

He sees his mother outside the sheriff's station all those years ago, chewing her thumbnail until it bled, praying to a God she didn't even like. He sees his father walking fairgrounds after midnight with a flashlight and a tire iron. He sees himself at sixteen, useless, guilt-sick, willing to cut open the whole world if Tessa might crawl out of it.

"I know," he says into Nadine's hair. "I know."

"You don't!"

"I do."

She twists enough to look at him.

He sees the hatred in her eyes. Honest hatred. Clean hatred. The kind that keeps a person standing when sorrow wants them dead.

"She's right there," Nadine says.

Nolan looks at Lissy.

The girl is crying now, not from fear of the Finder.

From seeing her mother.

That's what weakens her.

The black shape behind her swells.

It pushes forward.

Lissy slides one inch toward the street.

Nadine sees it and screams her daughter's name.

That helps it too.

The broken window frame cracks wider.

The Finder's mouth stretches.

"Found," it says.

Not in Tessa's voice this time.

In Nadine's.

Nadine goes still in Nolan's arms.

The thing laughs with her voice, soft and wet and intimate.

"Found you," it says again.

Lissy's knees buckle.

Nolan lets Nadine go and shoves her backward into Rinn's arms.

"Keep her away!"

Then he runs at the window.

He doesn't have a plan. Plans are for people who have time and facts and tools better than a dying lighter. Nolan has none of that. He has guilt. He has fear. He has an old dog trying to follow him into hell.

He has fire.

He slams the lighter against the edge of his T-shirt until flame catches cotton. Heat bites his fingers. He holds the burning fabric out in front of him and jams it into the broken window, against the fluttering remains of the posters, against the wet black seam where the laundromat stops being a place and starts being a throat.

The Finder strikes.

Something catches Nolan's wrist.

Cold floods his arm.

Not cold like winter. Cold like absence. Like every warm thing in him suddenly remembers it's temporary.

He sees Tessa.

Not a trick. Not the Finder wearing her voice. He sees her at eleven, standing under fairground lights with a paper bag of kettle corn in one hand, her hair frizzed from humidity, her face turned up to him.

Then he sees her after.

Under the bed.

Hands over her ears.

Shaking when the phone rings.

Screaming when their mother tapes a school photo to the fridge because the glossy paper makes a sound when it curls.

He remembers that now.

The photos.

How Tessa hated photos after she came back. Not just being photographed. Photos themselves. Magazines. Posters. Catalogs. The newspaper. She'd turn them facedown, rip them up, slide them under sofa cushions. Their parents called it trauma. The therapist called it association.

But Tessa knew.

Of course she knew.

"Nolie," she whispers.

This time the voice comes from inside him.

He sees his sister at twenty-three, sitting across from him in a diner, stirring coffee she never drinks. She says, Sometimes missing isn't the worst part. Sometimes found is when it follows you home.

He'd thought she meant memory.

He'd thought lots of wrong things.

The Finder pulls harder.

Nolan's shoulder hits the broken frame. Glass cuts his arm. The burning strip of shirt smokes against blackness, but the thing doesn't burn like paper. It sizzles. It recoils. It hates flame, but it's too close now, too fed, too many eyes, too many prayers, too much desperate wanting.

Behind him, Brindle Creek erupts into motion.

People finally understand because fear is faster than belief.

They tear posters from poles. Rip them from storefront windows. Pull them down from bulletin boards and car windshields and school fences. Rinn shouts orders until her voice breaks. Pratt runs from yard to yard, kicking over decorative fire pits, dumping old grocery bags full of posters into flames.

All over town, Lissy Bell begins to burn.

And every burning face screams.

The sound multiplies until Nolan can't tell one voice from another. Lissy. Tessa. Howard Timple. Other voices too. Children. Men. Women. Dogs barking from somewhere far away and underneath everything, underneath the world.

Cricket bites the thing holding Nolan.

Her teeth sink into nothing and something.

The Finder shrieks.

Cricket hangs from its long black wrist, shaking her old head with every ounce of mutt fury left in her body.

"No!" Nolan yells.

The Finder flings her.

Cricket hits the side of a washer inside the laundromat and drops.

Nolan's heart stops in him.

She doesn't get up.

The world narrows to that.

Not the missing girl. Not the monster. Not the town. Not Tessa. Not guilt.

Cricket.

His dog lies on the dirty laundromat floor, one paw twitching once, then still.

Something hot and clean tears through Nolan's fear.

He grabs the broken edge of the window with his free hand, slicing his palm open, and pulls himself forward instead of back.

The Finder expects prey to fight away.

Not toward.

Nolan drives his burning shirt into its mouth.

The pale split opens around the flame.

For a second, he sees inside.

There are rooms in there.

That's what breaks his mind a little.

Rooms.

A fairground bathroom with wet tile. A basement with yellow insulation hanging from the ceiling. A motel room. A school hallway. A hunting blind. The back of a van. The crawl space under a church. Little rooms, lost rooms, rooms where nobody comes in time.

And faces.

Not dead.

Not alive.

Pressed into the dark like flowers in a book.

Tessa is there.

Older than eleven.

Younger than death.

She looks at him.

Nolan can't hear anything now. The world has become one long note. But he sees her mouth move.

Not your fault.

The fire blossoms.

It catches something deep inside the Finder, something dry and ancient and packed full of all the names it has stolen. The thing releases Nolan's wrist. It tries to pull back, but Lissy turns and grabs it with both hands.

A nine-year-old girl grabs the dark and holds it in place.

Her face twists with pain.

Nolan reaches for her.

"Come on!"

She shakes her head.

"Lissy!"

She looks past him.

At Nadine.

Nadine has broken free of Rinn. She stands in the street, hands over her mouth, eyes ruined.

Lissy smiles at her mother.

It is the saddest thing Nolan's ever seen.

Then she turns back to the Finder and presses both palms against its chest.

The laundromat ignites.

Not slowly.

All at once.

Every poster, every receipt, every lint-clogged dryer vent, every bulletin board notice, every scrap of paper in the place goes up in white fire. Heat punches Nolan backward through the broken window. He lands on the sidewalk hard enough to crack his skull against concrete.

For a while, there's only red.

Then shouting.

Hands grab him.

Rinn's voice. "Get him back! Get him back!"

Nadine screaming.

Pratt crying.

Somebody saying the hydrant's on, get the hose, get the hose.

Nolan rolls onto his side and tries to crawl toward the laundromat.

Toward Cricket.

Rinn pins him down.

"My dog," he says.

His voice sounds far away and stupid.

"Nolan."

"My dog's in there."

"You can't."

"My dog's in there."

Rinn's face crumples, but she doesn't let him go.

The laundromat burns hot and bright and wrong. The flames inside are white at the center, blue at the edges. Shadows slam against the windows from within. Not people. Not anymore. Shapes. Arms. Mouths. Hands with too many fingers. They hit the glass, the walls, the ceiling, trying to find another way out.

All across town, fires burn in barrels and grills and driveways.

The screaming thins.

One by one, the voices go out.

The last voice is Lissy's.

It doesn't scream.

It laughs.

A small laugh.

A girl's laugh.

Normal for one impossible second.

Then the laundromat roof collapses.

The blast knocks everyone flat.

After that, rain comes.

No clouds.

No thunder.

Just rain falling straight from a clear black sky, hard and cold, hissing against the wreckage.

By morning, the laundromat is a black shell.

The official story starts forming before the ashes cool.

Gas leak.

Electrical fault.

Mass panic.

Carbon monoxide hallucinations.

Howard Timple is missing, presumed dead in the fire. The sheriff's department takes statements until the statements stop making sense and then stops taking them. People learn quickly how much truth costs. They trim their stories. They trade the impossible for something survivable.

A man disappeared.

A building burned.

A missing girl is still missing.

That's enough horror for most people.

Nolan says almost nothing.

His wrist is blackened where the Finder grabbed him, the skin bruised in the shape of too many fingers. The EMT wants him transported. He refuses. Rinn doesn't push. She sits beside him on the curb with soot on her face and blood drying under one nostril.

For a long time, neither of them speaks.

Then she says, "Your dog saved lives."

Nolan stares at the smoking ruin.

His throat closes.

Rinn clears hers and looks away. "I'm sorry."

Nadine Bell stands across the street wrapped in a blanket. She hasn't stopped looking at the laundromat. Nolan expects her to hate him forever.

She probably will.

But as dawn grays the sky, she walks over to him.

Her face is empty now in the way only fresh grief can make a face empty. Like everything human has stepped out for a minute and might not find its way back.

She stops in front of Nolan.

"You saw her?" she asks.

Nolan nods.

"At the end?"

He nods again.

Nadine swallows. "Was she scared?"

Nolan thinks of the flames. Lissy's hands against the dark. That last small laugh.

"Yes," he says.

Nadine closes her eyes.

Then Nolan says, "But she was brave."

Nadine folds over like someone has cut her strings. Rinn catches her before she hits the ground.

Nolan looks away.

He watches the telephone pole at the corner.

The missing poster is gone. Only four rusty staples remain, catching the dawn light.

Three weeks pass.

Brindle Creek becomes normal in the aggressive way small towns do after something terrible happens. The laundromat gets fenced off.

Flowers appear near the chain-link for Howard, for Lissy, for nobody specific. A few people leave candles, though the rain keeps killing them.

No one puts up posters.

Not for lost cats.

Not for lawn care.

Not for church fish fries.

The poles stay bare.

Nolan buries Cricket in the backyard under the maple tree, wrapped in the old blue blanket she used to steal from the couch. He puts her favorite rubber bone in with her, even though she hasn't chewed it in years. Then he sits beside the fresh dirt until dark and doesn't go inside until the neighbor's security light clicks on.

He dreams of Tessa almost every night.

Not bad dreams.

That's what scares him.

In the dreams, she stands across the creek in her county fair T-shirt. She doesn't speak. She only lifts one hand, palm out.

Not waving.

Holding something back.

Nolan returns to work at the library because bills don't care about hauntings.

Mrs. Weikel hugs him and cries into his shoulder, then pretends she didn't. The library board sends a plant. Someone leaves a casserole on his porch with no name on it. He eats half of it cold over the sink.

Life continues in pieces.

The world is cruel that way.

One Thursday afternoon, Nolan shelves returned books in the children's section. He keeps away from the bulletin board near the front doors, even though it's still empty. He can feel it waiting. Bare cork. Silver thumbtacks. A place meant for paper.

A boy asks where the dinosaur books are.

Nolan shows him.

A woman prints boarding passes from computer three.

The copier jams twice.

Normal day.

At 4:12, the receipt printer at the checkout desk begins to chatter.

Mrs. Weikel looks up. "That thing's acting up again."

Nolan's hands go cold.

The printer keeps going.

Not a short receipt.

A long one.

The paper curls from the machine and spills over the desk in a pale tongue.

Mrs. Weikel reaches for it.

"Don't," Nolan says.

She freezes.

He walks toward the desk. Slow. Careful. Every sound in the library seems to step backward from him. Pages stop turning. The air conditioner clicks off. A toddler stops babbling mid-syllable.

The receipt paper hangs down almost to the floor.

Most of it is blank.

At the bottom, gray thermal smudges darken into shape.

A hand.

Small.

Pressed flat from the other side.

Nolan's heart kicks once, hard.

Then words appear beneath it.

Not typed.

Not printed clean.

Burn doors.

More gray marks bloom.

Another hand presses beside the first.

Bigger.

Too many fingers.

The paper starts to bulge.

Nolan grabs the whole curling strip and rips it free.

The receipt printer screams.

Every computer screen in the library flashes white.

Mrs. Weikel whispers, "Nolan?"

He sees the bulletin board near the entrance.

A single sheet of paper is pinned there now.

It wasn't there a second ago.

White paper.

Black letters.

No photo yet.

Just one word.

MISSING

The printer in Nolan's hand twitches.

Something presses from inside the receipt paper, trying to make room for its face.

Nolan doesn't wait.

He snatches the little plastic lighter from Mrs. Weikel's emergency drawer, the one she uses for birthday candles in the break room. He flicks it once.

Nothing.

Again.

Flame.

People start shouting when he sets fire to the receipt.

They don't understand.

They can't.

Not yet.

Nolan looks at the blank white page on the bulletin board as its center begins to darken. As an image starts pushing up from nowhere.

Not Lissy this time.

Not Tessa.

A new face.

A boy maybe.

Or a girl.

Hard to tell.

The paper breathes.

Nolan walks toward it with the burning receipt in his hand.

Behind him, every printer in the library wakes up.

At once.

The machines chatter and spit and scream.

White paper floods the room.

And from every fresh blank sheet, something knocks.

The Preacher's Wife

The storm comes crawling over the hills like something on its belly.

Merritt Cole watches it through the windshield of his pickup, both hands tight on the steering wheel, knuckles pale under the weak glow of the dashboard. The road out to the Harrowby place doesn't believe in straight lines. It bends around dead oaks, dips through gullies full of brown water, climbs again past fields gone wild with weeds. The tires hiss over wet asphalt. The wipers slap back and forth, back and forth, never fast enough.

He tells himself he's only doing church work.

That's all.

A welfare check. A casserole drop. A brief visit to an old widow whose husband died three days ago and who hasn't answered her phone since yesterday morning.

Nothing more.

The cardboard box on the passenger seat slides when he takes the next curve. Inside it, wrapped in foil, is a chicken-and-rice bake Lottie Crane insists is "good grief food," which is an ugly phrase but probably true. There's also a loaf of banana bread, a jar of peach preserves, and a sympathy card signed by half the congregation.

Mother Grace, we love you.

Mother Grace, we're praying for you.

Mother Grace, may the Lord hold you in His hands.

Merritt glances at the card and feels something cold under his ribs.

He sees Reverend Gideon hanging from the pantry beam.

Not in person. Merritt didn't find him. Deputy Hollis Kemp did. But word travels in a town like Abner's Crossing. It travels fast and hot and mean. By breakfast the next morning, everybody knows enough to lie and say they don't know anything. By noon, people say Gideon used his own preaching stole. By supper, somebody says his feet were bare. By the next day, another person says there was blood under his fingernails, as if he'd tried to claw the Lord's name out of the floor.

Merritt doesn't know what's true.

He knows Reverend Gideon Harrowby preached at New Mercy Chapel for forty-seven years. He baptized babies in a dented tin basin and married couples beneath a warped wooden cross. He shouted hellfire when he had to, whispered mercy when people needed it, and never once missed Sunday service until arthritis started folding him into himself.

He also knows the last sermon Gideon preached was wrong.

Wrong in the way a spoiled thing is wrong before you see the mold.

Merritt had been sitting in the third pew from the back, where he always sits now. Not too close. Not too far. Gideon stood behind the pulpit with both hands gripping the sides so hard the tendons rose like cords beneath his skin. Grace sat in the front row with her hat pinned neat, her gloved hands folded in her lap, her smile mild as butter.

Gideon stared past everyone.

"The devil doesn't always come with horns," he'd said.

The congregation went still.

"Sometimes he comes with soup after a funeral."

A few nervous laughs. One cough. Grace didn't move.

"Sometimes he comes with a hymn. Sometimes he comes with a hand on your shoulder. Sometimes he kisses your forehead and calls you sweet boy."

Merritt remembers the way Gideon's eyes found him then.

Just for a second.

Maybe less.

But Merritt remembers it because his stomach turned.

Then Grace smiled wider.

Now the Harrowby house appears through the rain, hunched at the end of the road behind a low stone wall and two lightning-split maples. It's small, austere, white once, gray now, with peeling paint and black shutters banging loose against the siding. The porch sags in the middle. The chimney leans as if listening. The windows are dark, but they don't look empty.

They look shut.

Like eyes pretending to sleep.

Merritt parks beside Reverend Gideon's old Buick. The car sits under the carport, slick with rain, windshield filmed over with old pollen and dust. Gideon used to wash that car every Saturday morning, even when his hands shook and the hose gave him trouble.

The wipers stop.

The world becomes rain.

Merritt sits there longer than he needs to.

Ruthie Bell crosses his mind for no good reason. Eight years old. Missing Sunday school last week because of nightmares, according to

Lottie. Bad ones. The kind that had her mother calling Mother Grace at all hours to ask for prayer.

Mother Grace has always been good at that.

Comfort.

Merritt looks at the dark house again.

If Grace is lying on the kitchen floor with a stroke, or a broken hip, or grief so heavy she can't lift the phone, he'll have to live with knowing he stood ten feet away and drove off because an old house scared him.

So he grabs the casserole box, tucks it under one arm, and steps out into the storm.

Cold rain hits the back of his neck. His boots sink into mud as he crosses the yard. The wind shoves at him, carrying the smell of wet leaves, old wood, and something faintly sour from under the porch. A shutter cracks against the house. Another answers. The whole place creaks and knocks as if it's full of people shifting their weight.

At the porch steps, Merritt stops.

There's a Bible nailed to the front door.

Not hung. Not placed.

Nailed.

A thick black iron nail has been driven straight through the center of it, pinning the book open against the wood. Rain swells the pages. Ink bleeds in blue veins down the door. The exposed verses are torn, but Merritt recognizes the rhythm from years of unwilling memory.

Though I walk through the valley…

The rest is scratched away.

Not crossed out. Scratched. Dug at. Gouged deep enough to tear through paper and into the door beneath.

Merritt's mouth goes dry.

He raises his hand to knock, then sees the knocker turned upside down. So is the little brass cross beside the bell. It hangs point-down, trembling in the wind.

He thinks of calling out from the porch. He thinks of going back to the truck. He thinks of leaving the food by the door and telling Lottie nobody answered.

Instead, because he's stupid or decent or too tired to tell the difference, he knocks.

Once.

Twice.

The sound disappears into the house.

For a while there's nothing but storm.

Then floorboards creak on the other side of the door.

Slow.

Deliberate.

One step.

A pause.

Another step.

Merritt tightens his grip around the box until foil crinkles under his fingers.

"Mrs. Harrowby?" he calls. "It's Merritt Cole. From the chapel."

The creaking stops.

Something scratches the other side of the door.

Low.

Near the floor.

Like a fingernail dragging through paint.

Merritt leans closer before he can stop himself.

"Mother Grace?"

The scratching rises.

Slowly.

From the bottom of the door to the middle.

Then higher.

Higher.

All the way up.

It stops right where a face would be.

A woman's voice, soft and thin, whispers through the door.

"Merritt."

His name sounds wrong in her mouth.

Not mispronounced.

Tasted.

He swallows. "I brought some food. The church wanted me to check on you."

Silence.

Then a little laugh.

It's so delicate he almost misses it beneath the rain.

"Oh," Grace says. "The church still wants things."

The deadbolt clicks.

The door opens inward.

Grace Harrowby stands in the dim hall wearing a faded blue house dress, gray wool slippers, and Reverend Gideon's black cardigan. The cardigan hangs off her bony shoulders and comes almost to her knees. One sleeve is stained dark near the cuff.

Her hair is pinned in a loose bun, but strands have escaped and cling to her cheeks in damp wisps. Her face looks smaller than Merritt remembers, all wrinkles and hollows, like the skin has been carefully folded over a skull too narrow for it.

But her eyes are still blue.

Pale, watery blue.

Human.

For one relieved second, Merritt feels ashamed.

She's an old woman. A grieving widow. He's standing on her porch in the rain, frightening himself with nailed Bibles and gossip and old sermons.

Then she smiles.

Her lips part too slowly.

Her teeth look strange. Wet, even.

"Merritt Cole," she says. "My, my. You got tall."

He gives a weak laugh. "I've been tall a while."

"Not to me."

The words settle badly between them.

She steps back and opens the door wider. The hallway behind her is dark, though it's barely evening. No lamps are on. The air inside smells of dust, stale rainwater, candle smoke, and something sweet gone rotten.

"Come in before you drown," she says.

Merritt looks past her.

On the wall behind Grace, every framed picture hangs backward. Wedding photographs, church picnics, baptism portraits, Gideon shaking hands with some mayor from twenty years ago. All turned to face the wall. Their brown paper backs stare out instead.

A wooden crucifix lies on the hallway table, snapped in two.

"You know, I can just leave this here," Merritt says.

Grace's smile doesn't change.

"You afraid of an old woman?"

"No, ma'am."

"Liar."

The word comes out quick, sharp, almost playful.

Merritt's skin tightens.

Grace turns and shuffles into the hall, leaving the door open. "Kitchen's this way."

The smart thing is to set the food down and leave.

Merritt steps inside.

The house closes around him with a soft wooden groan.

Immediately, the storm sounds farther away. Not quieter exactly. Farther. Like the rain has moved to another world and left him in this one.

The hallway floorboards complain under his boots. To the left is the parlor, full of old furniture buried beneath white sheets. To the right, the dining room sits dark and narrow, table set for two. Plates. Forks. Water glasses. Cloth napkins folded into triangles.

At the center of the table rests a silver communion tray.

Beside it sits a tarnished cup, black around the lip.

No wafers.

No little cups of grape juice.

Just teeth.

Merritt stops.

The teeth are arranged in a neat white circle on the polished silver.

Some are small.

Child small.

Grace's voice floats from the kitchen. "Don't dawdle."

Merritt turns away from the dining room and forces himself forward.

His heart beats too hard. He can hear it in his ears. He tells himself there's an explanation. Dentures maybe. Old keepsakes from some strange mourning practice. Gideon collected odd religious objects. Everyone knows that.

No one collects children's teeth on a communion tray.

He reaches the kitchen.

Grace stands at the counter with her back to him. A single yellow bulb burns above the sink, swinging slightly though no window is open. Beneath it, dirty dishes crowd the basin. Rain ticks against the glass. A strip of flypaper hangs from the ceiling, black with dead flies.

"Put it there," she says.

Merritt sets the casserole box on the table.

The kitchen is colder than it should be. His breath doesn't show, but it feels close.

Grace's hands rest flat on the counter. Long fingers. Knuckles swollen with age. The nails are yellow, thick, and curved.

"I'm sorry about Reverend Gideon," Merritt says.

Grace bows her head.

For a second, she's just a widow again.

"He was tired," she says.

"I know."

"No, you don't."

Her voice is soft.

Merritt says nothing.

Grace turns her head a little, not enough for him to see her face. "He prayed so loud at the end. Louder than he ever preached. Begged like a child. Isn't that funny?"

Merritt's throat tightens. "Mrs. Harrowby…"

"He said God wasn't answering."

The bulb swings.

Grace's shadow stretches across the wall, too thin and too tall.

"I told him maybe God was chewing."

Merritt takes one step back.

Grace laughs again.

This time it's not delicate.

This time it's sloppy.

He looks toward the hallway. The front door is no longer visible from here, only the dark mouth of the corridor and the backward picture frames lining it.

"I should go," he says.

Grace's shoulders tremble.

For one mad second he thinks she's crying.

Then he sees her hands moving.

She has something in her fingers.

Pink.

Wet.

Her tongue.

She pulls it from her mouth with both hands, stretching it down past her chin, past her throat, longer and longer like taffy warmed in the sun. It glistens under the yellow bulb. Her jaw opens too wide. Wider than any jaw should open. A clicking sound comes from somewhere deep in her face.

Merritt can't move.

Grace lets go.

The tongue hangs from her mouth, twitching against the front of her dress.

Her right hand drops below the counter.

When it comes back up, it holds a hatchet.

The blade is dark near the edge.

Merritt's mind finally tears loose.

"Grace," he says, but it isn't a warning. It isn't even a prayer.

She sets the tongue on the cutting board.

Raises the hatchet.

And chops.

The sound is small.

Almost organic.

Blood patters onto the floor like water from a faucet.

Grace turns around.

Her mouth is full of red. Her smile opens around the severed root of her tongue. For a moment, she can't speak. She only breathes through the blood, bubbling softly.

Then her eyes blacken.

Not all at once.

The blue drains away as if ink spreads beneath glass. The whites vanish. The pupils vanish. Both eyes turn slick and black from lid to lid.

Merritt backs into the table, knocking the casserole box to the floor.

Grace's neck stretches.

The skin pulls in ripples.

Her head begins to turn.

Slowly.

Past the point where bone should stop it.

Past pain.

Past life.

Her body remains facing the counter while her head turns toward him, one hundred eighty degrees, front to back. Her gray hair slips free of its pins and spills over the wrong side of her face.

She lifts one arm.

An elongated, wretched finger points at him. The nail comes to a piercing point.

"I see you," she says.

The words come out clear despite the missing tongue.

Then she singsongs, voice high and childish.

"Teeth of gnarl, smile to a snarl; eyes of black, a tongue of clack; a wrinkled soulless face, I ate the heart of Mother Grace."

Her black eyes hold him.

"You're next."

The wind explodes through the hallway.

Every backward picture frame rattles against the walls.

Grace's thick gray hair twists and flows around her head like it's underwater.

Merritt runs.

He makes it three steps before the hallway changes.

Not moves.

Changes.

The front door was straight ahead. He knows it. He walked in through it. The door with the nailed Bible and rain-swollen pages should be waiting at the end of the hall, crooked brass cross trembling beside it.

But now the hall runs longer than the house.

Longer than any house.

It stretches into a narrow tunnel of buckled floorboards and backward pictures, the walls pinching inward like the house is drawing a breath and forgetting how to let it go. The yellow kitchen light spills behind him, thin and sick. Ahead, darkness piles in layers.

Merritt's boots skid on wet wood.

Wet?

He looks down.

The floorboards gleam black.

Blood runs between them in little streams, coming up through the cracks. It bubbles around old nails. It beads on splinters. It smells hot and coppery, like pennies left in a mouth.

Behind him, Grace laughs.

It's not one laugh. Not really. It's a crowd of laughs pressed through one ruined throat. An old woman's chuckle. A child's giggle. A man's dry sob. Something low and animal underneath them all.

"Merritt," she calls.

Her voice comes from the kitchen.

Then from the parlor.

Then from upstairs.

Then from inside the wall beside his ear.

"Merritt Cole."

He runs harder.

Rain lashes the windows, but the sound is distant, buried beneath the creak of timber and the wet patter of blood dripping somewhere it shouldn't.

He passes the dining room again.

He doesn't look in.

Then he does, because something makes him. A tug behind the eyes. A hook in the brain.

The table is no longer set for two.

It's set for twelve.

Plates ring the long table, though the room isn't large enough for that many places. The silver communion tray sits in the center, piled higher now with teeth. The tarnished cup sits beside it, filled with something thick and black. Around the table, chairs are occupied by shapes beneath white funeral sheets. Each sheet sits upright, draped over the seated forms, their heads bowed toward the tray.

At the far end of the table is Reverend Gideon Harrowby.

Dead.

Hanging.

But also seated.

His body wears the black suit they'll bury him in tomorrow. The collar is buttoned tight. His neck is purple above it, circled with the raw mark of the preaching stole. His eyes bulge wetly from his skull. His bare feet rest together beneath the chair like he's being polite.

A Bible lies open in front of him.

His right hand lifts.

One finger points to the page.

Merritt can't stop himself from reading.

Not scripture.

A message scratched into the paper in shaky block letters.

DON'T LET HER COMFORT YOU.

The sheeted figures turn their hidden faces toward him.

Merritt stumbles backward, hits the hallway wall, and a framed photograph drops beside him. The glass shatters. He looks down and sees a baptism picture, but the faces are rubbed away. Only Grace remains untouched, standing beside the tin basin, smiling with both hands resting on a baby's head.

"Merritt," Grace sings.

Closer now.

He bolts.

The hallway snaps back to its proper length. The front door appears twenty feet ahead.

Relief punches through him so hard it almost hurts.

He reaches the door, grabs the knob, twists.

It doesn't move.

He twists harder. Pulls. Slams his shoulder into it.

The nailed Bible shakes against the outside of the door. The scratched-out Psalm flaps wetly, though no wind should reach it from inside.

"Come on," he hisses.

The deadbolt is unlocked. The chain isn't latched. There's nothing holding the door shut that he can see.

Behind him, a slow chop sounds from the kitchen.

Thunk.

A pause.

Thunk.

A pause.

Thunk.

The hatchet into the cutting board.

Or into something softer.

Merritt digs his fingers around the doorframe and pulls until pain lances through his wrists. The door holds.

A whisper slides across the back of his neck.

"You used to cry so pretty."

He spins.

Grace stands halfway down the hall.

No, not stands.

Her body stands. Her head is still turned backward, facing him over the wrong shoulder. Blood runs down the front of her dress from the black hole of her mouth. Her severed tongue dangles from her left hand like a dead worm. The hatchet hangs from her right.

Her smile shouldn't be possible without the tongue. Wet red gums. Teeth too many in the dark mouth. Teeth packed behind teeth, little jagged white points pushing through where her molars used to be.

Merritt fumbles for his phone.

His fingers are slick. He almost drops it. The screen lights, showing no service. Of course it shows no service. He jabs at the emergency call anyway.

Grace takes one shuffling step.

The floorboard beneath her bare slipper moans.

"You remember your mama?" she asks.

Merritt freezes.

Grace's head gives another tiny twist, bone popping like knuckles. "Sweet woman. Soft heart. Good heart. Warm heart."

"Shut up."

The words leave him before he thinks them.

Grace stops.

The hallway does too.

Even the storm seems to pause.

Her black eyes widen with delight.

"There he is," she whispers. "There's the boy."

Merritt's breath comes sharp and ragged.

His mother's face rises in his mind, not as she was at the end, wasted and jaundiced under hospital lights, but years before that. Standing in the kitchen with flour on her cheek. Laughing when he dropped a full carton of eggs. Singing off-key in the car. Pressing cold fingers under his shirt collar to make him shriek.

Then another memory comes.

The funeral.

He's fourteen. His suit doesn't fit. The church basement smells like ham, coffee, wet coats, and carnations. Adults keep touching his shoulders. Telling him she's in a better place. Telling him to be strong for his father. Telling him God has a plan, as if God sat at a desk somewhere drawing up cancer in blue ink.

And Grace.

Mother Grace kneeling in front of him.

Her gloved hands cupping his face.

Her breath sweet with peppermint.

"You poor lamb," she whispers. "Grief opens what love closes."

He remembers her thumb pressing beneath his sternum.

Not hard.

Just enough to hurt.

He remembers gasping.

He remembers her eyes looking almost black in the basement shadow.

"Don't," Merritt says now.

Grace's smile twitches.

"Oh, I took just a taste then," she says. "Just enough to mark the door."

"The door?"

Her long finger rises again.

Points to his chest.

"No," he says.

But the word is weak.

Because beneath his shirt, exactly where Grace touched him twenty-four years ago, a spot of cold begins to bloom. It spreads through muscle and bone, unfurling like a black flower.

Grace starts toward him again.

Merritt grabs the broken crucifix from the hallway table.

It's only half there. The lower piece snapped away, leaving Christ's tiny metal body bent at the legs. He grips it anyway, holding it out in front of him.

Grace stops.

For a heartbeat, hope sparks.

Then she giggles.

"Oh, sweetheart."

She raises the hatchet.

The bulb overhead bursts.

Darkness slams down.

Merritt swings the broken crucifix blindly. It connects with something soft. Grace shrieks, but the sound rises into laughter halfway through. Fingernails slash across Merritt's forearm. Hot pain opens there. He staggers sideways, shoulder-checks the wall, and knocks down another picture.

Lightning flashes through the front window.

For that white second, he sees Grace inches away.

Her head is turned forward again, but her face is sagging wrong, the wrinkles shifting like something underneath is trying to rearrange itself. Her mouth works around the bloody stump of tongue. The severed piece in her hand twitches like it's still alive.

Merritt throws the crucifix at her.

It hits her cheek.

Steam curls from the place it touches.

Grace screams.

This time there's no laughter in it.

Merritt doesn't wait. He dives into the parlor, trips over a sheet-covered chair, and crashes to the floor. Dust blasts into his nose and mouth. The room is dark except for lightning pulses and the glow from his fallen phone in the hallway.

He crawls.

Behind him, Grace's slippers scrape across the floorboards.

Scrape.

Pause.

Scrape.

Pause.

She's not hurrying.

That scares him worse.

Merritt scrambles behind an old sofa and clamps a hand over his bleeding arm. The parlor smells like mildew, candle wax, and old flowers. Sheets cover everything: chairs, tables, a piano against the wall. A portrait of Reverend Gideon hangs above the mantel, turned backward like the rest.

Something taps beneath the piano lid.

Three gentle knocks.

Merritt doesn't breathe.

Three more.

Tap.

Tap.

Tap.

Then a voice whispers from inside the piano.

"Deacon Cole?"

It's a child's voice.

Ruthie Bell.

Merritt's heart lurches.

"Ruthie?"

A hush.

Then, very softly, "Don't answer her when she sounds like somebody you love."

Merritt presses his fist against his mouth.

The piano lid rises by itself.

Not far.

Just enough for darkness to show between the wood and the keys.

A small hand slides out.

Pale.

Wet.

Fingers bent backward.

Merritt jerks away.

The hand feels along the piano top, searching.

From the hallway, Grace calls in his mother's voice.

"Merry?"

No one calls him that anymore.

No one living.

His eyes fill before he can stop them.

"Merry, baby, come here."

The parlor tilts.

His mother's voice is perfect. Not close. Exact. The worn softness. The little upward break at the end of his name. He can smell her hand lotion. Lavender and cheap soap. He can see the thin gold chain she wore even in summer, the one with the tiny cross that rested in the hollow of her throat.

"Merry, I'm cold."

Merritt squeezes his eyes shut.

Ruthie's voice whispers from the piano.

"That's not your mama."

Grace answers from the doorway, still wearing his mother's voice.

"How would you know, little mouse?"

The room goes colder.

Merritt opens his eyes.

Grace stands in the parlor doorway, but the body is changing.

Not transforming cleanly. More like a corpse being badly dressed from the inside. Her shoulders crack wider. Her spine pushes up beneath the cardigan in little knobs. Her gray hair lifts around her face in the storm-wind pouring through a house with no open windows.

She stares straight at the piano.

"Children shouldn't interrupt grace," she says.

Then she looks at Merritt.

Her voice slides back into that ruined sweetness.

"Come out from there. I haven't even shown you what your preacher left in the pantry."

Merritt's gaze flicks to the mantel.

There's a fireplace poker in the stand.

Black iron.

Heavy enough.

Maybe.

Grace notices.

Her smile spreads.

"Go on," she whispers. "Hit an old woman."

Merritt rises anyway.

His knees tremble. Blood runs down his arm and drips from his fingertips. His chest burns with that spreading cold mark. He grabs the poker and feels its weight settle into his palm.

Grace bows her head.

Like she's ready to receive communion.

"Bless me," she says.

Merritt swings.

The poker cracks against her skull with a sound like splitting wood.

Grace drops to one knee.

For one wild, holy second, Merritt thinks he's hurt her.

Then the split in her scalp opens wider.

Not bleeding.

Smiling.

A black eye rolls up inside the wound and looks at him.

Grace raises her face.

"Thank you," she says.

The house begins to sing.

Not exactly music, though.

It's the long groan of joists under strain. The high whine of wind through window cracks. The clacking shutters. The drip of blood in the hall. The thin metallic hum of the communion tray in the dining room, vibrating beneath its circle of teeth.

All of it gathers into one voice.

Low.

Hungry.

Churchlike.

Merritt staggers back with the poker in both hands. Grace stays on one knee in the parlor doorway, the split in her scalp peeled open like a second mouth. The eye inside it rolls wetly, blinking slow. Glossy. Patient.

"House knows hymns," Grace whispers.

The voice doesn't come from her mouth this time. It comes from the wound in her head.

Merritt's stomach convulses.

He swings again.

But Grace catches the poker.

Her hand snaps up impossibly fast. Her fingers close around the iron, and her nails scrape over it with a dry, chittering sound. Her wrist bends backward. Too far. Then farther.

"Temper, temper," she says.

She yanks.

Merritt loses his grip and stumbles forward. Grace rises, lifting the poker with one hand, and throws it aside. It spears through the sheet covering the piano and strikes a cluster of low keys.

The piano booms.

Deep, rotten notes roll through the room.

Under the sheet, something answers.

A small whimper.

Ruthie.

Merritt looks at the piano. "Ruthie, are you really there?"

Grace's face tightens with annoyance.

"Always checking," she says. "Always doubting. That's what killed Gideon. Faith turned into looking. Looking turned into seeing. Seeing turned into rope."

"You killed him."

Grace's head cocks.

Her scalp-wound eye stays fixed on Merritt while her black eyes slide toward the ceiling.

"Killed?" she says. "No. No, no, no. He climbed up all by himself. Old bones. Shaking hands. Bare feet on a pantry stool. Brave man, really."

Merritt's throat works. "Why?"

Grace's smile softens.

For half a second, the old woman comes back. The widow. The church mother. The one who kisses cheeks at Christmas and folds bulletins before service. Her face trembles with something close to sadness.

"He finally understood marriage," she says with a throaty laugh.

Then the softness rots away.

"He was meat tied to a witness."

The house-song deepens.

The sheet over the piano flutters. A hand presses up from underneath it. Small fingers push against the white cloth, stretching it into a pale little hill.

Grace turns sharply.

"Be still."

The hand freezes.

Merritt moves before he can think better of it. He lunges for the poker. His fingers close around the iron handle just as Grace shrieks and charges.

Not like an old woman.

Not even like a human being.

She comes low and fast, shoulders jerking, knees bending the wrong way beneath her dress. Her hatchet flashes in one hand. Her severed tongue swings from the other. Her gray hair lashes around her face. The eye in her scalp rolls madly.

Merritt rips the poker free of the piano sheet and swings upward.

The iron catches Grace under the chin.

Her head snaps back.

Keeps going.

Her neck folds until the back of her head touches her spine.

Still she comes.

The hatchet comes down.

Merritt twists aside. The blade bites into the sofa arm with a heavy thunk, splitting wood and upholstery. Dust bursts into the air. He rams the poker into Grace's chest.

Once.

Twice.

The second blow lands where a heart should be.

Grace gasps.

Her whole body locks.

Something inside her chest knocks back.

Merritt feels it through the poker.

Knock.

Knock.

Knock.

Like a fist from inside a locked coffin.

Grace's mouth opens. Her tongue-stump wriggles. A voice pours out, but it isn't hers.

It's Reverend Gideon.

"Merritt."

Merritt almost drops the poker.

The voice is hoarse, strained, familiar from the pulpit and basement prayers and too many funerals.

"Merritt, boy, listen."

Grace's black eyes look up at him. They're empty of mercy.

But Gideon's voice comes again.

"Pantry."

Grace's lips twist.

"Don't," she says, in her own voice.

"Pantry," Gideon groans. "Under the flour bin. The ledger. The names. Take the names out of the house."

Grace screams. Her chest caves inward around the poker, sucking at the iron. Merritt yanks it free with a wet pop and stumbles away.

"Liar preacher," Grace hisses. "Dead preacher. Rope-necked coward."

The parlor wall behind her begins to bulge.

Wallpaper puckers. Old floral print stretches outward like something is pushing from inside. Shapes press against it. Hands. Faces. Open mouths. The wall breathes in and out, each inhale dragging more cold into the room.

The house isn't just haunted.

It's full.

Merritt glances at the piano. "Ruthie?"

The child's voice comes thin from beneath the sheet.

"I'm not in the piano."

His blood chills.

"Then where are you?"

A pause.

Then, from far away, maybe upstairs, maybe under the floor, Ruthie whispers, "I'm hiding in the closet at home."

Grace laughs.

The piano sheet collapses flat.

Merritt understands then, not fully but enough. Ruthie isn't here. Not her body. Grace is reaching through something. Dreams. Fear. Prayer. Memory. The same way she reached into his mother's voice. The same way she marked him in the church basement.

He needs the pantry.

He needs whatever Gideon hid.

He needs to get out.

Grace lifts the hatchet again.

"Little Gideon always loved keeping records," she says. "Baptisms. Weddings. Burials. Burials most of all. Wrote them down like the writing made him clean."

The door to the hallway slams shut behind her.

Then opens again.

Not to the hallway.

To a church.

Merritt sees pews stretching into darkness. New Mercy Chapel, but wrong. Too narrow. Too tall. The ceiling rises so high the rafters vanish in black. Rain falls inside though there's no sky. Hymnals sit swollen in the pew racks. Candles burn with blue flames along the aisle.

At the pulpit, Reverend Gideon hangs from his preaching stole.

Bare feet turning slowly.

Behind him, the wooden cross is upside down.

Grace gestures with the hatchet toward the impossible doorway.

"Come to service."

Merritt backs away.

The dining room door is to his left. Beyond that, the kitchen. Beyond that, if the house behaves, the pantry.

Grace takes a step toward him.

He throws the poker at her feet.

Not at her.

At the floor.

The iron crashes down hard enough to splinter a board. Blood wells up through the crack like the house is cut. Grace screeches and recoils, not from pain in her body, but from pain in the thing around her.

Merritt runs for the dining room.

The sheeted figures at the table all stand at once.

Chairs scrape back.

Merritt slams into the first one. It weighs almost nothing. The sheet collapses around him, wrapping his face in old cloth that smells of cellar damp and corpse powder. Beneath it there's no body, only sticks tied together with rosary beads and hair.

He tears free.

The communion tray rattles. Teeth jump and clatter like hail.

Grace howls behind him, and the dining room window cracks from top to bottom.

Merritt barrels through the room, shoulder first, knocking chairs aside. Something under one sheet grabs his wrist. Thin fingers. Too many joints. He brings his elbow down hard and feels bones snap like dry twigs.

A child laughs beneath the cloth.

Not Ruthie.

Younger.

Hungrier.

Merritt reaches the kitchen and nearly slips in Grace's blood. The severed tongue lies on the floor now, inching along like a slug, leaving a red trail behind it. It pauses when it senses him.

Then it flips.

The cut end opens.

A tiny mouth forms there.

"Merritt," it says in his mother's voice.

He stomps on it.

The scream is terrible. High and wet and furious.

The lights in the kitchen flare bright.

For one instant, every surface reflects black eyes. The window over the sink. The blade of a butcher knife. The puddles of blood. The glossy foil of the spilled casserole on the floor.

Then the lights die again.

Merritt lunges through the kitchen into the pantry.

The pantry door is narrow, half open. It smells of flour, mouse droppings, old apples, and rope.

Especially rope.

He stops just inside.

The air changes.

This is where Reverend Gideon died.

The pantry is barely bigger than a closet, lined with shelves holding jars, cans, sacks of dry beans, old preserves clouded with age. A wooden stool lies tipped on its side beneath the ceiling beam. Above it, a deep groove circles the wood where the stole bit and tightened under the preacher's weight.

Merritt's breath comes shallow.

He doesn't want to look up.

He does anyway.

The beam is empty.

Of course it's empty.

But the shadow hanging from it remains.

A man-shaped darkness, long and swaying, feet pointed down.

"Merritt."

Gideon's voice again.

This time from the shadow.

Merritt presses a hand against the pantry wall to steady himself. "What is she?"

The shadow turns slightly.

The rope-shadow twists with it.

"Something we invited by mistake," Gideon says. "Then fed on purpose."

A crash sounds from the kitchen.

Grace is coming.

"I kept count because I couldn't confess," Gideon whispers. "I helped her call it holy until I saw what holy cost."

Merritt drops to his knees and searches beneath the flour bin. His hands scrape over dusty boards, mouse pellets, a dead beetle, a strip of cloth stiff with old blood.

"No, no, no," Grace sings from the kitchen. "Don't dig where husbands hide their sins."

Merritt shoves the flour bin aside.

The floor beneath it has a loose board.

He digs his nails into the crack and pulls. The board resists, then pops up with a squeal.

Inside the hollow space rests a wrapped bundle tied with twine.

He grabs it.

The moment his fingers touch the bundle, the house stops singing.

Everything goes silent.

No rain.

No shutters.

No Grace.

No breath.

Merritt unties the twine.

The bundle falls open.

Inside is a black leather ledger, a tarnished communion cup, and a stack of yellowed photographs.

The cup is the same one he saw in the dining room.

Or something like it.

The top photograph shows Grace Harrowby at maybe thirty years old, standing in front of New Mercy Chapel. She's beautiful in a hard, hungry way. Dark hair pinned high. White gloves. Smile wide enough to hurt.

Beside her stands a woman Merritt knows from old pictures.

His mother.

Young.

Alive.

Pregnant.

Merritt's lungs lock.

On the back, written in Reverend Gideon's tight script:

Anna Cole. Marked after first loss. Child reserved.

Merritt stares at the words until they swim.

Child reserved.

His hand shakes as he opens the ledger.

Names fill the pages.

Columns.

Dates.

Mother's name.

Child's name.

Loss.

Comfort administered.

Harvest status.

He flips pages too fast. The handwriting changes over the years, first neat, then cramped, then frantic. He sees names he knows. Whole families from town. Women who died young. Children who grew up angry, hollow, addicted, vanished, drowned, ruined. Not random tragedies. Not God's plan.

A system.

A feeding schedule.

At the bottom of one page, circled so many times the pen tore through, is his name.

Merritt Cole.

Beside it:

READY WHEN FAITH FAILS.

The pantry door creaks.

Grace stands there with the hatchet at her side.

Her head is upright again. The split in her scalp is wider, and more eyes shine from inside the red seam. Not human eyes. Not all the same size. Some blink sideways. Some pulse like wet beads.

She looks at the ledger in his hands.

For the first time, she seems afraid.

Not of him.

Of the book.

"Give that to Mother Grace," she says.

Merritt stands slowly.

His grief changes shape inside him.

It's still fear.

But rage enters it now.

Rage burns warmer.

Grace notices.

Her nostrils flare.

"Oh," she whispers. "There it is. Warm heart."

Merritt clutches the ledger to his chest.

"Did you eat my mother's heart?"

Grace's lips part.

A small black tongue grows from the stump in her mouth, slick and twitching.

"No," she says gently.

For one second, he almost believes her.

Then she smiles.

"She gave it to me."

Merritt hits her with the ledger.

He doesn't mean to. Not at first. He means to shove past her, maybe get to the kitchen, maybe find a window, maybe break it and crawl through the glass and rain and never stop running until the Harrowby house is a bad shape behind him.

But Grace says it.

She gave it to me.

And something old and boyish splits open in him.

Not fear.

Not even rage.

A fourteen-year-old's grief, packed tight for twenty-four years, suddenly finds its teeth.

The ledger cracks across Grace's face.

She staggers sideways into the pantry doorframe, black eyes flashing wide. A hiss slips from her mouth. The little tongue writhes between her teeth and curls backward like a burned worm.

Merritt swings again.

This time, Grace catches the book.

Her fingers sink into the leather cover. It smokes where she touches it. She screams and lets go, clutching her hand against her chest. The nails on that hand split down the middle. Black fluid beads from beneath them.

"Hurts," Merritt says.

His voice doesn't sound like his own.

Grace looks up.

The thing inside her looks up.

All those eyes in her scalp seam blink at once.

Merritt backs out of the pantry, one hand tight on the ledger, the other gripping the tarnished communion cup. He doesn't know why he grabbed it. Instinct, maybe. Or the shadow of Reverend Gideon still swaying from the beam and whispering without words.

Grace blocks the kitchen.

She lifts the hatchet.

"No more running," she says.

Behind Merritt, in the pantry, the shadow of the preacher jerks at the end of its invisible rope.

"Cup," Gideon's voice rasps. "Cup and names."

Grace's head snaps toward the pantry.

"Be quiet, husband."

The shadow kicks once.

The beam groans.

"Blood remembers," Gideon says. "Names bind. Burn what's written. Spill what's kept."

Merritt looks down at the cup.

Inside it, dark residue clings to the silver. Not wine. Too thick. Too black. It coats the bottom like old syrup.

Grace sees him see it.

Every cabinet in the kitchen slams open. Plates leap from shelves and shatter. Jars explode against the walls, spraying preserves like clotted blood. The floorboards ripple under Merritt's boots, trying to throw him down.

Grace comes at him.

Merritt ducks the hatchet.

The blade bites into the pantry shelf, splitting a sack of flour. White dust erupts between them, filling the air. For one second, Grace is a ghost inside it, all black eyes and open mouth and hair lashing in storm-wind.

Merritt throws the communion cup in her face.

The black residue splashes across her skin.

Grace shrieks so hard the kitchen window blows outward.

Rain bursts in.

Not normal rain.

It comes sideways through the broken glass, cold and hard, scattering flour into paste. The curtains whip. The yellow bulb swings wildly overhead. Grace claws at her face while residue sizzles into her wrinkles and runs into her eyes.

Merritt doesn't understand what he's done.

He only knows it hurts her.

So he runs.

He barrels past her into the kitchen, slipping in flour and blood and broken glass. Grace catches the back of his church jacket. Her nails punch through fabric and scrape his shoulder. He twists out of it and leaves the jacket in her grip.

The ledger stays under his arm.

He dives into the hallway.

The walls tighten. Picture frames leap from their hooks and smash at his feet. The backward photographs flip over one by one, showing faces with their eyes scratched out. Mouths in the pictures open and whisper his name.

Merritt.

Merry.

Deacon Cole.

Reserved child.

Warm heart.

He keeps moving.

The dining room door slams shut in front of him.

He hits it shoulder first.

It doesn't budge.

Behind him, Grace crawls out of the kitchen on all fours.

Her limbs are wrong now. Too long. Her elbows bend high like a spider's legs. Her head hangs low between her shoulders, hair dragging through blood. The hatchet is clenched between her teeth, blade jutting sideways from her mouth. The eyes in her split scalp shine like beads of oil.

She skitters toward him.

Merritt grabs the dining room doorknob and twists. Locked. No key. No mercy.

Grace spits the hatchet into her hand.

"Mothers give," she says. "Children owe."

Merritt slams his foot into the door.

Once.

Twice.

The old wood cracks.

Grace leaps.

He throws himself aside as the hatchet chops into the door where his head had been. The blade sinks deep. Grace yanks at it, snarling.

Merritt kicks the door again.

The cracked panel gives way.

He plunges through it, tearing his shirt, scraping his ribs, and tumbles into the dining room.

The sheeted figures are waiting.

They stand around the table, taller now, the sheets stretched tight over forms that are less like bodies and more like bundles of sticks, teeth, and old church bones. The communion tray spins in the center of the table. Teeth rattle in circles around it.

One of the figures raises a sheeted arm.

Under the cloth, something points to the ledger.

Another figure whispers, "Read us."

Grace claws through the broken door panel behind him.

"No," she snarls. "Don't you dare."

The sheeted figures speak together.

Not loud.

That makes it worse.

"Read us."

Merritt opens the ledger with shaking hands.

The pages flutter though there's no wind.

Names.

Hundreds of names.

Some old enough that the ink has browned. Some recent enough that he remembers them from church bulletins and prayer chains. All of them folded into the same awful rhythm.

Mother dies.

Child grieves.

Grace comforts.

Something feeds.

His mother's name pulls his eye again.

Anna Cole.

The sight nearly drops him.

He sees her in the church basement. Sees Grace's gloved hands. Feels the thumb pressing into his chest. Feels the cold mark beneath his sternum blooming again.

Ready when faith fails.

Maybe that's why the thing waits.

Maybe it can't take what remains closed.

Maybe faith isn't belief in God at all. Maybe it's the last door in a person that grief can't open by itself.

And maybe his has been hanging by a hinge for years.

Grace tears herself through the door and rises on the other side, splinters jutting from her shoulders and face.

"Put it down, Merry."

His mother's voice again.

Perfect.

Soft.

Pleading.

"Merry, please. You're scaring me."

Merritt's breath breaks.

The dining room flickers.

For a moment Grace isn't there.

His mother stands in her place, younger than he ever got to know her, wearing the yellow blouse from the egg-carton memory. Flour on her cheek. Smile trembling. Eyes wet with love.

"Merry," she says. "Come here, baby."

He almost does.

His body leans before his mind catches up.

Then the front window flashes with lightning, and in that split-second glare he sees the truth overlaid on the lie.

His mother's smile is too wide.

Her eyes are black.

Her hands end in long hooked nails.

Merritt shuts the ledger.

"No."

Grace's face collapses back into itself. His mother peels away like wet paper, leaving the old woman underneath. The thing inside her shakes with fury.

"No?" she says.

The dining room ceiling cracks.

A rain of dead flies spills down, pattering over the table, the plates, the teeth. The sheeted figures don't move.

Merritt looks at them.

"What do I read?"

The nearest figure turns its hidden face toward the fireplace in the parlor.

Merritt understands.

The thing doesn't want him out.

Not anymore.

It wants witness.

Grace screams and charges.

Merritt runs straight for her.

It's stupid.

It works because it's stupid.

She expects him to flee from her, so when he drives his shoulder into her narrow chest, she rocks backward. He smells rot, blood, peppermint, and spoiled communion wine. Her nails slice down his back, but he keeps pushing. They slam into the broken door together.

Grace chops down with the hatchet.

The blade buries in the floor beside his boot.

Merritt drives his knee into her stomach.

Something inside her belly bites him through her dress.

Actual teeth close around his knee.

Pain explodes up his leg.

He shouts and falls sideways, dragging free. Fabric tears. Skin opens. Grace laughs and raises the hatchet again.

A sheeted figure steps through the broken panel behind her.

It wraps both cloth arms around Grace's neck.

Then another joins it.

And another.

Grace shrieks, thrashing as the dead of the house cling to her. Sheets rip. Beneath them, Merritt sees no faces, only bundles of hair, rosary beads, old baby teeth, finger bones, and strips of yellowed church programs tied into human shapes.

"Mine," Grace screams.

The figures pull her backward.

Not enough to stop her.

Enough to give Merritt one chance.

He crawls into the hall, grabs the fallen iron poker, and limps toward the parlor fireplace.

Every step sends fire through his bitten knee. Blood fills his shoe. His shoulder burns. His forearm throbs. The cold mark in his chest pulses in time with the house-song, which rises again, louder now, frantic and furious.

The fireplace is full of old ash.

No fire.

Of course there's no fire.

Merritt looks around the parlor. Candles. There have to be candles. Houses like this always have candles.

On the mantel, beside the backward portrait of Reverend Gideon, sit two white prayer candles burned halfway down.

He snatches one.

No matches.

Grace roars from the dining room.

The sheeted figures fly apart, thrown against walls and furniture. One bursts open, scattering teeth across the floor like dice.

Merritt searches the mantel, the side table, his pockets.

Nothing.

Then he remembers his truck keys.

The little emergency lighter on the key ring. A stupid gift from Lottie after he fixed the chapel furnace one winter. "For when the pilot light goes mean on you," she said.

His keys are in his jacket.

His jacket is in the kitchen.

With Grace.

"Damn it."

The portrait above the mantel thumps.

Merritt looks up.

The frame has turned around.

Reverend Gideon stares down from the portrait, old and pale, eyes sunken, one hand raised in blessing. But the painted hand moves. Slowly. It points toward the piano.

The piano lid lifts.

The same pale little hand slides out.

Merritt stiffens.

Ruthie's voice whispers, "Not me."

The hand opens.

In its palm rests a matchbook.

New Mercy Chapel

Merritt doesn't ask.

He grabs it.

The hand withdraws beneath the lid.

The piano plays one soft note.

Grace appears in the parlor doorway.

She's torn open now.

Not metaphorically. Not spiritually. Open. The seam in her scalp has split down her forehead, over her nose, through her lips, and into her throat. Her face hangs in two halves, and behind it is a dark red passage full of eyes and little teeth. Something pushes forward from deep inside her, stretching her skin, trying to climb out.

The old woman's body is only a doorway.

And the thing is almost through.

"Merritt Cole," it says.

The voice is no longer Grace's. It's too large for the room. Too many throats. Too much hunger.

The walls sweat blood.

The cross in the impossible church beyond the hallway burns upside down.

Merritt strikes a match.

It breaks.

Grace smiles through her split face.

His hands shake harder.

He strikes another.

The flame flares.

Small.

Yellow.

Human.

Grace recoils.

Merritt lights the candle, then holds the flame to the ledger's first page.

For a moment, nothing happens.

Then the ink begins to scream.

The names curl black. Smoke pours upward, thick and oily. The sheeted figures in the dining room moan. The house bucks under Merritt's feet, and somewhere upstairs glass explodes.

Grace drops the hatchet and clutches her chest.

"No," the thing says. "Those are mine."

Merritt feeds more pages into the flame.

The ledger catches.

Fire runs hungrily along the columns.

Mother's name.

Child's name.

Loss.

Comfort administered.

Harvest status.

All of it blackens.

Merritt holds on even when the heat bites his fingers. Names flare and vanish. Ink bubbles. Leather cracks. Smoke fills the parlor with the smell of burnt hair and old sins.

Grace crawls toward him.

Her nails dig into the floorboards and drag grooves through the wood.

"Stop," she says.

This time it's Grace.

Not the thing.

Grace Harrowby.

Old. Afraid. Small inside the ruin of herself.

"Merritt," she whispers. "Please."

He hesitates.

That's enough.

Her arm shoots out and catches his ankle.

Her hand is ice.

The cold blasts up his leg, through his stomach, into the mark beneath his sternum. Merritt gasps and drops to one knee. The burning ledger tumbles onto the hearth, still aflame but not finished.

Grace pulls herself closer.

Her split face hovers inches from his.

Inside that opened face, the thing waits with all its eyes.

"Your heart's already open," it whispers. "Your faith failed years ago."

Merritt's vision grays.

He thinks of his mother's funeral.

The church basement.

Casseroles lined on folding tables.

Grace kneeling before him.

Grief opens what love closes.

He feels that thumb on his chest again.

The cold mark opens.

Not on his skin.

Inside him.

A door.

Behind it, something moves.

Grace smiles.

"There," she breathes. "There's my good boy."

Merritt looks past her to the hearth.

The ledger burns lower.

Not enough.

His mother's page remains visible near the back, untouched by flame.

Anna Cole.

Child reserved.

Grace's fingers press deeper into his ankle. His heartbeat slows. Each beat feels farther from the last.

He hears singing.

Not the house this time.

Not Grace.

A woman's voice.

Off-key.

Warm.

His mother in the car, singing along to some old radio song, laughing when she forgets the words.

Not a trick.

He knows because it doesn't ask him to come closer.

It doesn't ask for anything.

It just is.

Memory, not bait.

Love, not hunger.

Merritt reaches for the hearth poker with one numb hand.

Grace presses her mouth to his chest.

Her split lips peel back.

Teeth touch the mark beneath his shirt.

He screams and swings the poker into the burning ledger.

Ash and flame burst upward.

The poker catches the last thick section and flips it open directly into the fire.

His mother's page ignites.

Grace's mouth tears away from his chest.

The thing inside her screams with every voice it has stolen.

Merritt sees faces in the smoke.

Women.

Children.

Men.

Old and young.

His mother is among them for half a second, not as a corpse, not as the sick woman, not even as the memory in the kitchen. Just her face, smiling softly through smoke and flame.

Then she's gone.

The mark in Merritt's chest burns hot.

The cold flower withers.

His grief remains.

But it is his again.

Grace convulses.

Her body bends backward, knees cracking, spine arching until the crown of her head almost touches her heels. The eyes inside her split face pop one by one, spraying black fluid across the floor. The house shrieks. Floorboards buckle. The ceiling splits open and rains plaster.

Merritt drags himself away from her.

Grace rises into the air.

Not lifted by hands.

Pulled by the thing trying to leave.

Her dress flaps around her brittle legs. Her gray hair whips upward. The blackened tongue in her mouth lashes like a snake. Her hands claw at nothing.

"No," Grace says.

Again, only Grace.

Her blue eyes flicker through the black.

One second of human terror.

One second of regret.

Maybe one second of asking to be saved.

Then the thing rips out of her.

It doesn't come through her mouth.

It comes through every wound at once.

A black mass of eyes, teeth, wet hair, and folded hands tears itself free of Grace Harrowby's body and slams against the ceiling. It spreads there like a stain, gripping the plaster with a hundred long fingers. Its face is not one face but many, layered and shifting. Mother. Widow. Saint. Corpse. Child. Preacher. All of them smiling.

Merritt can't move.

The burning ledger collapses into ash.

The thing screams again.

This time the scream turns into prayer.

Backward prayer.

Words Merritt almost recognizes, twisted inside out, holy sounds chewed into blasphemy. The upside-down cross in the hallway church bursts into blue fire. The dining room table splits in half. Teeth scatter across the floor, chattering as they bounce.

Merritt grabs the candle.

Only a nub remains.

He throws it at the ceiling.

It hits the black mass.

For one impossible second, nothing happens.

Then the thing catches fire.

Not yellow.

Not orange.

White.

A hard, clean blaze that throws every shadow in the room backward.

The thing twists and peels away from the ceiling, shrieking, dropping burning pieces of itself onto the furniture. Each piece hits the floor and becomes a little mouth, snapping and smoking until it curls into ash.

The house catches.

Curtains first.

Then sheets.

Then the old sofa.

Then the backward portraits, one after another, faces hidden no more as fire eats through paper backing and photograph and frame.

Grace crashes to the floor in the middle of it all.

What's left of her is small.

So terribly small.

An old woman in a ruined dress, bones broken, face slack, eyes pale blue again and staring at nothing. Her hand opens. The hatchet lies beside it, blade dark, handle worn smooth by long use.

Merritt crawls to the hallway.

The front door stands open.

Rain pours beyond it.

Real rain.

The nailed Bible hangs from the wood, burning around the iron nail but somehow not consumed. The scratched-out Psalm blackens at the edges.

He drags himself over the threshold and falls onto the porch.

Cold water hits his face.

Behind him, the Harrowby house screams as it burns.

Not wood.

Not just wood.

Voices. Hundreds of them. Some terrified. Some relieved. Some laughing. Some sobbing. The sound pours up into the storm, and thunder answers hard enough to shake the ground.

Merritt rolls onto his back.

Rain fills his mouth.

He spits and coughs and laughs once, not because anything is funny, but because his body doesn't know what else to do with being alive.

Headlights bloom at the end of the drive.

A cruiser.

Deputy Hollis Kemp stumbles out, raincoat half on, flashlight jerking in his hand.

"Cole!" he shouts. "Jesus Christ, what happened?"

Merritt tries to answer.

Nothing comes out but smoke.

Hollis runs up the porch steps, sees Merritt's torn clothes, the bite in his leg, the burns on his hands, the house burning behind him.

His face goes slack.

"What did you do?"

Merritt grips the deputy's sleeve.

"Ruthie Bell," he rasps. "Check her house. Closet."

Hollis stares.

"Now."

Maybe it's the fire. Maybe it's the blood. Maybe it's the look in Merritt's eyes. For once, Hollis doesn't argue. He turns and barks into his radio, voice shaking.

Merritt lies back again.

The Harrowby house burns hotter.

Through the open doorway, past flame and smoke, he sees the dining room one last time.

The sheeted figures stand around the broken table.

Burning.

But not fighting it.

One by one, they turn toward him.

One by one, they bow their hidden heads.

Then the ceiling caves in and takes them with it.

The fire department comes too late to save the house, which feels right. Some things shouldn't be saved. Men shout. Hoses uncoil. Red lights pulse against rain and smoke. Someone wraps Merritt in a blanket that smells like plastic. Someone tries to ask questions. Someone else says ambulance.

Merritt keeps looking at the ruins.

Waiting.

He doesn't know for what.

A shape in the flames, maybe.

A black eye under the porch.

Grace's voice singing through the rain.

But nothing comes.

Near dawn, Hollis returns, pale and wet and shaking.

He crouches beside the ambulance where Merritt sits with his hands bandaged and his knee wrapped tight.

"We found Ruthie," Hollis says.

Merritt closes his eyes.

"Alive?"

"Alive." Hollis swallows. "In her closet. Just like you said."

Merritt breathes out.

Hollis looks toward the smoking bones of the house.

"She had words written all over the inside of the closet door."

Merritt opens his eyes.

"What words?"

Hollis hesitates.

Rainwater runs down his face.

Or maybe not rain.

In the gray dawn, it's hard to tell.

"She wrote them in crayon," Hollis says. "Over and over."

Merritt already knows.

Some part of him knows before Hollis says it.

Teeth of gnarl, smile to a snarl.

Eyes of black, a tongue of clack.

A wrinkled soulless face.

I ate the heart of Mother Grace.

Hollis shivers.

"There was one more line."

Merritt's chest tightens.

The place where the mark used to be throbs once.

Hollis looks at him.

"She wrote, 'It knows the deacon got away.'"

The first sunlight slips over the wet hills.

Behind them, the Harrowby house collapses inward with a final groan, sending sparks up like fireflies.

Merritt stares into the smoke.

For a while, he says nothing.

Then, from somewhere deep in the ash, something taps.

Once.

Twice.

Three times.

Like a fingernail on glass.

Like a child at a window.

Like something patient enough to wait.

The Smile Farm

The first thing Lorna Picket notices is that her brother smiles when he vomits.

Not a little twitch, either. Not a grimace mistaken for joy. It's a full, bright, commercial-grade smile stretched across Tobin's face while his hands clamp the bathroom sink and his shoulders jerk hard enough to rattle the medicine cabinet.

Blood splashes porcelain.

Dark red. Thick. Speckled with little pale bits Lorna doesn't want to identify.

Tobin coughs. Gags. Spits.

Smiles.

"Oh, Jesus," Lorna says from the doorway.

Her brother lifts one trembling hand, like he's trying to wave her off, like this is embarrassing but ordinary. Like he's thrown up after bad chili or cheap beer, not sprayed blood across her sink at eleven thirty on a Tuesday night.

"I'm okay," he says.

He isn't.

His teeth are perfect.

That's the second thing she notices, even though she's noticed it all week. She can't stop noticing it. They're too straight, too white, too even. They look poured into his mouth instead of grown there.

Before last Friday, Tobin had a chipped canine, a gray molar, and one front tooth that leaned over the other like it was tired from standing up.

Now he has the smile of a man in a billboard for mortgage refinancing.

Except his eyes don't match.

His eyes are wet and scared and sunk deep into a face that's lost ten pounds in five days.

"Tobin," Lorna says.

He coughs again. More blood threads down from his lower lip. It cuts a bright red line through the white curve of his smile.

"Really," he says. "I'm fine."

"You're puking blood."

"Stomach bug."

"That's not a stomach bug."

He laughs.

It comes out wrong.

Tobin used to laugh like a busted lawn mower, all choke and wheeze and sudden snorts. It used to embarrass him in restaurants and make Della laugh so hard she'd fall sideways against Lorna in the booth.

This laugh is neat.

Small.

Clipped.

Almost polite.

He wipes his mouth with the back of his hand, smearing blood across his cheek. His smile doesn't move. His lips are peeled back from his teeth as if invisible hooks have caught them at the corners and tugged.

Lorna takes a step into the bathroom.

Tobin flinches.

That scares her more than the blood.

"You need a doctor," she says.

"No."

"Then urgent care."

"No."

"Tobin."

"I said no."

The words snap out of him, sharp and panicked, but the smile stays. It makes him look cruel. It makes him look delighted to be scared.

In the hallway behind Lorna, the old house settles with a soft pop in the walls. Outside, crickets saw away in the weeds. The air conditioner coughs and kicks on, blowing warm air through a vent that smells faintly of dust and mouse droppings.

Della sleeps in the little bedroom at the end of the hall, one arm curled around a stuffed raccoon with a missing button eye. Her backpack sits beside the door, already packed for tomorrow.

Pink sweatshirt.

Library book.

Dental appointment card tucked into the front pocket where Lorna put it two weeks ago.

Smile Farm Community Dental Clinic

Free Care Day
Della Picket, 9:30 a.m.
Please check in with Mavis.

Lorna thinks of that card now, and her stomach goes cold.

Tobin sees her looking down the hall.

His smile widens.

Not by much.

Enough.

"Don't cancel," he says.

Lorna turns back slowly. "What?"

His fingers tighten on the sink until his knuckles show bone-white under the skin.

"Don't cancel Della's appointment."

The bathroom feels smaller all at once. The yellow light above the mirror hums. Blood drips from the faucet where Tobin has splashed it, one drop after another, like a lazy clock.

"I didn't say anything about Della."

"She needs it," Tobin says.

His voice has gone soft now. Almost tender.

"She's embarrassed all the time. Kids are mean. You know kids are mean. Dr. Tine can fix it."

Lorna stares at him.

The smile sits on his face like a wound somebody has forced open.

"Tobin," she says, "what did he do to you?"

Her brother's eyes fill.

His mouth keeps shining.

"I can't tell you."

"Why not?"

His chin quivers. His cheeks pull tighter. The skin at the corners of his mouth splits with tiny red lines.

"Because," Tobin whispers, "it'll hear me."

Lorna doesn't move.

The bathroom light keeps humming. Tobin keeps gripping the sink. Somewhere inside the walls, water ticks through old pipes, slow and patient.

"It?"

Tobin's eyes cut toward the mirror.

Not at himself.

At the space behind himself.

Lorna looks, too, because fear is stupid that way. It makes you obey whatever scares you most.

The mirror shows the bathroom, narrow and yellow-lit. It shows Tobin hunched over the sink with blood on his chin. It shows Lorna in sweatpants and an old propane company T-shirt, one hand braced against the doorframe, her hair coming loose from its clip.

Behind them, nothing.

Only the hall.

Only dark.

Then Tobin's reflection smiles wider than Tobin does.

Lorna sucks in a breath.

The reflection's lips peel back until they show gum. Too much gum. Wet, red, glistening at the edges. Tobin in real life groans and clamps one hand over his mouth, but the man in the mirror keeps smiling like someone posing for a family portrait at gunpoint.

Then the mirror fogs from the inside.

Not from steam. There's no shower running. No hot water. The glass clouds in patches, blooming gray-white over Lorna's face, over Tobin's shoulders, over the bathroom wall.

A word appears in the fog.

KEEP

Lorna steps back.

Another word drags itself beside it, written by nothing, each letter formed in a trembling smear.

SMILING

Tobin makes a sound that's almost a sob.

The mirror clears all at once.

His reflection matches him again.

Lorna's heart thuds so hard she feels it in her throat.

"No," she says.

It's the only word she has.

Tobin turns from the sink. His legs wobble. For a second, she thinks he's going to fall, and even after everything, even with his awful stretched grin and the blood on his teeth, he's still her baby brother. He's still the kid who used to trail after her through drainage ditches, asking if snakes can climb trees and whether dead people can hear thunder.

She catches him before he hits the floor.

He folds against her, too light, all sharp bones and fever heat. His smile presses into her shoulder.

"Don't let her go," he whispers.

Lorna grips the back of his shirt. "I won't."

His fingers clutch her wrist hard enough to hurt.

"No. Don't let her go, but don't tell her why. Don't say his name near her. Don't say Smile Farm where she can hear it."

"Tobin, what the hell is happening?"

He shakes his head against her. His breath comes in little clicking pulls through his teeth.

"It likes kids best."

The words drop into her like stones.

From the end of the hallway, bedsprings squeak.

Lorna freezes.

Tobin freezes, too.

"Mom?" Della calls, thick with sleep. "Is Uncle Tobin sick?"

Lorna closes her eyes for half a second.

Then she pulls away from Tobin and steps into the hallway, blocking the bathroom with her body.

Della stands in her bedroom doorway in an oversized sleep shirt with a cartoon possum on it. Her hair sticks up on one side. Her stuffed raccoon dangles from one hand by its tail. In the dark, she looks younger than nine. Much younger. Too small for the thing already reaching for her from tomorrow morning.

"Go back to bed, baby," Lorna says.

Della squints past her. "Why's the light on?"

"Your uncle ate something bad."

"I told him that gas station sushi was dumb."

Despite herself, Lorna almost laughs.

Almost.

Then Tobin laughs from the bathroom.

That neat little laugh.

Della's face changes.

She doesn't know why it's wrong. She only knows it is. Children hear the animal under the human voice. They hear the wolf in Grandma's nightgown.

"Uncle Tobin?" she says.

"He's fine," Lorna says quickly. "Go on."

Della doesn't go.

Her eyes drop to Lorna's shirt.

Blood has smeared across the shoulder where Tobin's mouth pressed against her.

"What's that?"

"Ketchup," Lorna says, too fast.

Della gives her a look. Even scared, the kid has no patience for bad lies.

"At midnight?"

"Go to bed, Della."

That lands harder than Lorna means it to. Della's mouth tightens. One crooked front tooth catches the hallway night-light, and Lorna sees the familiar motion before it happens.

Della lifts the raccoon and hides the lower half of her face behind it.

Shame.

Automatic.

Practiced.

The sight breaks something in Lorna.

She crosses the hall and kneels in front of her daughter. "Hey."

Della looks away.

"I'm sorry," Lorna says. "I didn't mean to bark."

"You did, though."

"I know."

"Is he really okay?"

Lorna glances back.

In the bathroom, Tobin stands with both hands over his mouth now, like he's trying to hold his face together. Blood leaks between his fingers.

"No," Lorna says quietly. "He's not."

Della's eyes widen.

"But I'm handling it," Lorna says. "That's my job."

"Is my appointment still tomorrow?"

The question comes soft.

Hopeful.

Terrible.

Lorna looks at her daughter's hidden mouth. Looks at the raccoon. Looks at the backpack by the door with the appointment card tucked inside.

"No," she says.

Della's face falls.

"But Mom..."

"No."

"You promised."

"I know."

"You said Dr. Tine helps people who can't pay."

Lorna's throat tightens.

From the bathroom, Tobin whispers through his bloody fingers.

"Don't say it."

Della turns toward him. "Say what?"

The hallway light flickers.

Once.

Twice.

Then every tooth in Della's mouth clicks together.

Hard.

Like something invisible has tapped them from the inside.

Della screams.

It's small and sharp and gone almost as soon as it starts, chopped off by her teeth snapping together again.

Click.

Click.

Click.

Her jaw works like a wind-up toy. Her eyes flood with panic. She drops the stuffed raccoon and clamps both hands against her cheeks.

"Mom," she says, but it comes out mashed and wet. "Mmmom, make it stop."

Lorna grabs her daughter's face.

Della's skin feels cold.

Not fever cold. Basement cold. Winter-ground cold. Her little jaw trembles under Lorna's palms, and every tooth in her mouth ticks in place, fast and delicate, like a hundred tiny fingernails tapping glass.

Behind them, Tobin lets out a strangled moan.

"Don't touch her mouth," he says.

Lorna looks back at him. "What?"

"Don't touch her teeth."

Della's jaw snaps again.

This time, one of her crooked front teeth twists.

Just a little.

Just enough.

Della's scream turns into a gag.

Lorna sees red at the gumline.

"No," she says. "No, no, no."

She scoops Della up, even though Della's too big to be carried that way anymore. Her daughter clings to her neck with both arms, face buried in Lorna's shoulder, teeth still clicking against themselves.

Tobin staggers out of the bathroom.

Blood shines on his chin, his shirt, his fingers. His smile is worse now. The corners have split wider, and the skin there has opened in thin red cracks, as if his face isn't built to hold so much happiness.

"He marked her," Tobin says.

Lorna backs away from him. "Who?"

Tobin's eyes flick to the dark kitchen at the end of the hall.

"His patients get marked before he finishes them," Tobin says. "The card. The name. The appointment. It's enough."

From somewhere in the house, a phone rings.

Not Lorna's cell.

Not the cheap cordless in the kitchen, either.

This ring is older. Metallic. A hard little bell with a rattle in it.

Della whimpers into Lorna's neck. "Mommy."

The ringing continues.

Tobin starts crying.

His smile never changes.

"Don't answer it," he says.

Lorna doesn't want to. Every nerve in her body tells her not to move toward that sound, not to follow it through the dark hallway, not to leave the warm patch of light outside Della's bedroom.

But Della's teeth keep clicking.

And with every click, that front tooth turns a little more.

Lorna sees it happen against her shoulder.

A slow correction.

A painless correction.

That's almost the worst part. Della isn't screaming from pain now. She's screaming because she can feel something helping her.

The phone rings again.

Lorna carries Della down the hall.

Tobin follows, whispering, "No. No, Lorna. Please."

The kitchen is dark except for the green stove clock and the strip of moonlight on the linoleum. Dirty dishes sit in the sink. A box fan rattles in the window, pushing warm night air around instead of cooling anything.

The ringing comes from the kitchen table.

There's a black rotary phone sitting in the middle of it.

Lorna has never owned a rotary phone.

It looks like something dragged out of an attic. Heavy. Glossy. The cord trails off the edge of the table and disappears into shadow beneath it, though Lorna knows damn well there's no phone jack down there.

The bell rattles again.

Della lifts her head.

Her mouth has gone still.

Slowly, she smiles.

Lorna's blood turns to ice.

It's not huge. Not yet. Not Tobin's peeled-back nightmare grin. It's just a sweet little smile on a sleepy child's face.

But Della isn't happy.

Her eyes are begging.

"Mom," she whispers.

The phone rings.

Lorna sets her daughter on the counter, keeping one arm locked around her waist. With her free hand, she snatches the receiver off the cradle.

"What?" she says.

For a second there's only breathing.

Then a man's voice comes through, soft and warm as a hand on the back of the neck.

"Mrs. Picket," Dr. Hollis Tine says. "You sound upset."

Lorna stares at the black phone like she might be able to see him curled inside it.

Della sits rigid on the counter, one hand clamped around Lorna's wrist. Her little smile trembles. It tries to grow. It tries to behave.

Tobin stands in the kitchen doorway, bleeding and grinning and shaking his head.

"No," he mouths.

Lorna's grip tightens around the receiver. "What did you do to my daughter?"

A soft click comes through the line.

Not static.

Teeth.

"Nothing permanent," Dr. Tine says. "Not yet."

Lorna turns, pressing the receiver hard to her ear. "You stay away from her."

"My dear, she's already on the schedule."

"I'm canceling."

"That's certainly your right."

The way he says it makes her stomach twist. Polite. Patient. Almost amused. Like she's a child threatening to cancel the weather.

Della makes a tiny sound.

Lorna looks down.

Her daughter's front tooth is straight now.

Perfectly straight.

The tooth beside it twitches in the gum.

Della's eyes squeeze shut. Tears slide down both cheeks, but the smile holds them hostage, lifting them into false little arcs of joy.

"Stop it," Lorna says into the phone.

"I'm trying to."

"Bullshit."

A sigh. Gentle. Disappointed.

"Mrs. Picket, I've served this county for twenty-three years. I've treated infections that could've killed grown men. I've pulled abscessed teeth from children whose parents couldn't afford antibiotics. I've given people back their dignity. Do you know what rotting teeth do to a person's spirit?"

"I know what monsters do."

The line goes quiet.

The kitchen feels too still. The box fan stops rattling. The crickets outside cut off, all at once, as if the whole yard has leaned in to listen.

Then Tine laughs softly.

"Monster," he says. "That's a comfortable word, isn't it? Makes the world simple. Makes you innocent."

Lorna looks at Tobin.

His blood drips onto the linoleum in slow, fat drops.

"You did this to my brother."

"I relieved your brother."

"He's vomiting blood."

"He drank too much for years. Ate poorly. Ignored pain. These things collect, Mrs. Picket. Misery is not imaginary simply because we learn to hide it."

Tobin grips the doorframe. His smile shines red.

"Ask him how he felt before," Tine says. "Ask him what it was like waking up with that dead tooth throbbing into his skull. Ask him how many nights he pressed whiskey against his gums because he couldn't sleep. I didn't create his suffering. I relocated it."

Lorna swallows.

On the counter, Della's next tooth slides straight with a soft, wet sound.

Her smile widens.

Her small fingers dig into Lorna's arm.

"Relocated it where?" Lorna asks.

Another click.

Another.

A wet, crowded chatter rises faintly behind Tine's breathing. Dozens of mouths working at once. Maybe hundreds. Teeth clacking glass. Tongues dragging over lips.

Tobin makes a low sound and sinks to the floor.

"Where?" Lorna says again, though she already knows.

"Somewhere useful."

"There's no useful place for pain."

"Of course there is," Tine says. "Away from the face."

Lorna wants to throw the receiver across the room. Wants to smash the phone with a hammer. Wants to grab Della and Tobin and drive until the gas tank runs dry.

But Della's smile keeps growing.

Her lips are beginning to pull tight.

"Let her go," Lorna says.

"She can still come in tomorrow. Nine thirty. We'll finish properly. No fear. No shame. No more hiding her mouth behind toys or sleeves or careful little hands."

Della sobs through her smile.

Lorna looks at the stuffed raccoon lying in the hallway.

"You've been watching her."

"I notice need."

"You notice weakness."

"Same door, different hinges."

The phone cord shifts under the table.

Lorna sees it now.

It isn't a cord.

It's black and slick and pulsing faintly where it vanishes into shadow. Like a vein. Like a root. Like something grown from the house under her house.

She backs away, pulling Della closer.

Tine's voice drops, still kind, still rotten with kindness.

"Bring her in, Mrs. Picket. Don't make me collect from home."

Lorna slams the receiver down so hard the bell inside the phone gives one frightened little chirp.

For half a second, nothing happens.

Then the phone rings again.

Della screams through her smile.

Lorna snatches the black phone off the table and hurls it at the wall. It hits beside the calendar from Miller Feed & Grain and breaks into three heavy pieces. The plastic cracks. The dial pops loose and rolls across the floor, clicking as it spins.

The ringing stops.

The thing under the table doesn't.

The black vein jerks once, hard enough to rattle the chair legs. Then it slides backward into the dark beneath the table, dragging broken bits of phone cord with it. It leaves a wet streak on the linoleum.

Tobin crawls away from it, heels kicking, one hand clamped over his mouth. Blood leaks through his fingers.

Lorna grabs Della off the counter.

"We're leaving," she says.

Della nods fast. Her teeth are too straight now. All of them. Even the little ones that still have that child softness to them. They shine in the dim kitchen like something newly installed.

Her smile is still there.

Small.

Wrong.

But not as wide as Tobin's.

Not yet.

Lorna runs to the hall closet and yanks it open. Shoes tumble out. A winter coat falls off its hanger. She grabs her purse from the hook and digs for her keys with one hand while holding Della tight with the other.

"Tobin," she snaps.

He's still on the kitchen floor, staring at the broken phone.

"Tobin, move."

"I can't go back there," he whispers.

"We're not going back there."

He looks at her then. His eyes are red and ruined. "You don't understand. Once he starts a mouth, he has to finish it."

Lorna finds the keys and grips them so hard the teeth bite into her palm.

"Then he can finish mine," she says.

Tobin's smile trembles.

"No," he says. "Don't say that."

But Lorna's already moving.

She gets Della's sneakers from beside the front door and shoves them onto her feet without tying them. The old porch light spills through the curtains, yellow and weak. Beyond the glass, the yard sits in moonlight. Their gravel drive. The rusted mailbox. The ditch full of weeds. Lorna's ten-year-old Kia parked under the mulberry tree.

Normal things.

Normal enough to make the nightmare feel worse.

Della leans against her, shaking.

"Mom," she whispers.

"I've got you."

"My face is tired."

Lorna looks at her.

Della tries to close her mouth. Her lips tremble, fighting to cover the teeth, but the corners keep pulling back. Her cheeks quiver with the effort. Tears drip off her chin.

"I can't stop," Della says.

"I know, baby."

"I'm not happy."

"I know."

"I don't want people to think I'm happy."

That does it.

That breaks the last thin thread holding Lorna together.

She kisses Della's forehead, fast and fierce, then throws the door open.

The porch boards groan.

Insects go silent.

Every light in the house behind her clicks off at once.

Della clings to her arm.

Tobin staggers out behind them, barefoot, bloody, still smiling like he's won a prize.

They get halfway across the yard before the Kia smiles at them.

The headlights flare on.

So do the interior lights.

So does the radio, loud with static and that soft, wet clicking underneath.

The front grille bends.

Metal pops. Chrome flexes. The black opening beneath the bumper stretches wide and crooked, pulling the license plate down like a lower lip.

Della buries her face in Lorna's side.

The Kia's horn gives two short beeps.

Cheerful.

Inviting.

Then all four tires hiss flat at once.

For one stupid second, Lorna just stands there holding her keys.

The Kia settles lower on its rims with a soft, tired sigh. The headlights burn bright. The grille keeps its warped shape, not quite a mouth now, but not nothing either. Static pours from inside the car, and under it comes Tine's voice, distant and pleased.

"Roads are dangerous at night, Mrs. Picket."

Lorna backs up, pulling Della with her.

Tobin turns toward the county road.

"Gilly," he says.

Lorna looks at him.

"Gilly's place," he says. "She's close."

"She's three miles."

"Better than here."

He's right, and she hates him for it.

Behind them, something knocks inside the house.

Once.

Then again.

Not at the door.

Under the floor.

Della makes a little squeaking sound.

Lorna pockets the keys, scoops her daughter up again, and runs.

Gravel bites through her socks because she hasn't put shoes on. She doesn't care. Tobin stumbles beside her, one hand pressed to his ribs, his bloody smile flashing in moonlight whenever he turns his head.

They cross the yard, cut through the ditch, and push into the Johnsons' cornfield.

The stalks rise tall around them, black-green and whispering. Dry leaves slap Lorna's arms. The dirt between rows is hard and cracked. Her breath comes hot in her throat. Della bounces against her hip, too heavy and not heavy enough, her little arms locked around Lorna's neck.

"Mom," she whispers.

"Don't talk."

"My teeth are humming."

Lorna almost trips.

"What?"

"They're humming."

Tobin makes a broken noise. "He's calling her."

Lorna keeps running. "Shut up."

"I'm sorry."

"Shut up and move."

They move.

The farmhouse where they live falls behind them. No lights now. No porch glow. Just a dark shape under the sky. Then, from somewhere beneath it, something starts laughing.

Not one laugh.

Many.

Thin laughs. Wet laughs. Little child laughs. Old man laughs. Women laughing like they've got mouths full of pins. They roll out across the field and chase Lorna through the corn.

Della presses both hands to her ears.

Her smile stays.

The worst part is how pretty it looks.

Perfect teeth. Perfect child. Perfect lie.

Lorna hates that smile so much she could claw it off with her bare fingers.

Ahead, Tobin drops to one knee.

"Tobin!"

He pitches forward and vomits into the dirt.

Blood splatters the roots of the corn.

Still smiling.

Always smiling.

Lorna grabs the back of his shirt and yanks. "Get up."

"I can't."

"You can."

His face twists, but only above the mouth. His eyes crush shut. His forehead wrinkles. His lips remain peeled back, obedient and awful.

"There's something in me," he says.

Lorna looks behind them.

The corn is moving.

Not with wind. There isn't any wind. The stalks part far back in the rows, one after another, like something low and broad is crawling through them.

Della sees it, too.

Her teeth begin to chatter again.

Click-click-click-click.

"Get up," Lorna says.

Tobin digs his fingers into the dirt and pushes himself upright.

They run harder.

By the time they reach the old irrigation ditch at the far edge of the field, Lorna's lungs feel skinned. The ditch is dry this time of year, six feet down and lined with rocks, bottles, and sun-baked mud. Beyond it is County Road 9, and beyond that are the scattered porch lights of town.

Gilly's thrift store sits another mile past the crossroads.

Lorna lowers Della into the ditch first.

"Careful."

Della slides, sneakers skidding on dust, and lands at the bottom with a grunt. Tobin follows, half falling, half tumbling, and hits one shoulder hard.

Lorna climbs down last.

The corn behind them goes silent.

Too silent.

Lorna turns.

At the edge of the field stands Mavis Droot.

White hair. Purple glasses. Flowered clinic smock. Sensible shoes sinking into the dirt.

Lorna recognizes her from the appointment card.

From Smile Farm's cracked little website.

From the woman who answered the phone when Lorna called to ask if free really meant free.

Mavis lifts one hand and wiggles her fingers.

"Evening, honey," she calls.

Her dentures click.

Then the corn behind her opens wider.

Dozens of mouths hang in the stalks like ripe fruit. Lips without faces. Teeth without heads. Tongues lolling wet and eager in the moonlight.

Every one of them smiles.

Mavis steps down into the ditch like she's coming into church late.

Her knees pop. Her shoes scrape dirt. Her smile stays sweet and patient beneath the shine of her purple glasses.

"You gave everybody a scare," she says.

Lorna backs Della behind her.

Tobin crawls backward on his hands and heels, blood dripping from his chin onto his shirt. "Don't let her touch you."

Mavis makes a sad little sound. "Oh, Tobin. You always were dramatic."

One of the mouths in the corn chatters.

Another answers.

Then all of them begin working their teeth together, not loud at first, just a dry, busy ticking. Like bugs in the walls. Like rain made of bone.

Lorna looks for a weapon and sees a broken bottle near her foot. She grabs it by the neck. The glass bites her palm, but she holds tight.

Mavis notices and sighs.

"That's how people get cut, honey."

"Take one more step," Lorna says.

Mavis stops.

For a moment, she looks almost amused. Then her face changes. Not much. Just enough for the sweetness to drain out of her.

"You poor thing," she says. "You think you're saving that child by letting her suffer."

"She was fine."

"No, she wasn't."

Della's fingers clutch the back of Lorna's shirt.

Mavis points one bent finger at her. "That baby hides her mouth when she talks. She's afraid to laugh. She's already learning how to make herself smaller so cruel people don't see where to stick the knife. Dr. Tine fixes that."

"He fixes faces," Lorna says. "Not people."

Mavis's dentures click once.

"That's where people live."

The mouths in the corn chatter louder.

Della whispers, "Mom, they know my name."

Lorna doesn't look back. "Don't listen."

"They're saying it."

"Don't listen."

But now Lorna hears it, too.

Della.

Della.

Della.

Not spoken by one voice. Spoken by hundreds of little wet pieces. A child's name chewed into the night.

Tobin lurches up from the dirt and puts himself between Mavis and Lorna. It's clumsy. Pitiful. Brave enough to hurt.

Mavis tilts her head. "Move aside."

"No," Tobin says.

His smile shines red.

Mavis's own smile fades for the first time.

Without it, she looks ancient. Hollow. Angry in a way that's sat inside her so long it's become part of her bones.

"You're not finished," she says.

"I know."

"You'll rupture."

"Maybe."

"You'll beg to come back."

Tobin spits blood at her feet. "Maybe I won't have a mouth by then."

Mavis lunges.

She moves wrong. Too fast for her age, too smooth, like something yanks her forward by wires threaded through her joints. Tobin shoves Lorna and Della aside just before Mavis hits him.

They go down hard.

Mavis lands on top, hands clawing at his face. Tobin screams through his smile as she hooks both thumbs into the corners of his mouth and pulls.

Skin splits.

Lorna hears it.

A soft, wet rip.

Tobin's scream becomes a bubbling howl.

Della shrieks.

Lorna swings the broken bottle.

It catches Mavis across the side of the head, slicing through white hair and pale scalp. Mavis jerks sideways, but she doesn't fall off Tobin. She turns slowly toward Lorna, blood running down her temple.

Her dentures slide loose.

Behind them, something inside her mouth moves.

Not a tongue.

A smaller mouth.

Pink. Toothless. Smiling.

Lorna hits her again.

This time Mavis tumbles back into the ditch wall. Dirt rains down around her shoulders. The mouths in the corn erupt into furious chatter.

"Run," Tobin gasps.

Lorna grabs Della's hand and scrambles up the far side of the ditch. Her socks slip. Rocks tear her feet. Della climbs beside her, crying silently now, still smiling that stolen little smile.

At the top, Lorna looks back.

Tobin is still in the ditch.

He's on his knees.

Mavis is rising behind him.

"Tobin!" Lorna screams.

He looks up at her, and for one second his eyes are his again. Scared. Sorry. Full of love.

Then he grabs Mavis around the waist and throws himself backward.

They crash into the ditch bottom together.

The mouths in the corn shriek.

"Go!" Tobin roars.

Lorna goes.

She hauls Della across County Road 9 just as the asphalt begins to pucker beneath their feet, softening into a long black grin.

The road tries to bite.

Lorna feels it before she understands it. The tar softens under her torn socks, warm and sticky, tugging at the bottoms of her feet. The yellow centerline curves, warps, pulls into a crescent. Gravel along the shoulder lifts like little teeth.

Della screams again, but the sound's changed. It comes out bright. Almost delighted.

That makes Lorna run harder.

"Don't look down," she says.

Della looks down.

The road opens beneath them.

Not all the way. Not enough to swallow them whole. Just enough to show something gooey and pink under the asphalt, something ridged and pulsing, something with spit shining in the cracks.

Lorna leaps.

Her left foot lands on the far shoulder. Her right heel catches in hot tar. Pain tears up her leg as the skin peels. She nearly drops Della, catches herself, and stumbles forward into the weeds.

The road snaps shut behind them with a flat, angry slap.

Across the ditch, Tobin screams.

Then Mavis screams.

Then they both stop.

Lorna doesn't turn around.

She can't.

If she sees him die, she won't move. She knows that as clearly as she knows her own name. She'll go back. She'll claw at Mavis. She'll get herself killed in the dirt while Della stands there smiling and crying and waiting to be collected.

So she runs.

The town sits ahead in scattered pieces. Porch lights. A blinking gas station sign. The dark square shape of Gilly's thrift store with its painted plywood sign reading SECOND CHANCE GOODS in peeling blue letters.

A dog barks somewhere.

Then another.

Then all the dogs stop at once.

Della's hand is slippery in Lorna's. Sweat or blood. Maybe both.

"Mom," Della says.

"Keep moving."

"Uncle Tobin…"

"Keep moving."

"Is he dead?"

Lorna can't answer. Her throat closes around the word.

Behind them, from the far side of the road, comes a wet clicking sound.

Not Mavis.

Not Tobin.

The mouths.

They're crossing.

Lorna glances back despite herself.

Dozens of them inch over the asphalt like pale slugs, lips dragging, teeth clacking, tongues pushing them along. Some still have scraps of gum attached. Some have silver fillings that catch in the moonlight. One wears a smear of pink lipstick. Another has a child's blue retainer snapped behind its teeth.

They chatter as they come.

Della.

Della.

Della.

Lorna yanks her daughter forward.

They hit the sidewalk outside the thrift store hard enough to jar Lorna's teeth. The front windows are cluttered with lamps, old prom dresses, crockpots, and a mannequin in a church hat. A paper sign taped inside reads CLOSED MEANS CLOSED, UNLESS YOU'RE BLEEDING OR BRINGING TACOS.

Lorna pounds on the glass.

"Gilly!"

No answer.

She pounds again.

"Gilly, open up!"

Della looks over her shoulder.

The first mouth reaches the curb.

Its lips pucker. Its teeth chatter. It smiles up at them from the gutter.

Then it whispers, clear as a person.

"Pretty girl."

Della goes still.

Lorna kicks it.

The mouth bursts under her bare foot with a hot, rotten pop.

Pain lances through her sole. Something sharp cuts deep.

Teeth.

She's stepped on teeth.

She screams and falls against the thrift store door.

A light comes on upstairs.

"Who the hell's breaking my glass?" Gilly Baines shouts from above.

"Gilly!" Lorna screams. "Open the damn door!"

A face appears in the second-floor window, round and furious beneath a sleep bonnet.

Gilly squints down.

Then she sees Della.

Then she sees the things crawling over the road.

The window slams shut.

Locks rattle below.

A bolt slides.

The front door flies open, and Gilly stands there in a faded nightgown, one hand gripping a Louisville Slugger, the other holding a can of wasp spray.

"What in God's crooked ass is that?" she says.

"Move," Lorna gasps.

Gilly moves.

Lorna shoves Della inside and falls in after her. Gilly slams the door just as three mouths hit the glass.

They stick there, suckered to it.

Smiling.

Chattering.

One slowly licks the window from bottom to top.

Gilly raises the bat.

"Nope," she says. "Absolutely the hell nope."

Gilly throws the deadbolt, then the chain, then a second bolt Lorna didn't even know was there.

The mouths slap against the glass.

Wet little impacts. Smears of pink and red. Teeth clicking hard enough to make the window buzz in its frame.

Della stands in the middle of the thrift store, trembling in her loose sneakers and possum sleep shirt, her smile bright under the emergency light above the register. She looks like a child forced to pose for a picture at her own funeral.

Gilly looks at her.

Then at Lorna.

Then at Lorna's feet.

"Your blood is on my rug," she says.

Lorna almost laughs. It comes out as a sob instead.

"Sorry."

"No, honey, don't apologize. I hate that rug." Gilly lifts the bat and points it toward the window. "I'm more worried about the dentures from hell trying to French kiss my storefront."

Another mouth hits the glass.

This one has gold caps. It opens and closes, open and close, open and close, like a fish on a dock.

Gilly sprays it with wasp killer.

The mouth shrieks.

Not loud through the glass, but high. Furious. Human enough to make Lorna's stomach knot. It drops from the window and lands on the sidewalk, twitching.

"Well," Gilly says. "Good to know."

Lorna limps to Della and grabs her shoulders.

"Look at me."

Della's eyes roll toward her.

"I'm scared," Della says.

"I know."

"My mouth keeps wanting to listen."

Lorna's hands tighten. "Listen to me instead."

"I'm trying."

Gilly turns from the window. Her face has gone pale under the freckles. "Lorna. Why is your kid smiling like she just heard the punchline to a joke nobody else gets?"

"Tine."

Gilly stops breathing for half a second.

Then she says, "That son of a bitch."

"You knew?"

"No." Gilly's jaw works. "Not knew. Suspected in the way you suspect milk's turned before you smell it. Folks come back from that farmhouse looking too damn pleased. Ruthie Teague smiles through migraines. Oscar Bell smiles when his arthritis locks his hands. My cousin Willa smiled all through her husband's burial until she passed out facedown on the casket spray."

"Their pain goes somewhere else," Lorna says.

A mouth thumps against the door.

Then another.

Then several.

One with black lipstick puckers tight.

The glass darkens with them, all those hungry little smiles pressed flat.

Gilly steps backward. "Where?"

"Under the farmhouse."

Della whispers, "In jars."

Lorna looks down.

Her daughter hasn't heard that from her.

Gilly hears it, too. "What jars, baby?"

Della's smile twitches bigger. Her eyes fill again, but her voice changes. Not much. Just enough to sound too careful.

"The talking ones."

Lorna kneels despite the pain in her foot. "Della?"

"They're lonely," Della says.

The smile gets wider.

"They want me to come down and sit with them."

Gilly mutters, "Oh, hell no."

She hurries behind the counter and yanks open a drawer. Pens spill. Rubber bands snap loose. She digs past a church bulletin, a roll of quarters, three screwdrivers, and comes up with a revolver so old it looks like something a bank robber dropped in 1932.

Lorna stares. "You have a gun?"

"I run a thrift store by myself on a county road," Gilly says. "I have three guns, two knives, bear spray, a tire iron, and one extremely mean rooster out back."

The mouths at the door begin to chant.

Nine thirty.

Nine thirty.

Nine thirty.

Della claps both hands over her ears.

Lorna looks at the clock above the register.

12:18 a.m.

Morning is still hours away.

Too close anyway.

"We need to get to Tine," Lorna says.

Gilly turns with the revolver in her hand. "That's the dumbest thing you've ever said, and I've heard you defend canned tamales."

"He's already got her. We can run all night and he'll keep reaching through phones and roads and God knows what else. Tobin said once he starts a mouth, he has to finish it."

"Tobin said?" Gilly's face softens. "Where is he?"

Lorna can't speak.

Gilly understands.

For once, she doesn't make a joke.

The lights flicker.

From somewhere in the back of the store comes a soft, polite bell.

Ding.

The kind that rings when a customer walks in.

Gilly slowly turns toward the rear hallway.

"That door's locked," she says.

Ding.

Della lowers her hands.

Her teeth click once.

Then she says, in a voice that isn't quite hers, "Mavis found the back."

Gilly raises the revolver.

"Behind me," she says.

Lorna pulls Della close, but Della's body doesn't move right away. Her head stays turned toward the rear hallway, tilted like she's listening to someone whisper from a long way off.

"Della," Lorna says.

Her daughter blinks.

Then she stumbles backward into Lorna's arms.

The bell rings again.

Ding.

From the front window, the mouths press harder against the glass. Their lips flatten. Their teeth scrape. Little threads of saliva run down in shining strings.

Gilly moves first.

She doesn't run. She walks with the stiff, angry purpose of a woman who's spent twenty years dealing with people trying to steal from donation bins and piss behind her building.

"Whoever's back there," she calls, "you picked the wrong damn night."

The thrift store stretches long and narrow behind the register. Racks of old clothes make shadowy aisles. Lamps with no shades lean on end tables. Porcelain angels stare from shelves. A row of used mirrors hangs along one wall, each one reflecting a different sliver of dark.

The back hallway is worse.

It leads to the storage room, the little bathroom, and the rear exit that opens into the alley by the dumpster.

Gilly stops three steps short of it.

Lorna smells it then.

Mint.

Iodine.

Damp cellar dirt.

Something scratches on the other side of the storage room door.

Not a hand.

Too many points.

A slow drag down wood.

Della whimpers, and her smile brightens.

Gilly glances back. "Lorna."

"I know."

"No, you don't." Gilly's voice lowers. "Your kid's teeth are glowing."

Lorna looks.

They are.

Not bright. Not like a flashlight. Just a faint pearly shine from behind Della's lips, as if moonlight is caught in her mouth and can't get out.

Della shakes her head, crying silently.

"I don't want them to," she whispers.

The storage room door shudders.

Gilly aims the revolver.

"Come on, then," she says.

The door opens.

Mavis Droot stands there with half her scalp hanging loose over one purple lens. Dirt coats her clinic smock. Her dentures are gone. Without them, her mouth has collapsed inward, making her chin and nose seem too close together.

Then the smaller mouth inside her mouth opens.

It has teeth now.

Tiny ones. Sharp as seed pearls.

It smiles.

Gilly fires.

The shot is enormous inside the thrift store. Della screams. The front glass cracks. The mouths stuck to it squeal and drop away.

Mavis's head snaps back.

For a second, Lorna thinks that's it.

Then Mavis lowers her face again.

There's a neat black hole in her forehead.

She looks annoyed.

"Well," Gilly says. "That's unfair."

Mavis comes fast.

Gilly fires again, but Mavis ducks under it and hits her in the chest with both hands. The revolver flies into a rack of winter coats. Gilly slams into the counter and goes down, knocking over a jar of buttons that scatter like little teeth across the floor.

Lorna grabs the closest thing she can find.

A brass lamp with a cherub base.

She swings it at Mavis's face.

The lamp connects with a heavy clang. Mavis reels sideways into a shelf of porcelain angels. They fall and break around her feet, wings snapping, faces cracking, little white hands flying everywhere.

"Get Della out!" Gilly coughs.

Lorna doesn't argue.

She yanks Della toward the front, but the mouths have started wriggling under the door. They squeeze through the gap like soft animals, flattening themselves until teeth scrape wood.

One pops through.

Then another.

Then five.

They scatter across the rug, chattering and snapping.

Gilly rolls onto her side, grabs the wasp spray from under the counter, and blasts them. The mouths shriek and curl in on themselves, lips blistering, tongues thrashing.

"Back way!" Gilly shouts.

"Mavis is back there!"

"Then pick a nightmare!"

Lorna turns Della toward the rear hall just as Mavis rises from the broken angels.

The old woman's face is caved on one side. Her human mouth hangs slack.

The little mouth inside it says, very clearly, "Nine thirty."

Della's whole body jerks.

Her teeth click.

Then she starts walking toward Mavis.

Lorna grabs her around the waist. "No."

Della fights her.

Not like a child tantrum. Not like fear.

Like a hooked fish.

Her sneakers scrape over the floor. Her arms reach out toward Mavis. Her smile stretches wider, showing gums now, showing that faint shine.

"Mom," Della sobs. "I can't stop."

Mavis opens her arms.

"There's a good girl," the little mouth says.

Lorna screams and drives the broken lamp forward, not at Mavis's head this time.

At the mouth inside her mouth.

The brass cherub punches between Mavis's lips.

The little mouth bites down.

Hard.

The metal bends.

Mavis howls. A sound like every dental drill in the world going off at once tears out of her. Lorna shoves harder until the lamp base jams deep, splitting the old woman's cheeks from inside.

Gilly appears beside Lorna with the bat.

"Move."

Lorna ducks.

Gilly swings like she means to knock summer clean into fall.

The bat hits the lamp.

The lamp drives through.

Mavis's face bursts backward in a spray of black blood, teeth, and something pale that looks like chewed gristle.

She drops.

Della collapses against Lorna.

The glow in her teeth dims.

For two seconds, nobody moves.

Then the cellar mouths at the front door begin laughing again.

Gilly looks down at Mavis's body.
Then at Lorna.
Then at Della.
"We're going to the farmhouse," she says.
Lorna nods, breathing hard.
Gilly picks up her revolver from the coats and checks the cylinder with shaking hands.
"Not because your plan's good," she says. "Because every other plan's worse."
They leave through the back because the front of the thrift store is alive with mouths clicking and clacking everywhere.
Gilly goes first with the revolver in one hand and the bat tucked under her arm. Lorna follows with Della pressed against her side, half carrying her, half dragging her. The rear hallway reeks of Mavis now. Rotten mint. Spoiled blood. That damp cellar stink that makes Lorna think of old potatoes left too long in a bin.
The back door hangs open.
The alley behind Second Chance Goods is narrow and choked with weeds. A green dumpster squats beneath the security light. Gilly's mean rooster, a red-and-black bastard named Mr. Knife, stands on top of an overturned milk crate near the steps.
He looks at the three of them.
Then he looks past them into the store.
Then he makes a low, furious sound in his throat.
"Not now," Gilly tells him.
Mr. Knife hops off the crate and follows anyway.
Nobody argues with him.
They cross the alley and cut behind the laundromat, keeping low beneath the windows. Gilly's truck waits in the side lot where she parks it every night because the thrift store alley is too narrow and too full of people leaving broken microwaves after hours.
The town sleeps around them, or pretends to. Lorna sees curtains twitch. A porch light blink off. A shape move behind the frosted glass of the Methodist church office.
People know.
Maybe not all of it. Maybe not the cellar or the jars or the little mouths crawling over roads.
But they know something is wrong.
They've known for years.

That thought makes Lorna's fear harden into rage.

Della leans against her, shivering. Her smile shrinks some, but it still sits there, stubborn and awful. Her lips tremble with the effort of fighting it.

"Mom," she whispers.

"I'm here."

"If I go there, am I going to die?"

Lorna wants to lie. She wants to say no with all the force in the world. She wants to put a mother's certainty over the hole in the night and make it solid.

But Della is looking up at her with tear-glazed eyes and that false little smile, and Lorna can't feed her another pretty lie.

"Not while I'm breathing," Lorna says.

Della nods.

Gilly glances back. "That's not technically an answer."

"It's the only one I've got."

"Fair."

They reach Gilly's old pickup behind the laundromat. It's a faded brown Ford with one blue door and a cracked windshield. A bumper sticker on the tailgate reads I BRAKE FOR YARD SALES AND REVENGE.

Gilly unlocks it.

Lorna stops. "What if it smiles?"

"Then we walk."

Gilly opens the driver's door.

Nothing happens.

No lights flare. No radio clicks on. No grille bends into a mouth.

Mr. Knife hops into the truck bed and settles like he's been invited.

Gilly points at him. "You scratch my toolbox, I'll cook you."

The rooster blinks.

Lorna gets Della into the passenger seat and climbs in after her. Gilly starts the truck. The engine coughs, spits, then catches with a roar loud enough to wake the dead and whatever's pretending not to be.

They pull onto the road.

For the first minute, nothing follows.

That's worse.

The Smile Farm sits twelve miles outside town, past soybean fields and cow pasture, at the end of a gravel lane lined with dead apple trees. Lorna's driven past it a hundred times. Everyone has.

White farmhouse.

Green shutters.

Hand-painted sign near the road with a smiling tooth wearing a straw hat.

Cute.

Harmless.

Charitable.

A nightmare wearing Sunday clothes.

Della stares through the windshield.

"They're louder now," she says.

Gilly's knuckles whiten on the steering wheel. "Who?"

"The jars."

Lorna puts an arm around her. "Don't listen."

"I'm trying not to."

"What are they saying?"

Della's smile twitches wider.

Her voice drops into a whisper.

"They're saying Dr. Tine's hungry."

Gilly hits the gas.

The old Ford shudders like it's offended by the request, then lurches forward. Headlights tunnel through the dark. Fence posts flash by. The road unspools ahead in a long black ribbon under the moon.

Lorna holds Della against her side and keeps one hand near her daughter's mouth without touching it.

The teeth glow again.

Faint.

Pale.

Wrong.

"They're saying other stuff," Della whispers.

"Don't," Lorna says.

Della swallows. Her smile stays fixed, but her eyes squeeze shut. "I can't help hearing."

Gilly leans over the wheel. "Then say it. Better out than rattling around in your skull."

Lorna shoots her a look.

"What?" Gilly says. "We're already driving toward Satan's orthodontist. Let's not pretend silence is saving anybody."

Della's voice comes thin and distant. "They're saying he doesn't eat food anymore."

Lorna's stomach tightens.

"They're saying he eats what people won't show."

Gilly mutters, "That's cheerful."

The truck rattles over a pothole. Della's head bumps Lorna's shoulder.

"They're saying he started with animals," Della continues. "Dogs with broken legs. Horses that needed shooting. He'd fix their mouths even though nobody asked. Then they'd stand in the pasture smiling while their bones healed wrong."

Lorna looks out at the fields.

For the first time, she notices the cows.

They stand along the fence in the moonlight, black and white shapes facing the road. Dozens of them. Maybe more. Every head turned toward the truck.

Every mouth open.

Smiling.

"Don't stop," Lorna says. "Do. Not. Stop."

"Hadn't planned on petting the livestock," Gilly says.

The cows begin walking.

Slow at first.

Then faster.

Their hooves thud in the dirt beyond the fence. Their jaws stretch wide, lips pulling back from big square teeth. One bellows, but the sound comes out like laughter stuffed through a wet trumpet.

Gilly presses the pedal down.

The Ford groans.

The cows run alongside the fence.

Della starts crying harder. "They're full."

"What?" Lorna says.

"The cows. They're full of it."

One cow slams into the fence. Wire snaps. Posts tilt. Another pushes through, ripping its hide open across the barbs, still smiling, still running.

Gilly swerves as the first cow stumbles into the road.

The truck clips its rear leg.

Bone cracks.

The cow goes down screaming laughter.

Della buries her face in Lorna's shirt.

More cows break through the fence behind them, spilling onto the road in a grinning herd.

In the truck bed, Mr. Knife loses his mind.

The rooster shrieks and beats his wings, hopping from one side to the other as cows chase the taillights with their impossible, happy faces.

"Gilly," Lorna says.

"I see them."

"Drive faster."

"This is faster."

A cow slams its head into the rear bumper.

The truck jerks.

Mr. Knife launches himself from the bed with a furious screech.

Lorna twists around just in time to see the rooster hit the cow's face claws-first.

Gilly yells, "That's my boy!"

The cow veers off, smashing into a ditch.

Mr. Knife vanishes in the dark.

Della lifts her head, horrified. "Your rooster…"

"He knows the way home," Gilly says, but her voice cracks.

They crest a low hill.

The farmhouse appears ahead.

White walls. Green shutters. Dead apple trees clawing at the sky. The hand-painted tooth sign rocks in the dark.

Except, there isn't any wind.

And the sign isn't rocking.

It's chewing.

The sign chews with its painted wooden mouth.

Up and down.

Up and down.

Chomp.

Chomp.

The smiling tooth in the straw hat splits along its cartoon grin, and something dark pulses inside the crack. Splinters jut like rotten teeth. The post creaks as the sign works its jaw at the night.

Smile Farm Community Dental Clinic

Free Care For Those Who Need It Most

Need.

That word sits in Lorna's head like a hook.

Gilly slows the truck.

"Don't," Lorna says.

"I'm not stopping. I'm trying not to plow straight into whatever fresh hell he's got planted in the driveway."

The gravel lane stretches between two rows of dead apple trees. Their branches lean inward, tangled overhead, forming a tunnel that looks too much like a throat. White blossoms hang from the black limbs even though it's the wrong season.

They're not flowers.

Lorna realizes what they are as the headlights catch them.

Teeth.

Of course they are.

Hundreds of little white teeth tied to the branches with red thread.

Baby teeth. Adult teeth. Molars. Canines. Long yellow roots dangling like nerves.

Della makes a choking sound.

Lorna pulls her close. "Don't look."

"I can feel them looking at me."

"They don't have eyes."

"They don't need eyes."

Gilly grips the wheel with one hand and raises the revolver with the other. "That right there is why I never had kids. Mine would say something like that and I'd put the whole house up for sale."

The Ford rolls under the trees.

The teeth begin to chatter.

Not all at once. First one branch. Then another. Then the whole lane fills with that dry clicking, a thousand tiny pieces of enamel tapping together in the dark.

Della's teeth answer.

Click.

Click.

Click.

Lorna grabs her daughter's chin before she can think better of it. "Listen to me."

Della's eyes roll toward her.

"You're Della Picket. You're mine. You're stubborn. You hate peas. You like possums because you say they look surprised to be alive. You cried when that ugly stray cat got hit by Mr. Portley's truck, then you called Mr. Portley a bald old turd under your breath at the funeral."

Della lets out a tiny, broken laugh.

It comes through the smile.

It sounds almost like hers.

"That's better," Lorna says, even though it isn't. "Stay with me."

"I'm trying."

The trees scrape the truck roof.

The Ford shudders.

Something drops onto the windshield.

A mouth.

It lands wetly, lips spread flat against the glass. Its teeth clack. Its tongue drags across the windshield, leaving a cloudy smear.

Gilly hits the wiper blades and the mouth jumps over them like it's doing hopscotch.

So she fires through the glass.

The windshield bursts into glittering cracks. The mouth flies backward into the dark, smoking.

Gilly squints through the ruined glass. "I'm taking that out of Tine's ass."

The farmhouse waits at the end of the lane.

It looks smaller up close than Lorna expects. Old white siding. Sagging porch. Green shutters. A rusted wheelchair ramp leading to the front door. Warm lights glow inside, soft and welcoming. A hand-lettered sign by the porch says PLEASE CHECK IN WITH MAVIS.

Mavis is in pieces on Gilly's thrift store floor.

Lorna hopes.

The cows stop at the mouth of the lane. They don't enter. They stand beyond the trees, panting and smiling, their huge eyes reflecting moonlight.

Gilly brakes hard beside a row of parked cars.

Lorna recognizes some of them. Ruthie Teague's blue sedan. Oscar Bell's dented pickup. Her own neighbor's minivan with the soccer ball decal. All empty. All parked neatly, like everyone's just inside waiting for a cleaning.

The clinic door opens.

Dr. Hollis Tine steps onto the porch.

White coat. Rimless glasses. Gray hair combed back. Suspenders visible beneath the coat. His face is calm, kind, and tired in the way men look when they want the world to thank them for all the harm they call sacrifice.

He smiles.

Not like Tobin.

Not like Della.

His smile is ordinary.

That makes it worse.

"Mrs. Picket," he calls. "You're early."

Gilly lifts the revolver.

Tine doesn't flinch.

"I wouldn't," he says.

"Lucky for you, I rarely take advice from men in porch lighting."

She fires.

The bullet hits Tine in the chest.

He rocks back one step.

Only one.

A dark spot spreads on his white coat.

He looks down at it with mild disappointment, like he's just spilled coffee. Then he looks up again.

Behind his lips, something moves.

Not teeth.

Lorna sees a second row sliding into place.

Then a third.

Della screams.

Tine sighs. "Violence always feels honest to frightened people."

"Shut up," Lorna says.

She throws open the truck door and gets out, pulling Della after her.

The gravel cuts her feet. Blood warms her soles. Her whole body wants to run the other way, down the tooth-lined lane, past the cows, past the road, past the town, past every place that's ever smiled at suffering and called it help.

Instead, she walks toward the porch.

Gilly hisses, "Lorna, what are you doing?"

"What he wants."

"Nope. Bad sentence. Hate that sentence."

Tine's smile softens. "Good. That's very good."

Lorna stops ten feet from the porch. "You want a mouth finished."

"Yes."

"Then take mine."

Della jerks against her. "Mom, no."

Tine's eyes brighten.

Gilly steps out of the truck. "Lorna."

Lorna doesn't look back.

"Take mine," she says again. "Leave Della's alone."

Tine studies her.

The teeth in the trees chatter faster.

"Maternal bargaining," he says. "It's one of the oldest forms of misery."

"Is it enough?"

"Oh, yes." His voice warms. "More than enough. Delightful, in fact."

He steps down from the porch.

Della clings to Lorna's hand. "No. Mom, no, no, no."

Lorna kneels in front of her.

Every second hurts.

Not the feet. Not the torn skin. Not the fear.

Her daughter.

That's where it hurts.

"Della," she says. "Listen to me."

"No."

"You're going to stay with Gilly."

"No."

"You're going to run if she says run."

"No."

"You're going to keep your real laugh. You hear me? Not his. Yours."

Della's smile trembles, bigger and smaller, fighting itself. "I don't want perfect teeth."

"I know, baby."

"I want my old ones."

"I know."

"They were mine."

Lorna presses her forehead to Della's.

For one strange second, she remembers Della at three years old, biting into a peach too big for her mouth, juice running down both arms while she grins with only half her baby teeth in.

Not perfect.

Not polished.

Not straight.

Just happy.

Real happy.

Lorna kisses her.

Then she stands and shoves Della backward toward Gilly.

"Run when I say."

Gilly catches the girl.

Tine comes closer.

He smells like mint, iodine, and cellar damp.

"You're making a noble choice," he says.

"No," Lorna says. "I'm making a mother's choice. There's nothing noble about it."

He reaches for her face.

His fingers are cool and soft.

The moment he touches her jaw, pain opens inside her.

All of it.

Not tooth pain. Not like a cavity or root or nerve.

Everything pain.

Every bill she can't pay. Every lunch she skips so Della eats. Every job interview where a man looks at her shirt and skirt instead of her eyes. Every night she lies awake counting dollars. Every time Della hides her mouth. Every time Tobin calls needing money she doesn't have. Every ugly little shame. Every swallowed scream. Every laugh she fakes at work so men don't call her difficult. Every hard thing she's packed behind her face because nobody wants to see a poor woman break down in public.

Tine inhales.

His eyelids flutter.

"Oh," he whispers. "You've carried so much."

Lorna's knees buckle.

His fingers tighten.

Della screams behind her.

Gilly shouts something.

The world tilts toward the farmhouse.

Tine's mouth opens.

It keeps opening.

His jaw drops too far, skin stretching at the corners. Rows of teeth unfold inside him, layered like a shark's mouth, wet and gleaming. Behind them is darkness. Behind the darkness, chatter.

So much chatter.

Hundreds of mouths.

Thousands.

They're not just under the farmhouse.

They're in him.

They're in the walls. In the trees. In the sign. In every smile he's ever forced onto a human face.

"Let go," Lorna whispers.

"I can't," he says gently. "You came willingly."

"No."

His fingers dig into her cheeks.

Her lips begin to pull back.

She feels it. That horrible invisible hook at both corners of her mouth. The tug. The command.

Smile.

Smile through it.

Smile so nobody has to know.

Lorna fights it.

Her mouth twitches.

Pulls.

Her lips peel from her teeth.

Della sobs, "Mommy!"

The word cuts through the pressure.

Not because it's sweet.

Because it's terrified.

Because it's real.

Lorna's right hand slips into her pocket.

Her keys are still there.

House key. Car key. Little grocery store tag. Tiny pepper spray canister Gilly gave her two Christmases ago after a man followed her to her car at the Dollar General.

Lorna closes her fingers around the pepper spray.

Tine leans closer, drinking her suffering through the shape of her mouth.

"You'll feel peace soon," he whispers.

Lorna smiles.

For real.

It startles him.

Just a flicker in his eyes.

That's enough.

She drives the pepper spray straight into his open mouth and empties it.

Tine shrieks.

Smoke pours from his throat. His fingers rip away from her face. He stumbles backward, choking, clawing at his lips as the rows of teeth snap and grind against each other.

The teeth in the apple trees scream.

The parked cars scream.

The cows scream at the end of the lane.

The farmhouse lights go red.

"Now!" Lorna yells.

Gilly runs for the porch.

Not away.

Toward it.

"Gilly!"

"Cellar!" Gilly shouts. "We end it or we're doing this bullshit forever!"

Lorna grabs Della and charges after her.

Tine twists on the gravel, still gagging smoke. His jaw hangs low, unhinged. Teeth tumble from his mouth in bloody handfuls, but more push through behind them.

Endless teeth.

Hungry teeth.

The front door slams open before Gilly reaches it.

Warm light spills over them.

Inside, the clinic looks like every place poor people are expected to be grateful in. Cheap chairs against the wall. A children's toy bin. Old magazines. A coffee station with powdered creamer. Posters of cartoon teeth holding toothbrushes. A bowl of stickers on the front desk.

Behind the desk, a hallway leads deeper into the house.

At the end of it, a door stands open.

Basement stairs descend into black.

The chatter rises from below.

Della covers her ears.

Her smile is gone now.

Gone.

Lorna sees her daughter's lips closed, trembling but closed, and almost drops to the floor.

Della's teeth are crooked again.

Not all the way. Not as before. But the front one has leaned back a little, stubbornly imperfect.

Mine, like Della said.

Lorna squeezes her hand.

Gilly looks over and sees it, too.

"Well, I'll be damned," she says. "Ugly teeth for the win."

The front door bangs behind them.

Tine crawls inside on all fours.

His white coat drags through blood. His mouth hangs open to his chest now, full of moving teeth.

"Downstairs," Lorna says.

"That's not usually the survival direction," Gilly says.

They go anyway.

The basement stairs are narrow and steep. The wood is damp under Lorna's bloody feet. The smell gets worse with every step.

Formaldehyde.

Rot.

Mint.

Old breath trapped too long in jars.

The walls sweat.

Halfway down, Della stops.

"I can hear Tobin."

Lorna freezes.

From below, under all the chatter, comes one voice.

Her brother.

Not laughing.

Not smiling.

"Lorna," he calls weakly. "Don't let him close the jars."

She moves faster.

The cellar opens wide beneath the farmhouse, much wider than the house above should allow. Brick walls vanish into darkness. Shelves stand floor to ceiling in crooked rows.

And on every shelf sit jars.

Hundreds.

No.

Thousands.

Glass jars filled with cloudy yellow fluid. In each one floats a mouth. Some fresh and red. Some gray. Some tiny. Some old. Some with lipstick. Some with braces. Some with missing teeth. Some with gold. Some with tobacco stains. Some with lips sewn partly shut.

Every mouth smiles.

Every mouth chatters.

The sound hits Lorna like hail.

Della screams and presses her face into Lorna's side.

Gilly gags. "Nope. I take it back. This is worse than upstairs."

At the center of the cellar stands a dentist's chair.

Old leather. Metal arms. Rusted foot pedal. A tray beside it holds instruments that look too sharp and too eager. Pliers. Picks. Wires. Curved needles. A hand drill with a bone handle.

On the far side of the chair, Tobin hangs against the wall.

Not by ropes.

By smiles.

Mouths cling to him everywhere. His arms. His neck. His shirt. His face. They suck at him like leeches, all grinning, all feeding on whatever misery Tine has shoved into him.

His own mouth is torn at the corners, but his smile has finally broken.

His lips sag.

Blood pours down his chin.

He sees Lorna and tries to laugh.

It comes out as a cough.

"Hey," he says. "You look awful."

Lorna sobs once. "You idiot."

"Yeah."

Gilly raises the revolver and starts shooting jars.

Glass explodes.

The mouths fall out in wet slaps, shrieking as they hit the floor. The cloudy liquid hisses and steams. Freed mouths crawl in blind circles, snapping at nothing, then collapse into twitching piles of gum and tongue.

The shelves shake.

Above them, Tine howls.

"No," he roars from the stairs. "No, no, no!"

His voice isn't kind anymore.

Good.

Lorna grabs a metal stool and smashes the nearest shelf. Jars tumble, break, spray the floor with yellow fluid. The mouths scream.

Some scream in voices Lorna recognizes from town. Oscar. Ruthie. Mrs. Larch from the school office. The man who bags groceries at Miller's and always says it's a beautiful day even in February rain.

Each broken jar changes something above.

The farmhouse groans.

The clinic walls crack.

Gilly fires again and again until the revolver clicks empty. Then she uses the gun like a hammer.

Della stands frozen at first.

Then a tiny mouth with braces crawls toward her sneaker and whispers, "Pretty girl."

Della looks down at it.

Her face goes still.

Then she stomps it flat.

"Shut up," she says.

Lorna's never been prouder of anyone in her life.

Tine reaches the cellar floor.

He no longer looks fully human. His body is stretched thin under the white coat. His jaw splits his neck. Teeth stud the inside of his cheeks, his throat, even the palms of his hands. Every wound in him smiles.

"You think suffering disappears because you break the vessels?" he snarls.

"No," Lorna says, smashing another jar. "I think yours starts."

The broken mouths on the floor turn toward him.

All of them.

The intact jars stop chattering.

Silence falls in pieces.

Tine looks around.

For the first time, he looks afraid.

One mouth crawls toward him.

Small. Pink. With one baby tooth.

Then another.

Then a dozen.

Then hundreds.

They move across the cellar floor, dragging themselves through fluid and glass, whispering, clicking, smiling. They've held everyone else's pain for years. Maybe decades. Maybe longer than Tine himself. Maybe the house has always needed someone in a white coat to feed it.

Now they smell the keeper.

Tine backs up.

"Stay away."

The mouths keep coming.

He tries to climb the stairs, but Gilly swings the bat into his knee.

His leg snaps backward.

Tine falls.

The mouths reach him.

They latch on.

His screams shake dust from the rafters.

They bite his hands first. His fingers. His palms. The smiling wounds there. Then his face. His throat. His open jaw. They crawl inside his mouth by the dozens, pushing past his teeth, chewing, sucking, reclaiming every stored scream.

Lorna grabs Della and turns her away, but Della has already seen enough.

Maybe too much.

Maybe exactly enough.

Tobin groans.

Lorna runs to him and rips mouths from his body. They come loose with wet pops. Gilly helps, cursing and swinging at any that snap back.

"Hold still," Gilly says.

"I'm trying," Tobin says.

"You're doing it wrong."

"Sorry."

"Stop apologizing while bleeding. It's annoying."

They free him from the wall as Tine thrashes behind them.

His screams change.

They rise high, then higher, then become a bright, cheerful laugh.

Not because he's happy.

Because his face won't let him tell the truth anymore.

The cellar shelves collapse.

Jars burst by the dozens. Fluid runs across the floor in ankle-deep streams. The farmhouse shudders overhead. Something heavy crashes upstairs. The clinic bell rings and rings and rings.

Gilly points toward the stairs. "Time to stop admiring our work."

Lorna gets one arm under Tobin. Gilly takes the other. Della leads the way, slipping in blood and fluid, her crooked teeth clenched, her face her own.

They climb.

Behind them, Tine laughs and laughs as the mouths eat him alive.

The stairs shake.

Halfway up, a hand grabs Lorna's ankle.

Tine.

Or what's left of him.

His fingers are mostly bone. Teeth sprout from the knuckles. His ruined face tilts up from the cellar dark, mouth packed full of other mouths, all chewing, all smiling.

His eyes lock on Della.

"Appointment," he gurgles.

Della turns.

For one sick second, Lorna thinks the pull is still in her. That the word has hooked her by the teeth.

But Della steps down one stair.

Then she spits in Tine's face.

"I'm canceling," she says.

Gilly brings the bat down on his wrist.

The hand breaks apart.

They run.

The clinic above is coming down. Posters curl off walls. Dental chairs fold in on themselves like dead insects. The toy bin vomits teeth across the floor. The front desk splits, and beneath it Lorna sees roots as black as phone cords pulsing up through the boards.

They burst onto the porch as the farmhouse begins to scream.

The whole house smiles.

Windows bend. Siding curls. The porch rail splits into long white slats. The front door stretches wide behind them, and for a moment Lorna sees the house's true mouth. A black cellar throat. Teeth made of beams. A tongue of red dirt and roots.

Then Gilly's truck explodes.

Not from fire.

From mouths.

The windshield pops outward. The grille screams. Tires burst. The whole thing collapses in a heap of metal and wet chatter.

"Damn it," Gilly says. "I liked that piece of junk."

The apple trees along the lane start tearing themselves from the ground.

Their roots writhe like black veins. Their tooth-fruit chatters. The cows beyond the lane bellow laughter.

Lorna looks around for escape.

None.

Then a furious screech splits the night.

Mr. Knife comes out of the dark like a feathered demon, riding the back of one of the grinning cows.

The rooster's claws are buried in the cow's neck. His wings beat wildly. The cow bucks, crashes through the tooth trees, and slams into the porch steps.

The steps splinter.

The farmhouse screams louder.

Gilly stares. "I'm giving that rooster my house."

The cow collapses near the porch, still smiling, legs kicking.

Lorna sees the gap it has made in the lane.

"Go!"

They run through the broken trees.

Teeth rain from branches. Roots snap at their ankles. Tobin falls once, and Lorna nearly goes down with him, but Gilly hauls them both upright with a strength that feels impossible until Lorna remembers rage counts as muscle.

Della runs ahead, ducking under a whipping branch.

The hand-painted sign lunges at her, split mouth opening.

Della grabs a fallen fence post and swings.

She hits the smiling tooth square in its cartoon face.

The sign cracks in half.

It lets out one final wooden shriek and falls into the ditch, chewing dirt.

They reach the road as dawn stains the horizon gray.

The cows stop at the edge of the lane.

The mouths stop, too.

The farmhouse behind them folds inward, slow at first, then all at once. Porch. Roof. Walls. Clinic. Cellar. Everything drops into the ground with a roar like a thousand people exhaling.

Dust rises.

Then silence.

Real silence.

No chatter.

No teeth.

No smiling thing hidden beneath the world.

For a while, nobody speaks.

They stand barefoot and bloody on Route 6, watching the place where the Smile Farm used to be.

Tobin wipes his mouth with the back of his hand.

His lips are torn. His cheeks are raw. His teeth are still too white, but his smile is gone.

He tries to form one.

Can't.

Then he starts crying.

Ugly crying. Open-mouthed. Snotty. Shaking.

Lorna pulls him in with one arm and Della with the other.

Gilly stands beside them, holding the bat over one shoulder, nightgown torn, hair wild, face streaked with blood and cellar fluid.

Mr. Knife limps out of the ditch, missing half his tail feathers.

Gilly points at him. "Don't you look smug."

The rooster looks extremely smug.

By seven in the morning, the sheriff's department arrives.

Then the fire department.

Then half the town.

They find nothing under the collapsed farmhouse but a sinkhole full of broken glass, old roots, and hundreds of teeth. No bodies. No jars. No Tine. No Mavis.

Pastor Teague stands beside Ruthie at the edge of the road, pale and shaking.

Ruthie isn't smiling anymore.

Neither are a lot of people.

Some cry. Some scream. Some touch their mouths as if greeting old wounds. Oscar Bell drops to his knees and sobs into his ruined hands. Mrs. Larch laughs once, a real laugh, then looks shocked by the sound and starts laughing harder.

Lorna watches all of it from the back of an ambulance while an EMT wraps her feet.

Della sits beside her with a blanket over her shoulders.

Her teeth are crooked again.

Not quite the same as before. One front tooth still stands straighter than it used to, a small reminder, a tiny theft. But when Della sees Lorna looking, she bares them in a fierce little grin.

Not Tine's.

Hers.

"Looks good," Lorna says.

Della snorts. "Liar."

"Yeah."

They sit there together as the sun comes up over the fields.

For a moment, the world looks almost gentle.

Then Tobin walks over with bandages at both corners of his mouth and a paper cup of water in one hand.

He looks exhausted. Hollowed out. Alive.

"Doctor says I need stitches," he says.

Gilly, sitting on the ambulance bumper with Mr. Knife in her lap, says, "I've got a sewing kit at the store."

Tobin looks at her.

"She's kidding," Lorna says.

Gilly pauses. "Mostly."

Della laughs.

It's small. Wobbly. But it's hers.

Lorna hears it and feels something inside her loosen, something that's been clenched for years.

Across the road, workers stretch yellow tape around the Smile Farm ruins. The old tooth sign lies in the ditch, cracked down the middle, straw hat splintered, painted grin split apart.

A deputy steps on it by accident.

The sign's broken mouth twitches.

Just once.

Lorna sees it.

So does Della.

So does Gilly.

Nobody else does.

Lorna stands, ignoring the EMT's protest, and limps across the road.

She picks up a shovel from the fire crew's pile of tools.

The deputy says, "Ma'am, you can't be over here."

Lorna looks at him.

He steps back.

Smart man.

She raises the shovel and brings it down on the sign.

Again.

Again.

Again.

Until the smiling tooth is nothing but painted splinters in the dirt.

When she's done, she's breathing hard.

Her feet bleed through the bandages.

Her hands ache.

Her mouth hurts from not smiling.

Good, she thinks.

Let it hurt.

Some things are supposed to show.

Behind her, Della says, "Mom?"

Lorna turns.

Her daughter stands in the road with the blanket around her shoulders and her crooked teeth catching the morning light.

"Can we go home?"

Lorna looks toward town. Toward their dark little house. Toward the broken Kia and the blood in the bathroom and the phone pieces on the kitchen floor. Toward all the ordinary nightmares waiting to be cleaned up.

Bills.

School.

Work.

Grief.

Pain.

Life.

She nods.

"Yeah," she says. "We can go home."

Della slips her hand into Lorna's.

This time, when she smiles, it fades when it's done.

And that's the most beautiful thing Lorna has ever seen.

About the Author

Christopher Winterberg's debut collection of short stories, Twisted Sanity: Stories Beyond Reality, enjoyed literary success. While he has not been published in any reviews, quarterlies, journals, periodicals, or elsewhere, he looks forward to those opportunities. Never having been labeled as one of the most famous writers of any generation, era, or century, he has received zero literary awards. He does, however, look forward to those in the future, if warranted. You can find out more about Christopher at chriswinterberg.com.

If you're daring and wish to, you may contact Christopher Winterberg either through a post on his website, or at info@chriswinterberg.com.

www.ingramcontent.com/pod-product-compliance
Lightning Source LLC
LaVergne TN
LVHW010647110826
845149LV00014B/2983